The Incomplete Sorcerer

Brian Ardel

blue ocean press

tokyo – florida

Published by: blue ocean press, an imprint of Aoishima Research Institute
U.S. (Main) Office
P.O. Box 510818
Punta Gorda, Florida 33951

807-36 Lions Plaza Ebisu
3-25-3 Higashi, Shibuya-ku, Tokyo, Japan 150

Email: contact@blueoceanpublications.com
URL: http://www.blueoceanpublications.com

ISBN: 978-4-902837-36-0

Cover Art by MaryRose Arciero

Table of Contents

Prologue

The old men worked in unison to carry the man up the mountain. They struggled with his weight, their own exhaustion and the steepness of the trail. As one tired body began to falter, another stepped in to shoulder the load. By the time they reached the top of the mountain, all had supported the unconscious man. The weight of what they had done, and what they were about to do, was thus evenly distributed amongst them.

The men worked with great urgency. They wore gaudy multicolored cloaks, covered with strange designs. One was solid blue, adorned with yellow astrological symbols that wandered purposefully across the fabric. Another was purple, accented with black arcane figures that undulated rhythmically. The cloaks all had hoods which covered the faces of the men.

Their leader paused and pulled his hood back. His face was a mixture of emotions, filled with fear, anger and most of all sadness. "We must hurry!" he cried out hoarsely. "The time approaches. The alignment is nearly perfect. None of us will live long enough to see the heavens be this way again!"

They entered a cave carved out of the mountain's side by a long-forgotten earthquake. The jagged scar in the stone was wide enough for the whole procession to pass through without breaking rank. As they entered the mountain, a flock of birds that was following them began to cry noisily.

The old men carried their burden like pallbearers at a funeral. The stunned body was carefully laid on a rock outcropping, near the cave's back wall. The man sputtered as dust kicked up by the procession tickled his nose. He coughed, then began to stir and moan.

The men formed a semicircle around him. From under their hoods, they glanced at each other with nervous eyes.

"Catharvus, you have committed unspeakable crimes against the people of this vale," mumbled the man in the purple cloak. "For that, you must be punished. Though many feel that you deserve death, that is not our way. The danger you represent to the people of the valley is too great to ever let you walk among them again. It is our unfortunate task to make sure that you never spill innocent blood again."

"Catharvus, remember your crimes for all eternity!"

The man in purple nodded to his colleagues. "Let our combined might create that which will never be undone."

After a moment of reflection, the men bowed their heads, then began to whisper as one, their voices summoning energies long dormant. With the strength of their combined powers, a spell congealed.

A tired voice whispered the thoughts of the assembly. "It is finished. No man will ever break this alone."

The bearers of Catharvus' body crawled out of the cave, their heads hung low. What they had just done hung upon them like a leaden weight. An all-consuming sadness added to the fatigue that nearly overwhelmed them.

The afternoon sun shone over their shoulders, brightly illuminating the face of the man left behind. His dazed eyes squinted in its glare. He clenched them shut momentarily, then opened them, and looked around. Panic filled him. He began to scream.

"Noooooo," he wailed, his mournful voice echoing off the cave walls. "It shall not end this way. You cannot do this to me!"

From the perimeter of the cave, twenty-five voices joined in arcane chant, their incantation an answer to his challenge. The man who lay in the mountain continued to wail, but his screams were drowned out by the united voices of the group.

The moon slowly rose in the afternoon sky, its color an unnatural blue. The sun, influenced by the men's combined words, grew dim as the moon passed before it. People in the valley shuddered as the eclipse that formed threw darkness upon them.

As the chanting continued, brightly colored bolts of light raced across the surface of the mountain. The figure in the cave struggled for a minute, then went limp as the shadow of the eclipse fell upon him. A curse died in his throat, unspoken.

The chanting stopped. Silence hung heavily on the darkened air. The men raised their arms to the heavens. Shimmering bands of light seemed to form around their interlocked hands. Their leader nodded almost imperceptibly. All hands were pulled down in unison. The ground shook as the very heart of the mountain shifted. Rocks tumbled down its sides, throwing showers of pebbles on the men. Dust fell from the cave's ceiling as the shaking within the mountain intensified. A rumble, like nearby thunder, exploded as the mouth of the cave collapsed upon itself, throwing unending darkness behind it.

As the light vanished from his tomb, Catharvus' eyes drifted closed.

The men waited by the cave's mouth for a moment, then turned as one, and shuffled down the mountain.

CH 1

The night began like the thousands that had preceded it. Mist drifted off the mountain, rolling down its tree covered slopes until the valley below was buried under its nebulous embrace. The animals of the day settled down for a night of rest; the creatures of the night began to rise and stir. The villagers of Dragon Springs relaxed as the sun set into the mist.

The first sign that change was coming was the oppressive hush that blanketed the forest with the falling mist. The insects remained silent, their nocturnal recital seemingly put off for another time. Horses fidgeted in their stalls, their nostrils flaring as they glanced about with widened eyes.

As the sun fled the crimson sky, an unsettling heaviness filled the air. Darkness came rapidly. The gloom swallowed the last of the day's light, leaving villagers huddling nervously around their fires.

The moon rose into the sky, cutting through the mist like the blade of a warrior's sword. Throughout the valley conversation stopped as attention was riveted to the rising orb.

The moon was an evil moon. It was not the friendly guide to the late traveler, nor was it the silent witness to lovers embrace. It was a cold signal of approaching change.

The moon rose blue. Its light was chilling and unnatural. Children cried. Women pulled their shawls closer to their bodies as if the fabric could keep out the perceived chill. Warriors allowed their hands to fall on the hilts of their swords. The firmness of the steel was comforting, though the metal seemed cool, out of proportion to the night's temperature. Dogs howled. From the depths of the forest, feral voices answered.

As the omen of ill tidings rose into the sky, a faint halo began to form around it. Attention across the land was riveted onto the moon as it continued its ascent into the sky. Slowly, a shadow fell across the halo, then across the moon itself. The darkness grew as the shadow centered itself on the moon. The moon became muted as the eclipse's shadow engulfed it, leaving only the wavering corona visible.

The corona, its azure band slowly twisting in the night sky, threw out an unholy light that bathed the countryside. Children cringed in fear while adults averted their eyes to escape its light.

The ground succumbed to the pressures of the aligned moon and sun. It began to vibrate and tremble. Trees fell. Walls crumbled. A long-sealed cavern felt its first breath of new air as cracks formed in the rocks that made up its walls. The moon's light shone in through one of these cracks, falling on a dusty form. The light triggered a reaction that broke an ancient spell. Energy flashes raced across the body of Catharvus. The interior of the cave was bathed in flashing lights as the magical energies sizzled and crackled before leaving the wizard's body.

Dusty air was drawn in, a long still chest rose.

Dark eyes opened.

A resonant voice filled the chamber. "I live," it said.

The book, covered in decaying leather, rested on a rocky outcropping. The thick coating of dust that entombed it was testament to its age. Nearby, a crystalline ball and iron wand rested in equally dusty solitude.

Catharvus' hand, almost skeletal in its form, reached for the tome.

His hand was ancient, though not as old as the book. Its skeletal framework was gnarled and distorted. The skin that covered it was parchment thin, its sallow surface marred by brown splotches. The nails were twisted and overgrown, almost as if they sought to escape the yellowed skin of the fingertips.

His hand was attached to a sinewy arm. Vein and gristle showed through the translucent skin, except where a tattoo, now blurred and faded by the passage of time, nestled among the age spots. Though difficult to make out, the tattoo appeared to have once represented a bird. A jeweled dagger, drawn by a different hand, impaled the tattooed bird.

The rest of the wizard's arm was concealed by a tattered black cloak. Its surface was decorated with arcane symbols as well as a thick coating of dust and mildew. Bat droppings smeared its sleeves. Though its owner was beyond caring, it smelled of dampness and decay.

The being wearing the cloak looked far worse than the garment itself. He was human, or at least once was. His emaciated body was topped by a head devoid of hair. His face was skull-like, the underlying skeleton plainly visible through the tattered skin. His eye sockets were deep, the eyes within them sunken far into the bony rims.

His cadaverous appearance was disrupted by his eyes. They were not the pale lifeless orbs of the dead, but instead, the hate filled piercing eyes of the obsessed. His gaze was sharp, cold and unwavering.

He coughed. Puffs of dust escaped from his cracked lips. With great effort, he sat up, ignoring the complaints of his tortured joints. A chorus of creaks and snaps gave testament to the years he lay unmoving. He breathed deeply. Each fresh breath brought increasing strength to Catharvus.

He looked towards the light that bathed his face. It was blue, much like the last light he remembered seeing before the great sleep was imposed upon him. The moon shone through a man sized, jagged crack in the mountain's side. It was not where the original opening of the cave had been. Dust thrown about when the mountain walls splintered filled his cavern, cutting visibility down to near zero. He spat a wad of saliva off dusty lips and stood.

"It is time to leave now," he muttered.

The wizard reached for the book and cradled it against his chest. Bat guano from his cloak smeared its cover. He shuffled across the chamber, but came to an abrupt halt at the crack that made up its door. He turned and looked at the force that stopped him. A glistening chain bound him to the floor near his rocky bed.

He stooped to examine the chain. It was of no earthly blacksmith's manufacture. The links were made of polished diamond; they sparkled with a blue light in the dim chamber. Each link was thicker than a man's thumb, with no seams marring the mirrored surface. The first link merged directly with the room's stone floor. The last link of the chain attached to a flawless band that encircled the man's ankle. Kicking and twisting did not loosen the shackle.

The man saw a rusted sword lying on the cave's floor. He nodded approvingly at the crimson stains that covered the blade and hilt. Good, he thought, I took one with me.

He reminisced for a moment, remembering his final battle. His minions of elemental warriors and conjured monsters followed him into the valley below. They had overrun the villagers like a forest fire swept by a hot summer wind. All that stood before them was crushed. Catharvus feasted on the life forces of the men, growing even more powerful as each one died.

The old sorcerer nodded as the images of carnage came flowing back to him. Suddenly he shook his head like a horse trying to unsettle a biting fly, for memories of the battle's end had come back unbidden. He ground his fist into the palm of his hand. Nothing would have been able to stand in my way were it not for the Air Children, he thought. Their interference robbed me of victory. Dominance was my right. They stole that from me. I will escape. I must escape! The Air Children owe me for the glory that they have taken from me. They will pay for what they have done!

He reached for the sword, ignoring the stiffness in his back. The blade felt awkward in his hand, for this was not the class of weapons he was trained to use. He swung the sword, driving it down into the links of the chain. The sword shattered into a rusty cloud, leaving the wizard holding only its hilt. The chain remained unbroken.

The wizard sat on the floor of the cave, unmindful of the bat droppings piled there. He lifted the chain and set it upon a rock. Bracing himself, he lifted another rock and slammed it onto the chain. Both rocks crumbled. The chain glittered in the cave's dim light, its surface still perfect, its links unbroken.

Catharvus walked back to the rocky outcropping dragging the chain behind him, its soft jingling in sharp contrast to his labored breathing.

Years of imprisoned sleep must have addled my senses, he thought. What hath been wrought by magic, must be broken by magic. The Air Children, those spineless cowards, were unable to muster up the courage to kill me. How typical of their kind. Far kinder to banish me to a dreamless sleep in the stinking bowels of this mountain than to finish me. They could have assimilated my life forces. It would have given them great power. Leaving life in this shell of a body was a great mistake. It shall come back to haunt them as no nightmare possibly could. They will beg for the peace of death.

He opened the book, gazing at it fondly. My friend the spell book, he thought. You have waited alone all these years for my awakening. I need you. My brain is tired, I no longer remember my spells. I will use you. With your help, I will escape this cursed hell.

He read for some time, then closed the book. "Let's see if magical energies flow through this cavern," he mumbled to himself.

He spoke the ancient words while making complex gestures with his hands, then stooped down and grabbed a handful of dust from the floor. He stood up, raised his hand over his head, then let the dust slip through his fingers.

The dust fluttered earthward until it reached the level of his chest, then raced parallel to the floor as if caught in a stiff wind. Half of the dust broke off from the main stream and circled the diamond chain at dizzying speed. It then rejoined the other dust stream, widening it back to its original width. The dust then streaked out of the room, leaving Catharvus staring towards the passageway that it had departed from.

He lowered his hand and sighed. The energies are quite strong here, he thought. The Air Children chose their prison well. The chain glows with the spell powers of many men. Such combined magic will be even more difficult to overcome.

If magic is the secret of my imprisonment, he thought, then it surely must hold the key to my escape. I will have to use it if I ever hope to see the light of day shine across the fallen corpses of the Air Children.

He once again opened the book and thumbed through its stiff parchment pages. He stopped at a page ornately accented by the picture of a comet streaking across an indigo sky. The heading next to the picture read "Magic Missile."

Yes, it comes back to me now, he thought. The first part of the page contains the arcane recital. Its words evoke the proper magical energies. His fingers fondled the ornate letters at the page's top, then slid down the page, his dirty nails leaving dark streaks on the paper.

The middle of the page now caught his attention. This part of the page contains the proper hand motions to focus and direct the magical forces, he thought. His hand lifted, then descended unto the lowest part of the page. He mindlessly tapped the parchment, muttering, "the final section contains the proper catalyst to convert the energies into magical force."

He began to read aloud from the opened page. His words hissed like dragon's steam as they passed over the twisted brown stumps that were his teeth. The sorcerer's hands traced complex patterns in the air as he spoke. He fell silent, enjoying the feel of the powers forming around him. The air shimmered as waves of the diffuse natural energies concentrated around his outstretched hands. He turned his palms upward, squinting into the intense blue light that he had wrought. The powers caressed his hands, tickling the skin like the static that fills the air after a lightning strike. Suddenly, he compressed the crackling energy between his hands until it formed a palm sized packet. He paused for a moment, enjoying his handiwork, then stooped to pick up a shard of rock from the cavern floor.

"Lovely catalyst," he muttered. "Feel the magical energies transform your mass into destructive powers."

He dropped the pebble into the hand holding the mystic energies. The blue light emanating from his clenched hand, instantly turned a blinding red. He whirled, the burst of speed in sharp contrast to his previous arthritic movements. His motion was unbroken as his arm cocked back, then let fly the pebble, now encapsulated by a crackling red halo.

He threw the energy cocooned catalyst towards the floor. It struck the diamond chain. A tremendous explosion issued forth, rocking the chamber. Chips of stone flew like shrapnel throughout the cavern, embedding themselves into the ceiling and walls. Through the magical energy harnessed by the spell, stone heading for the sorcerer was deflected harmlessly away.

The area of the spell's impact was devastated. Bedrock was pulverized into dust. A web of delicate cracks invaded the once solid stone floor. The diamond chain remained at the center of the explosion, perfect and unbroken. Pulling on it produced no slack for the imprisoned sorcerer. The chain remained firmly attached to the rock at the bottom of the hole.

The sorcerer repeated the spell, and again a tremendous explosion occurred. The chain held fast. The hole grew in depth, yet the chain remained anchored to the rock at the base of the hole. He fired two more spells. The chain remained unaffected.

Magic must be reforming the chain as quickly as my spells destroy it, he thought. Without magical fortification, nothing could stand up to the missile's explosions.

He shuffled over to the rock where his crystal ball lay. He looked into his spell book and chose another page. He mumbled strange words while his bony hands danced out complex patterns in the air. The magical energies crackled and glowed around his hands. With further manipulation, they formed a brilliant blue translucent cup. He picked up a handful of dust and sprinkled it into the cup. The dust acted as the catalyst and turned the magical container into a cauldron of fiery, swirling clouds. Into this he placed his crystal ball. The clouds immediately covered the ball, looking much like a mirror fogged by steam. The crackling died away, leaving the ball coated with maroon soot.

He picked up the ball and peered intently at its now opaque surface. His eyes narrowed as he spoke a single word, "Escape."

He put the ball back on the rocky ledge.

The maroon soot staining the ball's surface flared blindingly, then burst into flames. It burned, leaving clouds of thick smoke in the chamber. Catharvus hardly noticed the smell as he peered with watering eyes into the glowing ball. The white-hot crystal cooled as the flames died down. Its surface colors changed from white to red to pink, then finally glowed without color. As the color left its exterior, an image formed inside it.

The magician grabbed the ball, ignoring the sizzling sound that erupted as the hot crystal burned his flesh. He stared deeply into the orb.

The image of two men cutting wood in the forest flickered briefly, then died out.

For the first time since he awakened, the man smiled.

Alar leaned against a tree, relaxing as he gazed into the woods. How peaceful they looked in the light of day. Sitting next to him was a large man leaning sleepily against a tree stump. With exaggerated effort, the man rubbed a sharpening stone against his ax.

Alar tossed a pine cone at him. "Get up! Stop your loafing. If you don't stop toying with your ax, we'll be here all day."

The large man seemed unimpressed by the request. He gave his blade one more stroke with the stone, then looked up. "What's the hurry?" he said with a smile. "I have never seen you so eager to get started. Is there a serving wench waiting for you in town? Can it be that the thought of dancing and smelling fine perfumes excites you more than the company of your fellow woodsmen?"

"Of course it does," replied the laughing Alar. "Look at you! The thought of dancing with my donkey and smelling its fine perfume, excites me more than your company!"

Alar walked to Marcus, grabbed a handful of shirt, and pulled him to his feet. "What excites me most is the thought of sleeping in a real bed. An insect laden pile of pine needles does not make for a comfortable night's sleep. Besides, you snore like a cave troll!"

Marcus lifted his considerable bulk, moaning for theatrical effect. "Oh, to be young again," he said. "The energy you spend in a single day pursuing the fairer sex would heat my cottage for the winter."

He looked at Alar and chuckled. "If I hadn't promised your father that I would look after you, it would be easier to leave you here. Of course, you wouldn't last a night without my protection."

Alar looked up into the older woodsman's face and smiled. "If I wasn't teamed with my father's friend, the food would last far longer! To keep you in fodder, we must pack the provisions of a small army. And let's not forget the booze. I could float a boat in what you drank this trip."

Marcus looked at Alar with a pained expression. "No need to get personal. Who could be as perfect as you?" he asked, his voice filled with mock self-pity. "Look at the polished shell the gods have chosen to bestow upon you. It just doesn't look right. If you could only pack on a few pounds, you might grow to look respectable... like me."

The good-natured bickering continued as the men gathered their gear and started down the trail. Marcus, the older of the two men, was a jolly fellow. He carried an air of youthfulness that belied his fifty years. His girth bespoke the onslaughts of many a fine meal while his ruddy complexion hinted towards a working relationship with the bottle. His dress was typical for a woodsman, functional clothes made of coarse linen fabric. His shirt strained to hold back the expanding flesh of his ample abdomen though his shoulders also pulled the fabric taut. His large frame was topped by a head covered with wild gray hair. A salt and pepper beard framed his face. Though his physical presence was imposing, his eyes had the mischievous glint of a child's. A smile, currently a guilty one, was a permanent fixture on his face.

"Alar, did the bugs really keep you up last night?"

"You bet, I scratched half the night away. My bed was crawling with ants."

"Strange, mine wasn't. Do you think the sugar I sprinkled under your blanket had anything to do with it? I wanted to draw them away for my bed. You know, it worked!"

Alar stopped in mid-trail and stared at Marcus. "You laced my bed with sugar? I hope you fall into a pile of dragon droppings!" he swore as he swung a fist at the laughing man. Marcus blocked the blow, then fell to the trail, consumed by hysterics.

Alar smiled in spite of himself, kicked a few leaves at Marcus, then continued along the trail. He stopped at a small stream, one of the tributaries of the Dancing River. As he stopped to fill his canteen, he noticed the water's warmth. Even here, miles from the village, the effects of the underground steam vents could be felt.

Marcus approached silently, watching Alar stoop before him. He has grown up well, he thought. When he was a boy, he was nothing but trouble. As a man, he does the work of two.

Alar's frame, formerly thin, had solidified from the rigors of out woods work. He was angular and wiry, yet sported broad shoulders. His hair was long and curly, accenting his face as a frame does a painting. His features were fine boned, his eyes a deep green. The sun that deeply tanned him had lightened his once brown hair.

"Stop admiring yourself in the water's reflection," boomed Marcus, "there are no women here."

Alar stood, flicking water from his wet hands at Marcus, then crossed the stream, gracefully bounding from rock to rock. Marcus trudged after him, still laughing to himself.

"Marcus, your bugs were not the only reason that sleep eluded me. Have you ever seen the likes of last night?"

"No, my young friend, I have not. I will be a happy man if I don't see a repeat of last night's spectacle. I have seen much in my time, but nothing like last night's sky."

Alar agreed. "I feel the same way. It seemed that the very ground became cold and damp. For the first time in many years, I felt like a babe lost in the woods."

"You are a babe in the woods."

Alar ignored him and continued. "The trembling of the ground was like no earthquake I have ever seen, it sounded like an ax pounding against the mountains themselves. The shaking did not die down until the sun came up."

"I noticed it too," answered Marcus. "I am quite glad the sun rose this morning. I had my doubts about ever seeing it rise again. When the moon turned into a witch's eye, it tried to pull the Earth away from us. There are tales of the powers of the blue moon. After last night, I may just believe them."

Alar stopped for a moment. He looked at Marcus and spoke softly. "Though the moon is down, I still feel its presence. I know this sounds silly, but I can't shake the feeling that we are being watched."

Marcus laughed. "There are no ladies around here. We are alone in the woods. Rest assured, you are not being watched."

Hidden in the distance, dark eyes gazed unblinkingly at the two men. As Alar suppressed a shudder and looked up, their owner faded into the surrounding trees.

Catharvus paced in the grotto. Hatred burned inside him, his usual ill temper magnified by the indignities of imprisonment.

A great hunger gnawed at his insides. Using the spell book, he conjured up a meal of steaming food, ate a few bites, then spat out the mouthful. He threw his plate on the floor and resumed his pacing, his agitation growing with each step. Unmindful of where he walked, he trod upon the remnants of his meal. Vegetables and bits of mashed meat clung to his boots like seaweed to an ocean rock.

I have no taste for this food, he thought. It is disgusting to browse like an animal. This is not what I hunger for.

Catharvus reached inside his cloak, feeling for the hidden pocket. An audible sigh of relief escaped his lips as he felt the bulge within it. He withdrew an ornate dagger, his hands shaking as he fondled the knife. The dagger was made of silver, its blade remarkably untarnished considering the cave's dampness. The gemstones that encrusted its handle were priceless, wars had been started over items less valuable.

Catharvus spoke softly, his voice wavering with deep emotion. "They did not take you away from me. For that, I thank them." The dagger glowed weakly as the man spoke to it. Catharvus squeezed its handle, his hand relishing the warmth that radiated from its stones.

Catharvus knew that the spell book and orb were magically bonded to him. They could not be removed from his presence while he lived, for the magical forces would pull them back to him as surely as a magnet attracts iron filings. The dagger was another story. It came from a time before his magic. It possessed properties that he did not understand. Catharvus knew that it could not be magically protected. The thought of not owning it sent shudders down his twisted spine.

He thought back to the time he first saw the dagger. It lay forlornly at the bottom of deep mountain cave. An elfin skeleton, clothed in ancient garb, lay sprawled on the cave's floor, its outstretched hand reaching for the dagger. Judging by its position, the elf had fallen into the cave, then died while crawling towards the dagger.

Catharvus feared heights, yet felt drawn towards the knife. Overcome by the impulse, he climbed down the steep walls towards the cave's floor. He almost fell. Upon regaining his balance, he clung breathlessly to the sheer rock wall, his fingernails cracking as they strained to hold on.

His mind raced. Maybe the dagger was not worth the risks involved in getting it. The knife's blade deepened with pulsating waves of color. It seemed to be beckoning him. Driven by urges he couldn't seem to control, he took a deep breath to steel his nerves, then forced himself to resume his descent.

When he reached the cave's floor, he stepped over the skeleton and studied the dagger. The colorful gems seemed to call out to him. He reached for the knife and touched its handle. Powers flowed into him that changed the very fabric of his being. He felt as if the strengths of a thousand souls had flowed into his body.

He recalled the sensation. Never before had he possessed such energy. He kicked the skeleton aside and sprung against the cave's wall. In seconds, he had climbed out of the pit. He felt an intoxicating euphoria. That feeling had intensified and returned to him every time the dagger drew blood.

Catharvus' reverie was broken by the sound of scratching. The noise came from behind him, stopped, then restarted. Upon peering over his shoulder, he located its source. A small white mouse had snuck into the cave and was picking at the remains of his meal.

With movements that were imperceptibly slow, the sorcerer raised the dagger. As he turned towards the mouse, the blade began to glow. A soft pink color seemed to leach out of the handle and flow towards the tip, like sunset stained waters flowing down a river. The dagger's jeweled handle sparkled intently, almost as if the metal itself was becoming excited. The mouse, startled by the dagger's pink light, looked inquisitively at the mage. The hair on its back stood up as self-preservation instincts overrode those of hunger. It shuddered, then began backing away. With a lightning-like motion, the dagger seemed to launch itself from the wizard's hand. The blade's glow intensified noticeably as it neared the animal. It pierced the mouse's tail, pinning the squealing rodent to the floor. Though the wizard's spindly arms did not seem to possess the strength needed to throw it so hard, the blade lay buried deeply in the stone below the mouse. The creature screamed in fear, its nails scratching the ground as it tried to escape.

Catharvus smiled wearily, then walked towards the squirming rodent. He grasped the mouse by the nape of the neck, then roughly twisted the dagger out of the stone floor. The animal squealed from the pain, but for all its twisting and writhing, could not escape the wizard's grasp.

Catharvus pushed the mouse into his palm, exposing its underbelly. He nicked the mouse with the dagger, watching with anticipation as a drop of blood welled up from the shallow cut. He muttered ancient words while waving the dagger in the air. Energy lines formed, then coalesced at the knife's tip. The blade shined with the red-hot crimson light of a blacksmith's forge.

Catharvus dipped the dagger's glowing tip into the drop of the mouse's blood. The animal quivered, its eyes pleading. The wizard continued his chanting until the mouse stopped struggling, its body resting limply in his hand. In seconds, the mouse was cold to the touch.

The sorcerer looked at the fiery glow of his dagger. Its handle was hot, almost too hot for him to hold. Share some of that energy with me, he thought. If it were not for me, you would still lie in the dust of a forgotten cave.

Catharvus pulled back his sleeve. He ran the dagger across his arm until it reached the bend of his elbow. The skin there was crisscrossed by scars. Without hesitation, he plunged the dagger into his flesh. For a moment nothing happened, then the fiery red color of the blade faded as magical life energies left it and entered the sorcerer's pale arm. Catharvus' skin pinkened noticeably. He relished the warmth that flowed into his stiffened body. He felt energized and vital again.

He pulled the blade from his arm. It glowed a soft, lazy pink. Catharvus casually tossed the stiff body of the mouse over his shoulder, its life energies were now his own, he had no more use for it. The body landed in a crumpled pile near a rock.

Catharvus rolled the dagger in his hands. He spoke to the weapon as if it were a close friend. "When I free myself of this accursed chain, revenge would be ours. Together, we will bring forth the end of the 'Air Child' line. They will fall, and when their rotting corpses feed the beasts of carrion, the villagers will have no one to protect them. We will feast together!"

The dagger glowed an approving fiery red, its jewels glittering despite the caves subdued light.

The wizard sat down and opened his spell book. His memory of the spells was still foggy. Flipping through the pages intently, he paused, then smiled. His gnarled fingers tapped the page as he thought. "This is what I seek," he murmured. "It is time to let the good townsfolk of Dragon Springs know that Catharvus has returned."

Catharvus' spell book lay open to a page with a picture of an enlarging giant. Flowery writing spelled out the word Enlarge. The old man read eagerly, stroking his chin as he concentrated on the directions contained in the spell book. Catharvus' powers had not eroded with his years of enforced sleep, but his memory was foggy in places. Knowing the danger of a mistake, he opted to read his spell book like an apprentice, rather than risk having a spell misfire.

Catharvus began to recite the necessary words to visualize the magical energies. As the lines formed, he nodded approvingly at their green color. Following the book's directions, his hands deftly shaped and compacted the force lines into a fist sized mass. He smiled approvingly at the glowing packet that twisted in his hand, writhing like a bag of snakes.

He placed the swirling energy field carefully on the floor. The energies gave off an eerie glow as they whirled and danced before him.

Errant dust balls were sucked into the mouth of the spell's field. They popped out the base, enlarged to the size of watermelons.

Catharvus fished around in the pockets of his cloak. He withdrew the dried corpse of a spider from within its dusty confines. He stroked the brittle corpse, chuckling softly to himself. The spider's eyes stared blankly into his smiling face.

"Careful now," he muttered.

He stared at the swirling spell for a moment. After mentally measuring the distance between himself and the spell's mouth, he lofted the spider towards it. The sorcerer, not wanting to be crushed by his creation, dove backwards the moment the spider left his hand. The insect floated gently downward, picking up speed as the spell's suction drew it nearer. With a pop, it was drawn into the vortex.

A thunderous bang marked the spider's emergence from the base of the now used up spell. Clouds of dust billowed outwards as the spider carcass settled onto the floor. The mage ducked as two boulder sized dust balls floated by him.

As the dust cleared, Catharvus admired his handiwork. One end of the grotto was now filled by the body of an enormous spider. The head was lion sized. Its fangs could cover a man's hand and leave no flesh showing. If alive, the beast could easily eat a horse in one sitting. The creature's legs were as wide as a good-sized pine tree. They supported a body that must have weighed tons. The beast was covered by a glistening, black shell.

Catharvus walked to his creation and gave it a cautious push. The beast did not move. He pushed harder. Nothing happened. Catharvus' hand might as well be straining against the base of the mountain. The old man rapped his knuckles against the shell. A solid sound resonated back at him.

Catharvus slapped the animal in the face. "Can you hear me?" he yelled. The spider's multitude of black, grapefruit-sized eyes remained closed and lifeless.

"Time to animate it," Catharvus grunted. With growing anticipation, he thumbed through his spell book until he found the page bearing the Raise the Dead spell. He chanted arcane words and drew faint energy lines from deep within his body. The drain of his vital energies was immediately apparent. His shoulders stooped and his face paled as the energies left him.

Catharvus compressed his removed energies into a shimmering cloud. After exhaling, he inhaled, drawing the apple sized cloud back into his body. He walked to the spider and knelt in the dust before it. Cradling the animal's lifeless head in his arms, he pressed his lips against its mouth. How amusing he thought, kissing this spider will give me more satisfaction that kissing a tavern full of maidens.

Shrugging his shoulder, he exhaled, forcing both breath, and life into the giant insect's lungs.

The shell rose slightly, but nothing else seemed to happen. Catharvus stepped back a pace and stared at the spider. The animal's huge eyes slowly opened. It remained stiffly at attention.

Bringing the monster to life had drawn away much of Catharvus' vital energies. He stood wearily for a moment, then staggered back another pace. Drained of all strength, he slumped to the ground exhausted. Fatigue pulled intently at his eyelids as he fluttered between the worlds of sleep and awakedness. He barely saw the dark form moving towards him.

How long it has been since I have eaten, the spider thought. Prey lies before me. It is small and sickly, but will temporarily fill the emptiness in my gut.

The spider's leg brushed against a rock. The clatter of the stone as it skidded across the cave floor startled Catharvus. He shook himself awake, saw the spider, and began frantically back peddling across the grotto.

The spider was nearly upon Catharvus and gaining by the second. The sorcerer realized that he would not have time to consult with the spell book. Memory alone will have to do. He chanted frantically, waving his arms as he ran. A small brown disk of magical energy began to form in his right palm. The chain drew taut, stopping his escape.

The spider leaped towards Catharvus, knocking him to the floor. He groaned as the monster's weight slammed against him. Lying in the remains of his dinner, he knew that death was seconds away. He struggled, but could barely move. One of the spider's claws gripped his arm, tearing into the sallow flesh. Blood oozed from the wound, mixing with the dust and debris on the cave's floor.

Giant mandibles clicked in the air like monstrously large scissors. Coal black eyes focused on the sorcerer as he squirmed to avoid the jaws that snapped before him. The spider began to salivate. Thick globs of saliva dripped onto the sorcerer, stinging his eyes and gagging him with their odor.

The monster's jaws closed on the wizard's face and pressed against his flesh. The jaws, capable of splintering a large tree, pressed lightly into his flesh, but did not cut through. The brute is toying with me, Catharvus thought. It treats me like a house cat with a sparrow!

The knowledge that death was soon to occur, and that it was at the hands of one of his own creations, drove Catharvus to near insane levels of anger. With his fury came the strength of desperation. He ripped his arm free of the monster's claw, ignoring the bolts of pain that shot into his shoulder. He slammed the palm of his hand across the spider's forehead, activating the spell that he still held there. Spitting the thick saliva from his mouth, he shouted the word, "Obey."

The disk of magical energy flared brightly. The jaws clamping across his face continued to grip him, but did not tighten further.

The spider's weight was forcing the air from Catharvus' lungs. He felt the world beginning to spin as his vision dimmed to near darkness.

With all his remaining breath he yelled, "Get off me!" The words emerged in a hoarse whisper.

For a moment, nothing happened. Gradually, the pressure on the sorcerer's face decreased. The mandibles were opening! The monster stood up, then backed to the corner. It froze motionless as if awaiting further instructions.

Catharvus stood up shakily. He wiped his face on his sleeves, an action that only succeeded in smearing long streaks of mildew across his cheeks.

The spider stood at stiff attention, his body motionless, but his eyes fixed hatefully upon Catharvus. The wizard spat at the animal and laughed. He slapped the spider across the face.

"Try to eat me, you miserable bug."

He kicked at the spider, his boot glancing off the animal's armored shell.

No amount of abuse would sway the spider. It remained frozen in the grotto's corner, as immobile as one of the cave walls. Its eyes blazed with a fury that increased with each blow that the wizard rained upon it.

Catharvus laughed. "You await orders, my pet." He threw a rock at the animal that struck the side of its face. A trickle of purple blood dripped down, pooling in a viscous puddle at Catharvus' feet. "Move two paces back, you are soiling my living quarters."

The spider backed up, its eyes remained locked on the sorcerer as it moved. Catharvus nodded approvingly. He walked up to the beast and examined its mandibles. "Open you jaws," he commanded. A gap slowly formed between the spider's fangs. Catharvus put his hand between them and stroked their serrated surface. The animal's muscles quivered as it thought about snapping its jaws shut on the man that tormented it.

"Do not trifle with me!" Catharvus yelled. "You will not be pleased to find out the penalty for opposing my will." The spider started to snap its jaw shut, but stopped when an almost unbearable pain gripped the base of its skull and throbbed in time with its heart beat.

After a moment, the animal gave up its attempts, and stared hatefully at the man.

Catharvus whirled on his heels, purposefully exposing his back to the monster. He grabbed the crystal ball and approached the spider. It waited patiently, its muscles frozen like some oversized temple statue.

The old man repeated the crystal ball activation spell, this time shielding his hand with the sleeve of his gown. The fabric resisted the heat of the magical fire. He spoke the word "escape," again bringing up the images of the two woodsmen. The sorcerer held the ball in front of the spider's face, its eyes studied the men in the orb.

While the spider stared at the wavering image, the mage uttered commands.

"Seek..."

"Watch..."

"Kill."

The spider shuffled out of the cave and headed towards the forest.

Six freshly chopped trees lay at the woodsmen's feet. A small clearing was developing in what had previously been solid forest. Marcus was breathing heavily, his brow glistened with sweat. Alar looked none the worse for wear. His golden hair, tied in a braid behind his head, swung rhythmically as worked. He was neither sweating, nor breathing heavily.

Marcus winked. "You better take some time off. You look like you need the rest."

Alar smiled then resumed his assault on the tree. He grunted as his ax struck the bark, sending chips flying in all directions. A few more strokes left the tree standing upright, balanced precariously upon a slim pedestal of uncut wood. He looked up at the tree, then placed a finger against it. With a gentle push, the tree began its fall earthward.

"Down you go, my leafy friend," said Alar. "Marcus, your tree is the same size as mine. Why is it that yours is still standing?"

Marcus attacked his tree with renewed vigor. It soon joined its companion on the ground.

"Young man, you are a novice. Alar, try to stop showing your youth. I understand that you still do not appreciate the finer aspects of logging, but try to hide your inexperience! A true back woods master works with style, not speed. Logging is not a race, and anyway, what's your hurry? Do you have a pressing engagement back at the village? I know it can't be a new date. I have heard from reliable sources that there isn't a skirt you haven't chased left in the entire realm. I am sure that Dragon Springs will wait for you to get back."

Alar smiled as he shrugged his shoulders. Marcus always seemed to have a perfect comeback.

The woodsmen cut the trees into manageable sections. They knew that a wagon would arrive later that day to pick up the pieces and bring both the wood and the woodsmen back to the village.

Alar's ax soon brought down another tree. He paused for a second as the tree bounced on the forest floor before him.

"Cut out that loafing, you lazy cuss," barked Marcus.

Alar shot him a withering glance, then shouldered his ax, and walked to the upper part of the fallen tree.

"Don't get your underwear in a bunch," laughed Alar, "I'm looking for some healing moss. I hear that the supply in the village grows low."

Alar pulled back the branches at the tree's top. He knew that this was the only place that the moss grew, and though it was rare, its medicinal properties made it worth looking for. His search was rewarded when he found a small patch clinging to the tree's bark. Alar gently peeled the curly brown bit of fuzz off the tree and marveled that something that looked so plain could save lives. The village healer would be quite pleased to receive this natural treasure.

Alar had just placed the moss in his pouch when he heard a mournful squeaking noise. It disappeared before he could find its source. He stopped and listened closely. The squeaking started again. This time it lasted a bit longer, and he was able to home in on its source. It was coming from the middle of the fallen tree. Alar walked toward it and gently pushed the branches apart where he had heard the noise. It took his eyes a minute to adjust to the darkness, but when they did, he saw a small collection of twigs and straw. Two tiny heads peered out from it and stared back at him. They were baby birds that squeaked pleasantly at Alar as they stared at him with frightened eyes.

"It's a bird's nest," he chuckled, as he motioned for Marcus to come and look.

The chicks in the nest saw Marcus approaching and started peeping with fear. A sparrow, watching the two men from the trees, flew to the ground and fluttered in front of Marcus, trying desperately to draw him away from her children. The big man shoed the bird aside and looked over Alar's shoulder.

"They are baby sparrows," he said, as he stroked his beard. "I'm not really hungry, and anyway, they're too small to eat. Leave them be."

Alar shot him an amused glance. He pulled the bird's nest from the fallen tree, being careful to keep it intact. Ignoring the sparrow's desperate fluttering, Alar carried the babies towards a large tree at the end of the clearing. The mother bird following him, despondently chirping. He balanced the nest in one hand and climbed a crooked oak tree. He tucked the nest into a sheltered fork near the tree's top.

Marcus watched the rescue operation while slowly shaking his head. "That old oak is gnarled and twisted," he muttered. "It doesn't pay to cut it down. The chicks will be safe there."

"Well, now that you're done saving all of the forest's wildlife, would you mind coming down here and doing some work? Why is it that I have to do everything around here?"

Alar chuckled, then scrambled to the ground. The sparrow flew towards her now relocated nest. She perched for a minute besides it, making sure that nothing was amiss. When everything appeared to be all right, she stepped upon the nest's edge, then nestled down. She chirped contentedly as she drew her young to her breast.

Alar smiled and picked up his ax. He swung it at another tree.

"Marcus, you wouldn't really have eaten those babies, would you?"

"Not without proper seasoning..."

Dark eyes watched from the forest. A head nodded as their owner backed deeper into the brush.

Alar bundled the last of the wood, then set himself to the task of packing his gear. Marcus did likewise. Once packed, they turned towards the trail. They would clean up in the stream, then wait for the wood wagon to take them back to the village.

Marcus turned around slowly as he walked. He gazed up at the distant mountains, their purple walls rising in sharp contrast from the sea of forest green below them.

"Isn't it all beautiful, Alar? Being this close to nature makes the hours of labor worthwhile. I have loved this forest since I was a boy. I remember when your father first took me out to learn the ways of the woodsmen. I was a child then, much like you were on your first trip. Of course, I created far less trouble than you did! Do you recall the events that took place?"

Alar grimaced. He looked for ways to distract the big man, but none were readily apparent. Neither food, nor alcoholic spirits obliged him by appearing, no matter how much mental energy he expended trying to make them materialize.

Marcus sensed Alar's embarrassment and pressed onward.

"It seems to me that you were a young man of no more than seven. Of course you had already begun to look more like a noble woman's dance partner than a man of the woods, but we took pity on you and took you with us anyway."

"I remember the day well. You left with us at day-break. You were excited, but looked more than a little scared. I think that our company's looks didn't help."

"We were a group of maybe a dozen men. Ah, what a sight we must have been. The Orc wars had come to a close, and many of its veterans had returned to the village to resume their lives. Some of those men were still fighting the battle in their dreams. They were a rough bunch."

"We broke trail and entered a dark part of the forest. The trees fell before us. Despite your tender years, you swung that tiny hatchet like a warrior."

The large man's voice softened as he told the story. Though he tried his best to cover it, both pride and affection suffused his gruff baritone.

"By the early afternoon, your hands had become blistered. You were sweating and panting, your back was lathered like a racing stallion's. I had never seen you so tired. Despite your fatigue you pressed onward. You would not quit until the rest of the men did."

"Being the kind and gentle soul that I am, and fearing the wrath of your father, I decided that it would not do to bring home his son, dead from overwork."

Alar smiled, remembering how determined he had been to make Marcus proud of him. No amount of work would have made him quit that day! Alar also knew what part of the story was sure to come. He glanced around the trail, looking for any distraction, but alas, none presented themselves.

Marcus watched his companion out of the corner of his eye and chuckled to himself. After a painfully long pause, he continued.

"I figured the best way to save your life was to convince the others in the party to quit work. Once again, intelligence was rescuing youth. I broke out a fine bottle of distilled spirits and called the boys together to help me find out what the bottom of the bottle looked like. If I remember, I even asked you to join us."

Alar rolled his eyes, but Marcus ignored him.

"Anyway, you didn't join us. Other adventures awaited you. Should I continue my story?" chuckled Marcus.

Alar flushed slightly and shrugged his shoulders in much the same manner an oxen would when asked if he wants to plow the fields.

"You do want me to continue," he said with much emphasis on the word 'do'.

No reply.

"Good! Then I will! Let's see now. What happened? Oh yes, I remember. While we drank and relaxed, you wandered off into the woods to explore."

Marcus fought to keep from laughing. "You always were a bit on the brave side."

"If my memory serves me correctly, you heard a rustling coming from deep within the thicket. A lesser man would have avoided trouble and gone the other way. You, being a born adventurer, had to check it out. Working your way farther and farther into the dark forest, you homed in on the source of the sounds. You found something interesting, didn't you?"

Alar didn't answer.

"I'm talking to you son. What did you find? Surely you are not old enough to use failing memory as an excuse. What was in the thicket?"

Realizing that he had no means of escape, Alar reluctantly answered.

"I looked into the thicket and saw a unicorn colt. Its coat was a soft, tawny yellow. It had the largest brown eyes that I have ever seen. By the gods, it was beautiful. The colt was no more than three feet long and even shorter than I was. What I remember most of all was its golden wings. They glittered like precious metal, yet were gossamer thin."

Not willing to let his quarry off the hook this easily, Marcus cut in. "What was the unicorn colt doing when you found it?"

"It was trapped in the underbrush, I think."

"Did it look distressed?"

"Well, not when I first found it," admitted Alar. Despite himself, he was beginning to grin broadly.

"I remember now," replied Marcus. "You rescued the little colt. You dragged it, snorting and kicking, from the underbrush. Unfortunately, that is where its mother had placed it for safe keeping."

"The events are vividly returning to my memory," the big man boomed. "You pulled the baby unicorn from its lair to rescue it. It did not know that it was being rescued and let out a series of cries that sounded like a dragon birthing an egg sideways. Equally excited, you bellowed along with it. We heard the commotion and figured that you were being eaten by some monster with poor culinary tastes. Unfortunately, we arrived at the scene of the 'rescue' at the same time as the colt's mother did."

"What happened next Alar, my memory fades a bit?"

"I fought the winged mare," murmured Alar.

"Didn't quite catch that."

"I fought the horse," Alar sheepishly replied.

"Not so," laughed Marcus who was trying his best to keep his voice as stern as a judge's. "You were charged by the mare who ran at you, her horn lowered menacingly. She thundered towards you with eyes bulging and nostrils fairly spouting with steam. If I remember correctly, you turned tail and ran, squealing like a piglet as you fled."

"I saw what was happening and knew that I must save you. Despite my fatigue, I charged towards you as fast as my considerable bulk would allow. It was a heroic effort, but I couldn't reach you in time to protect you from the unicorn mare. She was enraged, as well she should be. You were attacking her colt!"

"My heart was filled with great sorrow. My best friend, a man who was like a father to me, gave me his son to teach. On his first trip, I allow him to get skewered by a fairy horse. What would I tell your father? I turned towards you to give you my last goodbyes."

"A lesser child would have given up, but not you. Always the tricky one, you dodged towards me, trying to pawn your problem off on me. The horse would have nothing to do with me, and adjusted its angle to follow you. I dove in front of the horse, trying to slow it down, offering myself as a target. It found you considerably more appealing, spread its wings, and took to the air. It flew over me, so closely that the wind off its back rustled my shirt and hair."

"Once past me, the horse swooped in on you, aiming its horn at your tiny behind. An instant before it was to have holed you, you tripped on a tree root and went flying. The unicorn's horn scraped under your belt and stuck there. The horse wheeled upwards into the air, screeching as it flew. Its colt, not wanting to be left out of the fun, charged after it and took to the air."

"For reasons that only the horse knows, it suddenly decided to take pity on you. Maybe it was the first example of your now legendary ability with women, I don't know. The flying mare flew in rapid upwards spirals until it reached the tree tops. It pushed you into the top of the tallest pine in the realm, then backed off while you clung to the tree like a dwarf does to a pot of gold."

"The mare hovered while the colt circled you twice, snorting and pawing at the air. They then flew off, leaving me with the problem of getting you down."

Alar grinned, his embarrassed flush fading.

"That was quite an introduction to the art of woodsmanship." Alar winked. "Once again let me thank you for opening a bottle when you were supposed to be watching me."

"You should have joined the party. You were punished for your snobbery!"

Alar smiled. He seemed to lose himself in thought for a moment. His eyes went blank as his thoughts took him far away. "I have no anger towards the unicorns," he said. "They were only trying to protect themselves. What I remember most is the softness of their coats and the beautiful deepness of their eyes. They took me flying. I was terrified at the time, but strangely, I enjoyed it. I still dream of it. Not a night goes by when I do not take to the air in my sleep. I would like to fly again though preferably without a horn scratching my bottom!"

Both men laughed. They talked animatedly as they walked the trail.

The men were so engrossed in their conversation that neither one heard the soft rustling sounds behind them. A shadowy figure followed them, keeping well off the trail. It watched them with eyes as black as burnt bone.

As Marcus and Alar walked onward, two figures burst out of the trees and blocked their path. They were Orcs though they were dressed more like bandits than soldiers.

Alar's eyes narrowed as he took in the sight of them. They were a mangy, but solid pair. The bigger of the two stopped in front of Marcus. He was about five feet tall, and very heavily muscled. By the way he gave orders, it was clear that he was in command. He was wearing a well-traveled breast plate, and had a matted, drooping mustache that covered a mouthful of pointed yellow teeth. He carried a slightly notched and rusted sword, the tip of which was now resting against the soft part of Marcus's throat.

The other Orc was slightly smaller, and far more nervous. He fought unsuccessfully to control a tic that rhythmically contorted the left side of his face. He fondled a greasy dagger as he scampered about.

Both had skin that was gray and crisscrossed with scars. Blood stained the clothing of the smaller one.

The beady black eyes of the smaller Orc flitted from Marcus to Alar. "Well, my human friends, You two must be a brave man indeed. You are deep in the woods, alone and unarmed. It is not like your kind to travel in such small groups. What is to protect you from the evil creatures that lurk out here?"

His face spasmed as he spoke, sending a shower of saliva in Alar's direction. Alar recoiled, causing the larger Orc to burst into laughter. His breastplate, an ill-fitting affair probably scavenged from a soldier's grave, rasped and grated against his skin as he laughed.

"We are woodsmen, working the nearby clearing," said Marcus, abruptly ending their hysterics. "We have no quarrel with you. Let us pass."

"I am Zerep," replied the larger Orc, his eyes now deadly serious. "Nobody tells me what to do. I will let you pass if it so suits my purpose. Right now, it does not. Shut up! If you speak again, the next noise you make will be your death scream." He looked at his smaller comrade. "Theeb, take their gear."

Theeb scampered towards Alar and grabbed his pack. He tried to pull it out of the woodsman's grasp, but Alar held tight.

"Do not trifle with me," roared Zerep. With a subtle twist of his wrist, he turned his sword, starting a trickle of blood flowing from Marcus' throat.

"Last warning human," he sneered. "Next time the blade runs him through. Let go of the pack, now!"

Alar's green eyes blazed with hatred, but his grip slowly loosened.

Theeb quickly relieved Marcus of his gear, then searched both men for hidden weapons. "They carry nothing," he yelled.

While Theeb searched, Zerep kept his blade lodged against Marcus' throat. He seemed to enjoy the sight of the dripping blood, for his smile grew with the swelling of each drop that formed.

"Check their packs," the larger Orc suggested. He spoke to Theeb, but he never took his eyes off the blood dripping from Marcus' neck.

Theeb gibbered to himself as he tore open the bags, throwing their contents about. A loaf of dark bread, some hard cheese, a few cloth rags, and two terra cotta jugs soon lay on the trail.

"Garbage!" yelled Zerep. "Not a single coin or gem!"

Theeb picked up the bread and sniffed it. He took a tentative bite, grimaced and threw the loaf into the bushes. "Yuck. Grain, not meat!" The taste of the cheese sent his face into convulsions of twitching. "This is rotten, I wouldn't give it to a pig!"

Both Orcs unstoppered the jugs. Zerep raised one jug to his lips, his sword never wavering as he drank. He spit a mouthful of clear fluid on the ground. "Water," he said with disgust. He smashed the jug against a tree.

Theeb was guzzling the contents of his jug when Zerep cuffed him. "Give it here," he demanded as he grabbed the jug. He tilted the jug back, draining it of the last of Marcus' ale. He tossed it into the bushes, then looked down the blade of his sword at Marcus.

"Ahhh," he said, wiping a long-nailed hand across his mouth. "That was of some value. Too bad for you that there was so little left."

Marcus raised his eyebrows in an expression of mock sorrow.

Zerep looked down at the wreckage of the two men's packs. "We must take something. "We have traveled far to reach this wretched spot. Our long journey has made me quite tired and hungry."

Zerep frowned. His brow wrinkled, breaking loose a bit of crust that had lodged there. His gray lips turned downward in an exaggerated frown, but his eyes sparkled with glee.

Theeb had heard this type of conversation before and was rubbing his hands together in anticipation. His face danced in a near continuous spasm.

"What might we take? What shall be the reward for our efforts?" pondered the larger Orc. "Theeb, watch the fat one for me."

Theeb drew his dagger and walked over to Marcus. He made a great show of flashing the greasy blade in front of the man's face. Once he had sidled over to the big man, he reached up with a filthy hand and dipped it into the blood that was congealing on Marcus's neck. His finger smeared the blood, tracing a dotted line across Marcus' throat. He then withdrew his blood-stained finger while smacking his lips greedily. He placed the bloody finger in his mouth.

"Tasty," he said. All I have to do is to run my dagger across the lines. There will be much blood for me. That is good. That is good. Poor Theeb gets thirsty in the hot sun!"

Zerep watched his partner taste Marcus' blood. "I don't think the other human is as delectable. He looks a bit scrawny compared to your corpulent specimen."

Zerep spun his sword blade idly. He looked at Marcus as he spoke, but watched Alar out of the corner of his eye. The Orc suddenly whirled, striking Alar on

the temple with the flat of his blade. The blow stunned
Alar. He staggered backwards as his vision wavered and
dimmed.   Dizziness overcame him as he fought to
maintain consciousness. His eyes fluttered shut as he
collapsed to the forest floor.

The Orc straddled the fallen man's chest and
pulled a dagger from his belt.

"Ears are tasty," he said. "Unlike Orcs, you
humans have no hair on your ears. It looks disgusting,
but makes the flesh most tender. I believe that is what I
like most about your kind."

Marcus suddenly began to stagger around. He
looked quite queasy as he whimpered to the Orcs. "You
must stop this. This is a crime against nature. I cannot
bear to see this! Don't make me look!"

The smaller Orc gibbered with excitement at his
captive's distress.

"But look you shall, human. I want you to watch
as I carve each delectable slice. Orcs have fine table
manners, you know. You will not go hungry. I am sure
that we will let you enjoy some of his tasty flesh before
we kill you," he laughed. Marcus looked like he was
about to vomit. Theeb jumped about. "Of course, we
would feed it to you raw!" he yelled. "Cooking can
destroy the meat's subtle flavor."

Marcus shrieked, then collapsed limply against the Orc. His face was pale, his eyes closed. Marcus' considerable weight caused the Orc to stagger. Theeb relaxed his grip on the woodsman, letting him fall to the ground.

"Weak hearted swine," the Orc spit out, as he watched the man fall. "What are you worried about? We wouldn't eat you. I hate fatty meat anyway."

"Fat?" roared Marcus as he hit the ground and rolled to his feet in one fluid movement. "This is solid muscle! Taste it, you cowardly vulture."

As he spoke, he moved with a speed and grace surprising for so large a man. He lowered his shoulder and crashed into the orc with a bone shaking thud. Marcus grabbed Theeb's dagger arm with both hands and twisted as his full weight landed on it. The crack of breaking bone echoed through the woods.

Theeb cried out in pain as Marcus ripped the dagger out of his now useless hand.

Marcus sprung to his feet and leapt towards Zerep. The big Orc cursed, jumped up from his dazed prisoner, and dodged out of the big man's way. He sheathed the dagger and redrew his sword in one fluid motion.

The two circled each other warily. Marcus tossed the dagger from hand to hand as he stalked the Orc. Zerep swung his sword in a whistling arc, trying to behead the crouching man. The rusty blade, still stained with Marcus' blood, barely missed. The steel passed close to Marcus' head, far closer than he would have liked. A wisp of gray hair fluttered to the ground, cleaved off by the Orcish blade. The momentum from the swing twisted the Orc. As Zerep's body turned with the blade, Marcus saw an opening. He darted in, grabbing his opponent in a bear like grip. Marcus squeezed hard, noting with satisfaction the grunt that involuntarily escaped the big Orc's lips.

"Drop the sword now," he yelled. Zerep continued to struggle. Marcus squeezed harder. An Orcish rib snapped with a sharp popping sound. Zerep screamed in pain and let his sword fall to the ground. Marcus released him and watched as he collapsed to the forest floor. The Orc knelt before Marcus, his head bowed as he gasped for breath.

Marcus backed away from the Orc, sliding its sword with his foot. He stooped to pick it up, never once taking his eyes off Zerep.

He tapped the Orc's neck with the flat part of the sword. "I have your weapons. Leave now and do not return. No more blood will be spilled. If you stay, you will lose more than just your weapons."

The Orc looked up at Marcus with astonished eyes.

"I tried to kill you, yet you let me live? If the roles were reversed, I would watch while Theeb killed you slowly."

"That is not our way."

Zerep nodded, slowly breaking into a smile.

"My fat friend, it should be," he said as Theeb, his right arm still hanging limp, smashed a rock into the back of Marcus' skull.

The unexpected blow knocked Marcus senseless. As he lay unconscious on the trail floor, Zerep kicked at his unprotected ribs. Alar heard the sounds of the beating filter through the fogs of unconsciousness. He forced himself to open his eyes, and immediately regretted the attempt, as his head throbbed mightily. With blurred vision, he took in the scene before him. Zerep was pounding away at his defenseless friend.

He saved my life, thought Alar. I must do something to help him!

Alar tried to stand, but was still dazed from the blow to his head. The world spun before him, and he fell back to the ground. Alar sat up and began to crawl towards his friend. Zerep watched as Alar struggled to reach Marcus. He walked to the younger man, pushed him on his back, and stooped low to taunt him.

"Your friend sleeps like a baby. You are too stunned to stand, you stagger like a drunken fool. You humans are pathetic. Hunting squirrels would be more challenging. Well, at least you two will feed us well."

Alar again tried to get to his feet, but the Orc stopped him by stepping firmly against his chest.

He turned towards Theeb and spoke. "Get rope and firewood. I will bind them, then we shall burn them alive. Maybe we can cook the fat off the older one."

Theeb sat on Alar's chest as Zerep bound Marcus' wrists and ankles. Zerep then turned his attention to Alar. The big Orc knelt and tied him securely. As he stood up to admire his work, he saw something at the end of the trail. Stretching forward, he sniffed intently at the gentle wind that blew towards him.

"What is it," whimpered Theeb?

"Humans. I would know that smell anywhere. There are many of them! They approach on some kind of wagon. It is hard to know for sure, but judging by the strength of their scent, it won't be long until they get here.

Theeb swore loudly. His facial twitching reached a new level of intensity.

Zerep squinted his eyes and stared at the approaching men. "The villagers must be coming to gather the wood that these fools cut. They will be here soon. This is so unfair, the hunger in my belly grows."

Zerep drew his dagger from its sheath. He knelt on Alar's chest. The cobwebs cleared from Alar's head as he fought against the Orc's weight. He stared at the dagger and struggled frantically against his bonds. Zerep grabbed him roughly by the face while he held his dagger above Alar's throat.

"Look at me," he yelled. "Look into my eyes. My face will be the last thing you see as a living being. I want you to take my image with you into the underworld."

Alar was not looking at the Orc. Instead, he blinked his eyes rapidly, desperately trying to focus on the shadowy form that stepped out of the woods behind the Orc. The figure was murmuring and waving its hands in a serpentine manner.

"Look at me you sniveling coward," Zerep thundered.

The Orc slid his hand to the man's hair, grabbing a handful. He yanked on it, tilting Alar's head backwards, exposing his throat. His bloodshot eyes locked onto Alar's. He smiled, then plunged the dagger downward.

Alar's world exploded into sparks as blinding waves of color engulfed him. The dagger flew from Zerep's hand and landed harmlessly on the ground near Alar's feet. Zerep's weight remained on Alar's chest, but his grip on the man's hair seemed to loosen. Alar wiggled and forced himself into a sitting position.

The Orc tumbled off him, landing on its back on the forest floor. Zerep's eyes stared lifelessly upwards. Where previously a breastplate had been, there now was a smoking mass of molten metal. His chest and torso were missing, replaced by smoldering, charred flesh.

Theeb shrieked and ran off into the woods.

With Herculean effort, Alar struggled free of his bonds. He stumbled to his feet. and ran to Marcus. His friend lay face down, bleeding from a scalp wound, but did not appear to have been stabbed. Alar picked up one of the shredded rags from the forest floor and dressed Marcus' wound as best as he could. He untied the ropes that bound him. With a gentle shake, he brought the big man back to consciousness. Marcus looked up and saw Alar's concerned face. He weakly smiled and with Alar's help, pulled himself to a sitting position.

"Nice going sport," he said. He started to rub the back of his head where the rock had struck him. "What a hangover. Remind me, no booze, ever again."

"If you hadn't guzzled down three fourths of the ale, the Orc's might have left us alone!"

Marcus shrugged, then winced as the action started his head pounding again. He looked at the smoldering remains of the Orc and raised his eyebrows in a most impressed manner.

"When did you learn that trick?"

"I didn't do it. I was lying flat on my back, trying to keep from gagging from the smell of our gray friend. Besides, you know how I hate magic. It must have come from over there," he said as he pointed down the trail.

There was no one to be seen on the trail except for the men on the wagon rounding the corner in the distance.

The wagon full of villagers soon arrived.

Alar called out to his friends as he worked on Marcus' wound, "Boys, come quickly and help me! We were attacked, and Marcus is hurt."

The burly woodsmen jumped out of the wagon and rushed to Alar's side.

"By the love of the forest god's, what happened here?" a bearded mountain of a man asked.

"We ran into two orcish bandits," answered Alar. "Rolf, hold pressure on Marcus' wound for me. I am feeling a bit dizzy."

"Well, you ought to feel dizzy. Look at the lump that is forming on your forehead. Get in the wagon now, I will take over here."

"Thanks, my good man," Alar sighed. "I think that the sooner I get horizontal, the sooner my head will stop throbbing!"

Alar crawled into the wagon and watched some of the bigger woodsmen carry Marcus to the wagon.

"We ought to put you on a diet," grunted Brokus. "You weigh more than a two-hundred-year-old pine tree!"

"When is the last time you got a fat lip from a two-hundred-year-old pine tree?" asked Brokus' cargo.

While Marcus was being loaded onto the wagon, some of the other men helped by collecting Alar and Marcus' belongings.

"You men are injured, and need medical attention," observed Joseph, the group's leader. "The cut wood can wait. I say we turn this wagon around now, and head back to the village. We will come back later for the logs, and we will carry swords as well as axes. Who knows how many more of those mangy gray skinned orcs are waiting for us in these woods?

One of the men in the wagon had some training in the healing arts. His name was Burnsie. He had stout arms, and hair the color of Alar's, though much less of it. He removed the crude dressing that Alar had applied and examined Marcus' scalp wound.

Burnsie whistled softly as he probed the laceration. "How'd you do that?"

"Trying to knock down a tree with my head," replied Marcus through clenched teeth.

Ignoring him, Burnsie set to work. He flushed the wound with water from his canteen.

"This water is from Dragon Springs, it will help purify the wound."

He opened his bag of supplies, took out a soft cloth and dried the wound. He looked in his pouch, and cursed softly.

"Damn, I am totally out of Velvet Moss. Alar, did you find any of that brown moss on the trees you were cutting? I used up the last of it yesterday."

Alar groaned as he pulled himself to a sitting position. He reached for his pouch and pulled out the two bits of brownish fuzz. Burnsie gratefully took them, shredded them into a fine powder, then added enough water to make a thick paste. He pressed the polstice into Marcus' scalp wound. The big man flinched.

"Brace yourself," Burnsie scolded. "You are acting like the biggest baby in the village. I am going to sew the wound edges closed. This may hurt a bit."

Marcus' eyes opened wide with fear as he sat bolt upright. "Burnsie, I thought you were my friend. You can't do this to me! I won't be able to stand it! I'll need something to deaden the pain."

Alar had to bite his lip to keep from laughing. He had been around Marcus long enough to recognize his acting.

One of the other villagers reached into his pack and pulled out a bottle of distilled spirits. "Here you go Marcus," he said, his brow wrinkling with concern. "Try some of this. It might help dull the pain."

Marcus stretched out a wavering hand and took the bottle. He shot a wink at Alar, then drained half the bottle in one swallow."

"Ahhh," he said. "I feel better already. Burnsie, you may begin sewing, just keep the medicine nearby!"

Burnsie set to the task of pulling the wound edges together. He used a forged needle and cotton thread to close the wound and stop the bleeding. Marcus fussed and whined on a regular basis, but his friends didn't seem to mind. The procedure had to be stopped twice for Marcus to reload on anesthesia.

Burnsie smiled as he watched his patient latch onto the bottle. "Oh that I were a wizard. Knowledge of magic would really help now. A few seconds of a 'Healing Spell' would fix your scalp and save our drink. If that didn't work, at least I could throw a 'Silence' spell on you!"

Alar shook his head. "Your magic sure helped earlier. You blasted that Orc seconds before he would have killed me. Since when did you expand your studies into the magical arts? I always thought that you were content to be a healer."

"It wasn't I," laughed Burnsie. "You know me better than that. If I could harness magic, the first thing I would do is to figure out how to turn base metal into gold. When you see me slaving besides you in the fields, you know that I haven't mastered the magical arts."

"Well then, which of you did it?" Alar demanded. "Who killed the orc, and saved my life? Which of my fellow woodsmen has been keeping his knowledge of the earth energy arts a secret? Who is the sorcerer in our midst?"

Murmurs of denial arose among the men.

Joseph, the oldest man on the wagon spoke up. "Alar, none of us knows magic. This area hasn't seen magic for generations." With his flowing white beard, Joseph looked more like a magical scholar than a woodsman. He was quite knowledgeable in historical lore. It seemed appropriate that he answer Alar's questions.

"Joseph," Alar asked the old man, "my father does not speak highly of magicians or magic. For as long as I can remember, he has told me that it is nothing more than the tool of evil tricksters. Does magic exist outside of tavern shows? Is it ever used for good purposes?"

"Yes, my brave friend, it does, or at least it did exist. The sect of the 'Air Children' lived here many years ago. Legend says that they started off as a group that was more closely linked to the land than the rest of the villagers. They studied nature and learned to control its forces. Their group practiced the arcane arts in the forests, avoiding unnecessary contact with the other villagers. Over time, they became powerful magicians."

"They were rarely seen, but they were a good lot. They seemed to know just when they were needed, and would appear seemingly out of the air itself. They healed us when we were injured, then disappeared back into the woods to remain unseen until the next time that their services were required."

"Did you know that it was the Air Children who added magical fire to the waters of Dragon Springs? In ancient days, the waters were icy cold. As you know, they now flow steaming hot all year round. Even during the coldest part of the winter, we count on that spring for heat and unfrozen water."

"What drove them away," Alar asked?   "My father says they killed many people, then left in shame?"

"I do not know the reason they left," he answered. "Legend has it that one of their kind strayed from the chosen path. His deeds were so horrible, that the Air Children banished themselves so that their kind could never cause harm to innocents again. It is not known where they went, or if they still live. Generations have gone by since anyone has seen one of them. It is said that they will one day return, if the need is great. I, for one, would be happy if they did."

Alar listened to Joseph's words attentively, but shook his head in involuntarily disagreement. His father's stories of evil magicians raining death onto misbehaving children still rung in his ears. Nightmares of mystical spells wrenching life from his helpless body haunted him for as long as he could remember. causing even now, the dream caused him to shudder as if a cold wind had blown across his neck. Joseph saw him grimace and shook his head sadly.

Marcus' surgery was now over. He sat up and gingerly touched his wound. It was now neatly sewn and dressed. He returned the empty sprits bottle to its former owner, and smiled. "Thanks," he laughed, "that almost made the procedure worth doing!"

Marcus turned around to face Alar. He wobbled slightly, but was smiling like a dragon in a pen of sheep. His graying hair, always unruly, now sported a sparse patch where the Orc's sword had grazed him.

"Glad to see you're with us," Alar laughed. "Nice haircut!"

Marcus' reply was drowned out by a hideous, nonhuman scream that floated down the trail. The men looked back, but could see nothing. Rolf snapped the reins, and the wagon thundered towards the village at a gallop.

The giant spider prowled the woods looking for the two woodsmen it had seen in the magician's crystal orb. The "Obey" spell controlled its mind. It had no choice but to kill Alar and Marcus. Before it could kill them, it had to find them.

The orders did not please the spider. Great hunger gnawed at it. It had lain a withered corpse in the sorcerer's cloak for years. It was now alive and healthy. It desperately wanted food!

It homed in on the clearing where the men had been chopping wood. As it approached the spot that the sorcerer had sent it to, it noted that others had been in the area. The scent of warm-blooded flesh clung to the trees and bushes surrounding the clearing. Something had hidden in the shadows of the trees. Judging by its scent, it hadn't bathed in some time.

The spider stopped to examine the ground before it. The grass and leaves were pushed aside as if two thick bodies had passed that way. Its primitive mind flashed a caution signal. It ignored it. The hunger inside, coupled with the sorcerer's orders, had removed its normal wariness.

The spider began to move forward again, its hunger growing with each step. When it reached the clearing, it would find the men, watch them, and eat them all in the same moment's time. It must follow Catharvus' orders to seek, watch, and kill. Its orders said nothing about how long it must spend seeking and watching.

The trees rustled to its left. Something was coming, and judging by the noise it was making, it was either very clumsy, or moving in a great hurry. The spider crouched in the underbrush, its muscles tensed to strike.

Theeb ran as fast as his gray legs would carry him. The image of Zerep's death burned in his mind. In the span of one moment, they had gone from triumph to tragedy. What kind of trickery did the humans use to kill his comrade?

He burst through a thicket of bushes, then stopped dead in his tracks. Before him lay a monster drawn from the depths of his worst nightmare. It was two tons of bristling, jet black evil, watching him with clusters of eyes the size of drinking mugs.

He stared at the abomination, his muscles frozen in fear. The little Orc grabbed his dagger as the spider leapt through the air and slammed him to the forest floor. Theeb thrust at it with his knife, but the blade bounced uselessly off the spider's hard shell.

The spider's mandibles opened widely, and it began to salivate. Staring at its helpless prey, the spider crouched downward until its mandibles encircled the orc's neck. Theeb kicked and fought with all his strength, but couldn't escape. As the mandibles glistened in the dappled light of the forest floor, Theeb began to shriek with the terror of one who sees his own grave open before him.

The spider snapped its jaws together. The serrated edges of its mandibles made a clicking noise as they cleaved the flesh of Theeb's neck, snapped his spine, then interlocked neatly in its center. A high-pitched whistling sound continued for perhaps ten seconds as the Orc's lung muscles obeyed its brain's final order and continued to force air through a throat that was no longer there to scream.

The spider greedily sucked the juices out of the Orc's head, then leisurely turned towards the body for a full meal.

The wizard gazed into his crystal sphere, then screamed in frustration. His careful plans were unraveling before his eyes. The foretelling orb had shown the woodsmen when he questioned it about escape. He had sent the spider to kill the men and drag their corpses back to his prison. Instead of having the bodies of the woodsmen, he had nothing. He remained chained in a cave like an animal, still suffering from the Air Children's punishment.

He held his dagger up to the light. Curse my luck, he thought. First wandering Orcs nearly steal the men away from me, then my insect stops the chase for a roadside snack. Nothing is working! When will these delays cease?

He looked at the dagger, then spoke to it. "We shall escape, my friend. You and I will leave this place, and when we do, nothing will stand in our way!"

He gazed back at the crystal ball, letting his mind wander.

Magic was used in freeing the woodsmen, he thought. The residual traces look like Earth energies. An Air Child must be involved. I saw none in the orb's scan of the woods, but that is not unexpected. A good sorcerer can block his image from the orb.

"They must still be in the area," he sighed. The dagger's color darkened in response to his words.

Those miserable, pigeons continue to torment me, he thought. The fact that their race has survived surprises me. I am sure they haven't changed. Imagine, using the magical energies to cure snot-nosed kids and to heat bathing water. Their trifling is a perversion of the arcane arts.

He pulled up his sleeve and gazed at the tattoo that adorned his forearm. He brushed at the image of a bird, tracing its graceful outlines with his fingers. For a moment, hatred seemed to flow out of his body. He looked like a kindly, old man. His finger drifted down to the dagger that impaled the bird. It was drawn by a different hand. Its strokes were cruder, more hurried and sloppy.

The mage absentmindedly fondled his dagger. It again began to glow, its jewels glinting in the dim light of the cave. He placed the dagger against his forearm and studied it next to the image tattooed on his skin. The drawing matched the dagger in every detail.

"Not a bad likeness of you," he murmured.

A faint energy field formed around the dagger, then crackled as it flowed into Catharvus' hand. His back stiffened, his bearing changed. Hate seemed to suffuse every pore of his being.

He spoke to the dagger. "If the woodsmen prove an elusive prey, others can be used. Kill enough foot-soldiers and you will stop an army, just as surely as if you slay the general. It looks like the townsfolk will have to start dying. Pity, such a pity!"

He began to laugh. The dagger emitted a pulsating light that eerily matched his laughter.

The wagon with the woodsmen returned to the village of Dragon Springs at a full gallop. As they rounded the last bend in the road, Rolf began to rein in the horses. The sound of their throaty whinnying, added to the squealing of the wagon's brakes cut through the quiet air like a storm wind. From throughout the village, people came running.

Marcus' wife Barona, heard the commotion, and put down the sweater she was knitting. She joined the throng of townspeople that were milling around the wagon. When she saw her husband being helped from the wagon, a look of concern clouded her beautiful features. She hesitated for a second, then pushed her way to the front of the crowd.

"By the god's, look at you!" she yelled, as she stared at the bloody bandage that covered her husband's forehead. "Are you alright?"

"I think I am, my queen," Marcus replied, as he gazed into her hazel eyes. Mounds of dark curls framed her face, making her stare more penetrating. Her look of concern changed as she got close enough to smell the alcohol on his breath.

"You smell of alcohol again," she growled at him. "Let me guess, you got drunk and fell down. Probably cracked your head open on one of the logs you were supposed to be bringing back. Well, despite the bandage, and the alcohol, you look well enough to walk. Come with me, sir, you have some explaining to do."

With that proclamation, she grabbed her husband and dragged him through the crowd and towards their house. Alar chuckled as she heard Marcus desperately trying to explain the attack by the Orcs to his wife.

"It is the truth, I swear it!"

"Sure, and I suppose a lightning bolt flashed down from the sky to rescue you. No way Marcus! I have spent half of my life listening to your stories. Don't you think for a moment that I believe this one. I saw the bruises on Alar. You two probably got into a fight in a pub again. Didn't you? Honestly man, when are you ever going to grow up?"

Alar stepped out of the wagon as Marcus and Barona turned a corner and walked out of sight. With Marcus gone, Alar took the brunt of the crowd's attention. He told his story to first on man, then another. When he had told all the people that gathered around the wagon about the attack, a fresh group gathered, and wanted to hear about the Orcs. Finally, it became too much, and Alar fled to the safety of his cottage.

Since they had survived an attack by Orcs, and since magic was mysteriously used, Marcus and Alar had become instant celebrities. Word travels quickly in a small town, and Dragon Springs was a tiny village. The story of the woodsmen's encounter with the Orcs was passed around faster than the rumors that started when Burnsie's twin daughters got drunk and passed out behind the stables. Uninvited guests dropped by Alar's home on a regular basis, both to offer support, and to hear the story first hand.

Days of constant attention from the curious townsfolk were starting to get to Alar. It seemed he had told his story to every man, woman and child in the village. He needed to get away from them for a while. The headache he was getting from the unwanted attention threatened to eclipse the one caused by the Orcish sword.

Alar needed some time alone, and he knew that he wouldn't be getting it in town. There was a place where even the most curious villager wouldn't follow him. Maybe his headache would disappear if he could make it there. Alar packed a light lunch, turned his back to the Dragon Springs fountain, then hiked out of town.

Miles away, dark eyes gazed approvingly into a crystal orb. Leave the safety of your friends, thought Catharvus. Travel to lonely places where I can more easily reach you. It seems your stupidity is even greater than your luck.

Alar walked on, unaware of the plans that were being made against him. He followed the water as it flowed from the springs and became the Dancing River. Being outdoors gave him great pleasure. The air smelled of greenness, and the murmuring sound of the water flowing over the rocks put his mind at rest. He hiked onward, following the current, letting his thoughts drift with the swirls and eddies of the water. As the river turned towards the mills, he let himself wander off the trail. Alar reached the rubble that separated the Dancing River from the base of the Dragon Spine mountains. He looked upwards, then nodded as his eyes focused on a spot far in the distance. He was soon climbing rocks and boulders as he worked his way up the mountain's side. He climbed until the sun shone high in the noontime sky.

When he looked down, the river was reduced to an iridescent ribbon glittering beautifully in the gorge below. On its banks sat his village. The hot springs caused the air behind the village to shimmer. From this vantage point, the view was breathtaking.

Alar turned away and resumed his climb. The sound of falling water came faintly from above. He worked his way towards it, knowing that he was nearing his destination. Disguised by a heavy growth of ferns and mossy fallen rocks was the opening of a cave. Water tumbled out of a cleft in the rocks twenty feet below the cave's mouth.

The cave had been a favorite place of Alar's since he was a boy. Hot water from the underground springs bubbled up a shaft in the rocks to a spot in the cave's roof. The water cascaded down from the ceiling, forming a natural waterfall. The waters collected in a depression in the cave's floor, producing a waist high pool. The magical properties of the spring's water kept the pool spotless. A delightful scent, like crushed wild flowers, emanated from the water itself. The water circulated through the pool, then overflowed the back wall and drained down the side of the mountain from the crack below the cave's entrance. The steaming waterfall could be seen from the village, yet few knew of the hidden cave, and even fewer had the athletic ability to manage the climb to get to it.

Alar had visited the cave often as a child. It had always been a special place for him, a place where he could go to get away from it all.

The events of the day before, coupled with the long climb, had exhausted Alar. He lay down behind a large bolder to rest and eat his lunch.

As he relaxed, he looked at the sky and daydreamed. His thoughts turned to flying, to floating unfettered by gravity's bonds. As if to punctuate his dream, a beautiful white dove banked out of the sky and flew into the cave above him. The creature did not see him as it wheeled in midair to navigate the vine choked entrance.

Alar finished his lunch. The rest had renewed his energy, he was ready to move on. The boulders of the steep cliff wall rapidly passed below his feet. He soon found himself outside the cave's entrance. Alar closed his eyes and inhaled deeply. The steam rising off the waters smelled so beautiful, he could easily believe he was standing by the bath of a regal princess.

As Alar approached the entrance of the cave, the noise of the falling water rose in volume. The water's noise blotted out almost all the noises from the village below. The unbroken sound of falling water was one of the things that attracted Alar to this place. He could bask in the tepid waters while their perfumed scent filled his head with delight. No outside sounds would distract him. The water supported his body in an almost sensual, weightless caress. In the world of the secluded cave, he was as close to flying as he could ever be.

Alar entered the cave. Years spent in the woods made his approach silent, though above the din of the falling water, it need not have been. He slipped through the tropical vegetation that flourished around the constant heat and moisture provided by the steam.

Alar stepped into the cave, temporarily blinded by the sharp drop off in light. When his eyes adjusted to the dimness, he gasped. He was not alone in the cave.

CH 14

Alar stared in amazement.

Before him, still unaware of his presence, was a naked woman! She was stunning. His breath caught in his throat as her beauty overwhelmed his senses.

Alar had seen his share of women. He had a social life that by any criteria would be called an active one, yet he had never seen anyone whose beauty remotely compared to that of the woman who stood in front of him.

She was stepping into the waterfall's pool, intent on bathing. Her skin was unblemished and pale. It shone in the cave's dim light with the luster of a fine pearl. She had a firm body with a narrow waist and well-proportioned breasts. She was slim, yet looked toned and muscular. Her shape reminded Alar of a statue he had once seen in the ruins of an ancient temple. She moved with the grace of a dancer as she entered the water.

The woman slowly slid into the pool, relaxing as her body sank beneath its shimmering surface. A sigh of pleasure escaped her lips as the warm waters surrounded her.

Flaming red hair, long yet tightly curled fanned out behind her, floating lightly on the water's surface. Still unaware of Alar's presence, she lay back, floating on the scented waters. She relaxed, letting the currents move her about the pool. As she turned in his direction, he got a good look at her features.

Her face was angelic. The alabaster skin was beautifully framed by the corona of fiery hair that floated around it. High cheekbones guided Alar's gaze towards her closed eyes. Lashes impossibly long and feathery interlaced, their tips curling like the petals of an auburn flower.

Summoning up his courage, he whispered to her in his most gentle voice. "Please do not be afraid. I did not know that anyone knew of this cave. I will leave now."

Her eyes flew open and gazed at Alar with astonishment. They were dark, sharply contrasting her pale complexion.

She looked up at him and smiled. Her teeth were perfect. They sparkled like the sun does when it shines on freshly fallen snow.

Alar felt his heart flutter. He stared at her wordlessly.

She laughed, her voice flowing melodiously like the waters of the fall behind her. "You don't appear to be leaving now, do you?" she spoke in a lightly accented tongue.

Alar had never heard an accent like hers before. He continued to stare, feeling embarrassed as a blush burned its way up his cheeks.

"I believe the opening of the cave is that way," she said as she pointed towards the vines behind Alar.

Out of the corner of his eye, Alar noticed the fullness of her cleavage as the water danced around the tops of her breasts. He forced his eyes away from her body and stared intently at her outstretched hand. On her forearm, clearly visible through the clinging drops of water, was a tattoo of a bird in flight. Alar was impressed with the artistry; the bird appeared so lifelike and gentle that he was tempted to stroke it.

Forcing the thought from his mind, he mumbled, "I was just leaving."

He turned to leave the cave, when he impetuously stopped, looked over his shoulder and smiled. "Will I ever see you again?" he asked.

The melodious laughter that followed lit his heart afire. "I think so," was her reply.

Feeling euphoric, he turned and left the cave. He was so self-conscious of his movements, he did not notice the large leather-bound book, the shoulder pack or the crystal orb resting against the far wall.

Alar waited outside the cave for some time. He knew that the woman in the cave would have to pass him if she was to go down the mountain. She was so beautiful and mysterious. He just had to see her again! Alar had hardly gotten over his surprise at seeing a naked woman in what he had considered his private cave when he had beat his embarrassed retreat. Now that he had some time to think about it, his mind fairly burst with questions to ask her.

Who was she, he wondered? Was she from Dragon Springs? He knew almost everyone in his village, and he had never seen her before. What was she doing in a hidden mountain cave, and how had she managed to get to it? Alar was an experienced outdoorsman, and the climb took him half a day. How could a stranger to the area get to the cave in less time than that? The cave didn't look lived in, and if she hadn't spent the night, how did she get into the cave without him seeing her climb in front of him? The rocky face of the mountain would not hide a climber, and Alar had scanned the area closely before he climbed.

Alar waited until he could no longer stand it. Despite his vigilance, he had seen no activity around the cave's entrance. Neither man, nor beast had left the cave in the hour he had been watching it. He began to worry about the mysterious stranger. Why hadn't she come out? Had she somehow become injured in the pool? Anxiety fueled his already powerful curiosity until he could stand it no longer.

He climbed up the trail, retracing his steps towards the cave's mouth. As he prepared to reenter the cave, he was startled when a small white dove burst from the cave's opening. The bird circled him twice, then flew off into the sky. Though it was difficult to see given the bird's speed in the air, it had unusual markings across its shoulder and chest.

Alar pushed the vines aside and stepped into the cave. When his eyes adjusted to the light they were greeted with the image of only empty walls.

Catharvus remained a prisoner of the Air Children's spell. Chained to the cave's rocky floor, he schemed of ways to get at the woodsmen. Catharvus watched Alar in the crystal orb, but lost his image when the orb began to shimmer, then went dim. Catharvus cursed mightily, but for the time being, could no nothing.

The spell that powered the foretelling orb had a marked limitation on it. That shortcoming was that the spell only lasted a few minutes. When the orb's magical energies wore out, the image in the orb would disappear. Due to the magical residual that clung to the sphere's surface, the spell could not be recast for about 15 minutes. To Catharvus, this seemed like a lifetime.

He recited the spell again and again, waiting for it to take. Eventually, an image came into focus. The sorcerer intently stared at the sphere, studying its surface. The orb showed a puzzled looking Alar leaving a vine choked cave. He looked around, seemingly searching, then shrugged his shoulders and started climbing down the side of a ravine. He was making good progress, but would soon face a steep incline. Catharvus shielded his hands with his cloak, then turned the orb slightly upward. The image panned upward as he adjusted the sphere. He scanned the rock face until he located a large boulder. The boulder was precariously balanced on a ledge made of crumbling rock. It lay directly above Alar.

There will be no escape for the woodsman now, Catharvus thought. The cave is too high above him, and the boulder's ledge won't support his weight. The rest of the rock wall is slick, and unsuitable for climbing. He will have nowhere to go.

Catharvus rubbed his gnarly hands together as he planned his attack. He broke into a smile as he made his final preparations. The sorcerer judged the distance between himself and Alar. He readied the spell energies, carefully following the book's instructions. The crackling magical energies collected by the mage needed the beard hair of a troll to catalyze them. Catharvus placed the energies on his crystal orb. He fished around in the pockets of his cloak and pulled out a small platinum box. He opened it and withdrew a single orange hair.

This is the only one I've got, thought the mage. My aim must not waver on this spell.

He straightened the coarse hair and dipped it into the energies that clung to the crystal ball. There was a flash of brilliant blue as a lightning bolt flew from the orb and whistled about the cave. The bolt followed the gaze of the sorcerer who guided it by shifting the focus of the crystal ball. Under his control, it streaked out of the cave, and headed towards the Dragon Spine mountains. The lightening screamed through the air, homing in on Alar. Air, roughly displaced by the advancing bolt, boomed and thundered noisily.

Alar heard the thunder and looked over his shoulder for approaching rain. All he saw was a burning spot in the distant sky that was rapidly approaching.

He scrambled to his left, trying to distance himself from the threatening horror. The bolt seemed to veer off its course and follow him. Alar scrambled to his previous position, watching with increasing unease as the fiery streak followed him back.

Alar climbed up the rocky slope, trying to make it back to the cave. The bolt was coming too quickly, he would never make it. A rapid glance to his right and left showed him no place to hide.

The bolt was seconds away from Alar when the orb flickered and went dim. The sorcerer screamed with rage. His voice, magnified by the cave walls, floated down to the village. The distorted moan sounded like the death howl of some tortured animal.

Alar felt the heat from the approaching spell. In desperation, he let go of the cliff wall. He began to fall. For a moment, familiar feelings of weightlessness encompassed him. As he began to fall faster, the pitch of the wind increased in his ears. Alar knew that this was no idle daydream of flying. He was falling rapidly downward, and would soon crash to the rocks below.

Alar snatched desperately at the exposed roots of a long dead tree whose corpse still clung to the cliff's face. He grabbed one, then grimaced as his arms and shoulders were yanked upward by the force of his deceleration.

The lightning bolt, now unguided by the sorcerer, hurtled towards Alar's last position. It struck the cliff twenty feet above him, showering him with sparks and dirt. The cliff wall itself shook from the bolt's impact. The force ripped out half to the tree's roots. Alar fell ten feet downward, still clutching the root tip. Some deeper part of the root system held, jerking him to a stop again.

Alar gasped for breath. He took in the situation and shuddered. He was hanging from a root that looked like it would rip out of the cliff face at any moment. He was dangling at least twenty feet from the nearest hand hold and had nothing but sheer rock below him.

Climbable rock lay above. The only way to get to it was to pull himself up the root. He could then work his way across the wall and hopefully reach an area of easier climbing.

Hand over hand, he pulled himself up, climbing the root like a rope. He was almost to the top of it when a shower of gravel fell on him as the root again slipped. A two-foot segment of his handhold ripped out of the cliff, sending Alar tumbling downward. Finally, some part of the tortured plant held. Alar's fall stopped with a jerk that was sharp enough to dislodge one of his hands.

Alar hung by one hand as he spun on the twisting root. With grim determination, he began to climb again. Sweat stung his eyes as he looked upward. His breath came in short gasps. He dared not stop as the root was frayed and looked like it would break any second.

"What more could possibly happen?" he muttered as he climbed.

Sand fell onto his face as the ledge above him cracked, then gave way. The boulder that perched there, was larger than a cask of ale. It shuddered for an instant, then spilled forward and began to bounce down the cliff.

Alar contemplated his plight. He was dangling by a spindly root from a sheer rock face. A quick glance down showed that to let go of the hand hold would mean a certain death. There was nothing below him that he could grab. The boulder was too large to try to fend off. If it hit him, it would either crush him or knock him from the cliff wall.

Alar kicked at the cliff wall, causing the root to swing like a pendulum. Not unlike a trapeze artist, he arched and bent until the root was swinging in dizzying arcs. He tried to time his swings to put as much distance between him and the falling rock as possible.

Alar gritted his teeth. His timing was off! The boulder hurtled towards him as he swung back towards it. It passed within a breath of him, lightly dusting him with sand as it fell. He was so close to the stone, he could actually hear the wind whistling off its surface.

As Alar fought for his life, distant lips conjured a spell. Dark eyes followed his every move. Unaware, Alar stopped his swinging and once more started to climb.

Suddenly, the root snapped. Alar's eyes locked on the end of the frayed root as he fell. He grabbed at a rock projecting from the wall. It was too small for him to hold on to. He bounced off it! There was no further chance for escape as he hurtled towards the ground below.

Defeated, he shut his eyes and concentrated on the weightless feeling of flight that was to be his last mortal sensation. The lightness coupled with the whistling wind in his ears relaxed him as he prepared for death.

Suddenly, Alar felt his skin crawl with pulsating energy. He felt distant and disoriented. The whistling sound of the wind disappeared.

Curiosity forced him to open his eyes. He was still tumbling through the air, but something was different. Instead of rapidly falling, he found himself drifting downward like a leaf tossed about by the Autumn breezes. He wafted and soared on the wind currents.

Alar lost himself to the feeling of flight. With eyes shut, he relished the feeling of weightlessness. He came to rest on the rocks below the cliff. He opened his eyes. He was alive! Suddenly, his body started to shake as if a cold wind blew upon it. He began to hyperventilate. Clutching at the rocks, he tried to get his run away breathing under control. He sank to his knees. The pounding in his chest finally slowed. When Alar stood up, his legs felt rubbery. He slipped on the mossy slickness of the rock and sat down ungracefully in the waters of the Dancing River.

He thought he heard melodious laughter coming from behind him. He turned around. No one was there.

Alar made his way back to the village, his head spinning with the events of the afternoon. He had gone for a walk to clear his mind. Unfortunately, he was left with more mysteries than answers.

Who was the beautiful woman in the cave? Her image kept returning to him, invading his thoughts. Her hauntingly beautiful voice and melodious laugh fascinated him as much as her physical appearance. She was a vision fit for dreams, and given her vanishing act, he was beginning to wonder if she was indeed a figment of his imagination. Her disappearance from the cave was physically impossible. Equally unlikely was her laughing voice at the bottom of the ravine. If she had managed to elude him at the cave, and had somehow beaten him to the ravine's bottom, why did she disappear before he could see her?

Alar was muttering questions to himself as he rounded the bend at the village's entrance.

"Now he's talking to himself," boomed Marcus' voice.

The big man was sitting on a rock by the side of the road drinking from a black glass flask. Alar was so preoccupied by the day's mysteries that he didn't see Marcus until he was almost upon him.

"I'll share my drink with you if you share your conversation with me," Marcus said. "Leave it to the younger generation to let you nearly get your head caved in by a gray skinned bandit, then leave you alone during your convalescence. If it were not for this fine potion of healing herbs, I don't know what shape I'd be in now."

"Sober, I bet," replied Alar. He stopped by Marcus and heaved a great sigh as he sat next to him. He took the flask from his friend and took a healthy swig from it. His eyes teared as he tried to swallow the volatile brew. Grimacing, he forced the liquid down.

As Alar was trying to regain the ability to speak, Marcus chuckled and took a hit from the bottle himself.

"Good medicine must be strong. This drink is strong, so it must be good medicine."

"Drunken logic," croaked Alar as he wiped the tears from his eyes. "That stuff could strip the varnish from a Troll's treasure chest."

Ignoring his remark, Marcus took another drink from the bottle.

"Ah... Good stuff. Alar, what has gotten into you? You are normally the confident one, yet now you look so confused."

"Too many strange things have been happening lately. I don't know..." Alar shrugged his shoulders, then continued. "First the rising of the witch's moon, then the strange sounds coming from the mountain. After years of safety in this area, we were attacked by Orcs, then rescued by magic. Today I saw a beautiful woman in the cave of the hidden waterfall. Before I could spend any time with her, she disappeared."

"What is so unusual about that?" asked Marcus. "It used to happen to me all the time. Good thing that I found a nearsighted woman!"

"Marcus, stop picking on yourself. I am the only one allowed to do that!" was Alar's laughing reply. When Marcus had stopped laughing, Alar continued.

"It was really strange. She was bathing in the pool when I first saw her. She was gorgeous! I backed out of the cave after we talked a short while. I sat outside the cave and watched its opening like a hawk. I know she couldn't have gotten out of it, yet she was gone when I went back in to look for her."

"Maybe she left through a secret exit in the cave," suggested Marcus helpfully.

"I doubt it. I have explored that cave since I was a boy..."

"You are still a boy," interrupted Marcus.

"Quiet or I'll take your bottle away!" scolded Alar.

Marcus' features assumed a hurt and slightly stunned look. He could not hold the posturing and broke into laughter.

"Anyway," Alar continued, "I know that cave like the inside of my cottage. There is no way out except for the entrance that I was watching."

"As I left the cave, I was attacked by unholy magic."

Marcus had stopped his clowning around and listened with rapt attention.

"A lightning bolt appeared out of the western sky and seemed to follow me across the cliff face. There is no doubt in my mind that it was aiming for me. I managed to just get out of its way, avoiding a crispy death by inches. I fell from the cliff as I was attempting to escape. The area I fell from is hundreds of feet above the ground. Instead of crashing onto the rocks below, I was somehow rescued by a spell that made me float to the ground as if I were weightless."

Marcus cut in. "That must have been a Feather Fall spell. As a child, I heard my parents speak of it when they talked of the magic of the Air Children. I wonder if they are back in the forest."

"If they are, I wish they would leave!" replied Alar.

"The accursed moon must have brought them, I wish it would take them away. These magical arts are evil and unholy. They start trouble which only multiplies with time. This area would be far better without wizards and witches throwing spells at each other and catching me in the middle."

"Alar, not all magic is evil. Tales abound of good deeds wrought by the arcane arts."

"Say what you will, I prefer to keep my distance from them. All my life, I have feared that I would die at the hands of a magic user. I have recurring nightmares about it. I do not run from mortal danger, but I truly believe that magic is different. There is no way that I can defend myself against it, except to avoid magic and its users at all costs."

A small bird burst from the tree behind Marcus and flew off down the road.

Marcus watched the bird as he slowly shook his head. "You can't be serious. Your dad used to scare you with threats of evil sorcerers. It was the only way to make you behave!"

Alar's glum expression did not change. Seeing seriousness cover the usually ebullient face of his friend, Marcus changed the subject.

"Say, what was this new girlfriend of yours wearing."

"Nothing when I found her, she was bathing."

Marcus nodded knowingly. "I see why she got away from you so rapidly. Self-defense!"

"Not true, I am always the perfect gentleman."

"And I am always the perfect example of sobriety," laughed Marcus as he made kissing sounds and took another swig from his bottle. "After she fought you off, what type of clothes did she put on."

Realizing that further argument on the subject would be futile, Alar thought for a moment. "I think that I saw a cream-colored gown in the cave. It may have had a hood on it."

"And what did this expert on the womanly art of self-defense look like?"

"She was a beautiful woman with red hair and dark eyes," replied Alar. "Why do you ask?"

"Because she is standing behind you."

Alar turned and looked at the woman who stood behind him. In the light of the sun, she was even more beautiful than she had been in the cave.

Her hair sparkled like a ruby held up to a blazing fire. She had dark eyes that were both thoughtful and gentle. She stared intently at Alar.

He stared back. Their eyes locked in an embrace that caused Alar's heart to flutter. Though his eyes seemed to be working well, his mouth surely wasn't.

"Um.... Ah.... Hhhhi..." he murmured.

Marcus roared with laughter. "Hello lovely lady is what he is trying to say. You see, he is shy around women."

Alar turned a shade of crimson that nearly matched the woman's hair.

Marcus' laughter rolled like thunder. He stopped briefly, then his face reddened as he tried unsuccessfully to keep from laughing. He staggered to his feet and started to walk away. "Please excuse me you two," he gasped between spasms of laughter. "I must leave now before I break a rib from laughing."

His cackling could be heard long after he was out of sight.

Alone now, Alar and the woman continued to stare at each other.

Alar's mind raced. He felt his heart pounding in his chest. Ten minutes ago, there were a million things that he wanted to ask her. Right now, he couldn't think of any.

"Hello," stumbled out of his mouth.

"Hello," was her soft reply. As she looked up at him, her eyes spoke volumes.

The woman was standing so close to Alar that he could feel the warmth of her body. Her perfume's gentle scent, soft and floral, reached him a moment later.

"Are you the woman from the cave?"

"You would confuse me for another?" Though her eyebrows rose in mock horror, the broad smile on her face showed the absolute lack of seriousness in her question. "You either have a short memory, poor eyesight, or are seeing so many women that you can't keep them straight!"

"Neither is the case," he semi-truthfully replied. "My memory and vision are both excellent."

They both smiled.

"How did you get out of the cave without me seeing you?"

"I was afraid. I was alone in the cave when I met you. You were a stranger. How could I have known your intentions?"

Alar was so taken by her beauty that the evasive answer almost sufficed. The part of his brain that was still unaffected by the hormonal surges that were buffeting the rest of him, remained unsatisfied with her answer.

"But how did you escape the cave? I watched it for almost an hour."

She pouted. The soft beauty of her face sent fresh ripples into the tidal wave of emotion that was building in Alar's heart.

"Your mind must have been elsewhere. I left the cave through the vine covered opening in front. I passed right in front of you. I saw you clearly as I left. You must not have been watching as closely as you thought you were."

She smiled again. The vision of her looking up at him pushed Alar's mind to other thoughts.

"My name is Avais. What is yours?"

"Alar."

A wagon loaded with supplies trundled down the road. Its approach broke the reverie that engulfed the two.

Alar blinked, then touched Avais softly on the shoulder.

"Come. We block the road. It is long past meal time. You must be weary from your travels. Would you permit me to buy supper for you?'

"I thought you would never ask."

While Alar and Avais dined, the sorcerer paced in the cave. He had failed to kill the woodsmen twice. Neither the lightning bolt, nor the spider had harmed his intended victims. He remained a prisoner in the cave, chained to a dusty rock.

The foretelling orb had shown the woodsmen's picture when he had asked it about escape. Though the orb was known to talk in riddles, he had never known it to be wrong. For Catharvus to escape, he somehow needed Alar and Marcus. Killing them and having the spider bring their corpses to him seemed the easiest way to accomplish this. He suspected that the humans were receiving magical help, but since the orb did not send him the image of the magic user, he couldn't identify their benefactor. Not knowing who was interfering with his plans infuriated him even more.

He paced relentlessly in the cave, stopping each trip only when the chain drew tight against his leg. In frustration, he pounded on the chain with a rock. The rock crumbled. He let fly two magic missiles against the chain without producing so much as a scratch on the polished diamond surface.

Catharvus sat down heavily on the rock and stared at his feet. The shackle that linked him to the chain rested snugly against his ankle.

As he pondered his bonds, he shook his head slowly. The chain is unbreakable, he thought. That I have proven. Its link to the rock cannot be destroyed. I have not yet received the bodies of the woodsmen that the orb tells me I need to escape. I lay here rotting in this dank cave, still suffering the punishment meted out by those accursed Air Children."

He drew up his sleeve and stared at the tattoo that adorned his left forearm. The faded picture of the bird was drawn in a gentle and flowing hand. The dagger that impaled it was crude, clearly the work of another artist.

He pondered his tattoo. The mark of the Air Children, he thought. It was quite a feat to carve the image of the dagger into my own skin. It is a good thing that we weren't marked on our backs! How I detest them.

His eyes glazed as he sunk into deep thought. I can't believe that I once followed their path. The years have reduced it to a faint memory. From the time I found the dagger, I realized that they led trivial lives. They used the Earth's energy to cure the petty ills of the villagers. Only I knew the true worth of magic, to obtain power!

First, I perfected the use of the dagger on animals. Brief bursts of energy were mine, but I stole no knowledge from their worthless corpses. The villagers soon fell before me; only the need to keep my activities secret from the Air Children elders prevented their wholesale slaughter. It did not matter. The knowledge of the locals was so limited, it wasn't worth the effort of killing them to obtain. True power only came to me when I took the life of my first magic user.

He chuckled to himself as he thought of the murder. The fool! She thought that I was interested in her, that I wanted to love her. It was easy enough to play along, wooing her like some mindless teenager. When she lay in my arms, I cut her throat. Her power and knowledge lifted me above the others. I killed them one by one, growing stronger with each victory. They did not even know that the assassin was one of their own. The idiots. Alas, I was young and foolish. I let my head swell with self-confidence. I enslaved them instead of killing them all. That mistake defeated me. Now I pay my penalty, entombed in the side of a mountain, instead of ruling from its summit. I will escape. I must. When I do, I will not repeat the errors that were my undoing in the past.

He looked again at his shackles, then at his forearm. He reached down and grasped the leg shackle with his fingers and idly spun it around his leg. It was not too tight, it glided smoothly.

This may be my way out, he thought. Though I detest the thought of degrading myself by changing into their form, it just might make escape possible. This band would slip off a leg that was smaller than my own.

He leafed through the spell book, then stopped.

This spell, I do not need to look up. I have done this change enough times to be able to do it in my sleep. He looked at the figure of the bird on his arm. It is hard to believe that I once voluntarily traveled in that perverted form, he thought.

He spoke the magic words, spitting out each word as if it were poison. His hands danced in a practiced manner, channeling the now visible magical energies into a glowing pink ball. He held the ball in his right hand, noting the radiant colors that filled the cave.

On his belt, the dagger began to glow with a startling intensity. Its blade and handle became red hot, burning the magician despite his cloak's protective abilities.

Feeling the heat on his flesh, the magician dropped the pink spell energies as if they were a smoldering ember. The spell energies fizzled as they reacted with the dust on the cave's floor. The dagger immediately cooled, its color returning to normal.

The magician withdrew the dagger from his belt and stared at it. He smiled, noting the sensation of almost smug contentment that the blade seemed to emanate.

"Still jealous of that bird cult, my wicked friend. You need not be. I could no more rejoin them than I could grow long hair and birth children. My devotion to you is absolute."

He put the blade on the rock, then stood up and repeated his spell. He held the magical energies in his right hand as he turned to look at the dagger.

"This is only a temporary transgression my dear blade. I will use the old powers to escape this leg shackle, then we may be once more reunited in freedom. Stop your fretting, I will reclaim you soon."

Upon saying that, he slammed the magical energies onto the tattoo and was instantly transformed. Whereas before a wizened old man stood shackled to a diamond chain, a large, and rather ugly bird now appeared.

The bird was a vulture. Its black feathers were greasy and sparse. Its scaly legs were crusted in places, giving it a mangy, diseased look. The skin covering its head was devoid of feathers. Fleshy red growths dangled from under a beak that was impressive in size. The feathers on its chest were discolored. Close inspection of the area revealed that the pattern of Catharvus' tattoo now graced the bird's chest.

The vulture squawked loudly then took off.

The dagger, its glowing having ceased the second the transmutation took place, now faded into a cold gray color. If such could be said of a knife, it looked forlorn and lifeless.

The sorcerer flew his bird body swiftly in the direction of the cave's opening. He was jerked back to the ground by the diamond chain before he reached it. In his bird form, he examined his leg. Though it was no more than a few inches around, the diamond band still imprisoned it. The band had shrunken to conform to his leg's new size.

The vulture pecked at the shackle and chain, but did not succeed in loosening them. He fluttered around the room a few times, then stopped to eat the long dead carcass of the mouse he had previously killed. Before, he had drained its life energies, now he ate its flesh.

He strutted back to his spell book and stared at the leather cover. On the lower third of the cover was a faded imprint of a bird. Its stylized lines were almost obscured by mold and dirt.

The vulture hopped upon the table and pressed its chest against the book. The bird pattern on its chest matched the image on the book's cover. When the two met, a blinding flash of light flared in the room. It faded to reveal the sorcerer standing next to the book. He remained shackled to the chain.

He wearily sat down and picked up the dagger that was now glowed a cheerful red.

Alar sat with Avais in the village's only pub, The Dragon's Mouth Tavern. He gazed at her as she picked at her salad. The room was noisy. Woodsmen toasted and caroused at the bar, while the cook tended the fires and made clanging sounds in the kitchen. Though some may have thought that the noise level was like that at the base of a waterfall, all he heard was her.

Her bearing was mysterious. She seemed to speak in riddles. He couldn't identify her accent, or decipher half of what she told him, yet he hungered for her every word. Her clothes were different from any he had ever seen. Where the villagers wore sturdy, utilitarian garments, her silk gown was translucent, a soft and flowing thing of delicate beauty.

Alar averted his gaze for a moment, then let his eyes be drawn back towards her. She gave off an air of confidence, yet it was tinged with vulnerability. She simultaneously radiated power and timidity. Though her appearance was one of openness, he couldn't shake the feeling that she was hiding something from him. He had never known a woman who was even remotely like her.

"Where did you come from Avais? I don't recall seeing you before. What brings you to this area?"

Avais temporarily stopped wrestling with some unruly salad greens and looked up at him. She paused, choosing her words carefully.

"I am from a land on the other side of the mountains. I have been drawn to this area by forces that I cannot seem to control. I know that I am needed here. That is why I have come."

Alar raised his eyebrows in surprise. "The mountain chain goes on for many hundreds of miles. The mountains are too high to climb. Your journey must have taken a long, long time, yet you do not look road weary."

Avais shrugged her shoulders and smiled. "I should hope not!" she giggled.

Alar returned her smile, then discreetly looked her over. No, she does not look like a traveler, he thought. I know she has just bathed. I guess that explains why she has no dirt or grime upon her. But what about her clothes? They are clean, delicate and unwrinkled. I have never traveled and looked so fresh at the end of my journey. The only luggage she carries is a small shoulder pack, so it is not like she just changed into a new outfit.

Alar was puzzled. The pieces of the mystery did not fit. "How did you travel here Avais, in a coach, or on horseback?"

"Neither," she replied. Her voice sounded as sincere as Alar had ever heard a voice sound. "I do not like to travel with beasts of burden. Don't you feel that it is somehow unfair to enslave them? I enjoy being closer to nature. To travel silently, unmolested by the sounds of hoof beats, is to really know the land."

Though Alar was puzzled by her fresh appearance, especially if she had traveled by foot, he could not argue with her logic. He loved to walk the woods, alone except for the company of the forest creatures. He had always mistrusted horses, possibly due to his earlier experiences with the unicorn mare.

"Tell me about yourself, Alar," she asked. Her accent caressed each word as her tongue formed it. Alar's eyes rested on her mouth. Thoughts of lust intruded in his mind, displacing those of caution. As he stared at her, his suspicions melted away like a candle thrown into the glowing ashes of a camp fire. His attention was so fixed on her lips as she spoke that he almost didn't answer her question.

Caught in staring, he blushed fiercely, then smiled.

"I am a woodsman, he said. "I chop down trees. Not much else to tell, I'm afraid."

"That is the reply of one who has a lot to tell, but doesn't want to tell it," was her hurt response. She pouted. The expression started Alar's heart pounding again.

She leaned over the table and looked deeply into Alar's eyes. "You are blushing. Are you married and dining with me behind your wife's back, or are you just shy?"

"Yes, I mean no. Damn," he stammered. "You have me tongue tied like a young boy."

Alar was glad Marcus wasn't around. He knew how awkward his conversation sounded, and could just imagine the fuss the old man would be making. He half expected to hear his deep laugh erupt at any moment.

Blinking his eyes to refocus his thoughts, he tried again.

"I am not married, and never have been." Avais smiled pleasantly.

Alar was pleased that his tongue had seen fit to start working again.

"And you?"

"I have spent much time alone with my studies. I too, am single."

Alar was about to ask her about what she had studied when Avais cocked her head slightly and interrupted him. "Tell me of your parents, Alar. I bet they are wonderful people."

"I am the only son of Brenton, a senior woodsman from this town. They say my mother was a fine woman though I don't remember her. She died when I was quite young. Since my father was quite old, I spent a lot of time with Marcus, the man you met earlier."

"From what I have seen of Marcus, you should not only be a fine woodsman, but the town drinking champion," laughed Avais. "He seems to be a most happy man."

"He is at least until the next morning! Marcus is a wonderful man. I have never seen him angry, and it is rare to see him with a serious look on his face. Marcus has always been there when I needed him. He is like a father, and a best friend to me.

Alar continued. "As carefree as he appears, he would gladly give up his life for a friend. We were attacked by Orc's a few days back. I was wounded, and surely would have been killed were it not for his bravery."

Avais listened intently, her face showing no emotion.

"I imagine you must have been in quite a predicament."

"Well yes," replied Alar. "Even with his help, I was almost killed. Through treachery, the Orcs had us at their mercy. As my fatal blow was about to be struck, the Orc was killed by the missile of a magical spell."

Avais cut in. "It sounds like you owe your life to magic. Orcs can be quite nasty. They seem to enjoy killing for its own sake. When they take a prisoner, a funeral is sure to follow."

"I wish that we had never met the Orcs," muttered Alar, his eyes glazing over. "Before that moment, I had never seen magic. I almost believed that it didn't exist. Now, there is no doubt in my mind. I am filled with dread at the thought of its practitioners returning to this area."

Avais looked shocked. "Why do you say that, Alar?" The passion in her voice surprised him.

Alar's face took on a sad look. He seemed lost in his thoughts for a moment.

"I have always been a person who dreams a lot. My nights are filled with dreams of the most vivid colors. I remember my dreams after I awaken. It is frightening, but more often than not, the dreams come true." Alar's voice faltered.

Avais took his hand. "I also have dreams that predict the future," she said. "It is a trait shared by all of my people. Tell me of the dream you fear."

He took a deep breath, then began speaking again. His voice emerged a hoarse whisper as he struggled to express himself. "I am in a dark place. Friends of mine are in great danger, but I can't see their faces. Blood spills. The feeling of death fills the room. Strange energies appear before me. They cling to me. Difficult decisions tear me apart. I am not sure what to do. The energies grow brighter, they are all over me. My skin burns, I feel life drain out of me. There is a tremendous explosion..."

Alar blinked, then looked at Avais. "Some first impression I am making. I barely know you, yet burden you with tales of my night terrors. I am acting like a child running to his mother's bed after a bad dream. Forgive me."

Avais gazed deeply into his eyes. Her hand still held his. It felt warm and soft.

"I believe greatly in dreams," she said. "Don't forget, I am the one who asked you. Now tell me, what happens after the explosion."

Alar shrugged. "I wake up. The dream has come to me dozens, no hundreds of times. It never goes further than the explosion."

Alar swirled his glass, watching the tea spin about. "Since no magic had been seen in the realm for years, I thought I was safe. What doesn't exist, can't kill you. Now I know that magicians and their magic are back. It frightens me greatly. I must avoid them at all costs."

"Alar, all magic is not evil! It can be used in many ways that benefit man. Magic can and has been used by men of great virtue. Whole populations have thrived under its protection. Natural and supernatural disasters have been averted by its power. You must not judge an entire art, an entire lifestyle, by one cloudy dream."

Alar shrugged his shoulders.

"How can I not fear magic? My dreams have foretold events for years. I believe what I believe. Magic will be the death of me."

"Alar, if it were not for magic, the Orc would have been the death of you."

Alar sat back, squeezed Avais' hand and finished his tea. He again shrugged his shoulders as he shook his head.

"See what a bag of worms you open up with your questions! There must be more pleasant things to do than dwell on thoughts of death. Let's get out of here and enjoy some of the sunshine while the afternoon still lasts."

Avais nodded. As she started to get up, Alar reached for her shoulder pack.

"Let me take this for you," he said. "My, this weighs a ton! What do you have in here, a horse?"

Her eyes looked sad and distant as she replied.

"No, not a horse. Just a book. A large, important, and very old book."

Avais left the bar with Alar trailing close behind her. As they walked, her mind raced. She was troubled by his recurring dreams of death by magic. Was it truly prophetic? Would it act as a wedge between them? She did not know. She was determined not to let this one irrational fear get in the way, for she was greatly attracted to Alar, and she knew in her heart that she would need him.

The two walked together towards the town's gates, talking amongst themselves. Alar had calmed down enough to show his true personality. He was honest, warm and charming.

As they walked, each marveled at the similarities they shared. Their similarities made conversation easy. Both loved nature and the outdoor life. Both were gentle and caring. The fact that Avais had prophetic dreams drew her closer to Alar, as he had always thought that only he had dreams that foretold the future. Knowing that he was not unique with such an unusual burden took a load off his shoulders.

With similar easy going and friendly personalities, they soon talked like old friends just reunited. The more they talked, the more each was attracted to the other.

Avais was fascinated by the sound of Alar's voice, for it was strong, yet caring. She asked him countless questions, enjoying the conversation that they provoked. She remembered that Alar didn't care for horseback travel and thought this odd for a man.

"Alar, why don't you like to ride horses? Is it the noise and commotion they make, or do you dislike the animals in general?"

"A little of both, I'm afraid," was his reply.

In response to her puzzled look, he told her his unicorn story. He told the story accurately, without Marcus being present, he did not have to be on the defensive as he told it. She laughed when he told of his aborted flying experience on the horn of the enraged horse. She was especially interested in his admission that he had secretly dreamed of flying ever since that time.

"Alar, I too dream of taking to the air. To have the freedom of a bird in flight is something I often wish for. Since I was a little girl, I have secretly wanted to take to the wing. Many a time, my mind wandered from its Earthbound prison to soar with the creatures of the sky. I'm afraid my school work suffered because of it! Think how wonderful it would be if our bodies could follow all of our thoughts."

Alar nodded as he remembered how she looked, naked in the cave. He smiled at the idea of his body following those thoughts. As he dwelled on the image, he put his hand on her shoulder.

She saw the glint in his eye, and the barely suppressed smile. "What are you thinking?" she asked.

"With your figure, you are light enough to fly! A soft breeze could sweep you away!"

"Thank you for noticing. I hope you are not alluding to what you saw in the cave. A gentleman would have averted his eyes. Anyway, keep up the flattery, it will get you everywhere!"

Alar laughed with her. He lightly massaged her shoulder and was gladdened when she did not pull away from his touch. His heart fairly leapt in his chest when she leaned towards him, intensifying his pressure on her skin. He slowly spun her towards him. She did not resist.

"Where might this flattery get me?" he whispered, leaning closer to her.

"Trouble, big trouble," was her breathless reply.

Their lips met as they shared a delicate kiss. The two held each other tightly, savoring the moment. Their embrace was interrupted by the sound of a shrill scream.

Avais pulled away from Alar and took off in the sound's direction. Alar ran after her. She was surprisingly fast, easily outdistancing him. Such bravery, he thought as he raced after her. She is a woman who confronts the unknown instead of cringing in fear from it. How different she was from the other girls he had known.

Avais rounded a corner and slowed to a walk. A pitiful sight befell her. A merchant's wagon, dangerously overloaded, was stuck in a roadside ditch. A small donkey was hitched to the wagon, desperately trying to pull it back onto the road. The animal was lathered in sweat and straining mightily, but couldn't budge the heavy cart. So disproportionately large was the wagon, it was a wonder that the animal had been able to move it on level ground.

The owner of the wagon snarled at the beast. He was a nasty looking human who seemed to be a traveling vendor of some type. He was dirty and unshaven, his face adorned with a scar that zigzagged its way from chin to temple.

The man was beating the donkey with a whip, drawing long red welts upon its flanks. Blood dripped from the fresh cuts, staining the donkey's once white hide.

Desperate to avoid further whipping, the donkey threw itself against the harness, but the cart remained stuck. The man whipped the animal again and again. It lost its footing, collapsing in the harness. The man became more enraged at the beast and yelled at it to get up. When it didn't, he dropped the whip and began to pummel the cowering animal with his fists. The donkey thrashed and screamed as it was beaten in the dusty road, then shuddered as some type of fear induced paralysis overcame it. The livid man grabbed his whip and raised it to strike the helpless animal again.

Avais dove between the donkey and the man. She grabbed the whip with both hands. "Leave the poor creature alone," she pleaded. "He obviously can't move the wagon. We will help you lift the cart back onto the road."

The man was a good head taller than she and was strongly muscled. His swarthy complexion was accented by a thick layer of road grime. Grappling with him for the whip, Avais couldn't help but notice how badly he smelled.

"My name is Ortut, and the donkey is my animal. As is his nature, he is being lazy. If I let him get away with this now, he will be worthless in the future. I own the beast, I will treat him as I please. Get out of my way! Now!!"

Her hands remained locked on the whip. "I cannot permit you to abuse that defenseless animal. You will kill him before he could possibly move this wagon."

"I own the ass, he is mine to kill if I so choose. Move now, I will not warn you again."

Avais did not budge. She twisted her arms sharply, pulling the whip from Ortut's hand. While he watched in disbelief, she cracked the whip's handle across her knee, breaking it in two.

"Bitch," he screamed at her. The man's fetid breath nauseated her as he yelled in her face. "You deserve to be whipped like the stupid animal." Ortut sneered as he raised his left hand. "Who do you think you are? I have beaten my wife for far less than that!"

Avais did not flinch. Avais stared straight into his face, her dark eyes sparkling with defiance. "I pity your wife, for I would rather marry the donkey."

Alar rounded the corner in time to see Ortut strike Avais. He had unleashed a short backhand blow that caught her flush on the face. The blow knocked Avais off balance, causing her to tumble down the shallow embankment behind the road.

Alar dove at the man as red waves of rage overcame him. He slammed his fist into Ortut's gut, doubling him over. Short chopping blows followed, bloodying the man's face. Ortut was tall and more muscular than Alar, yet he retreated under the woodsman's furious attack. Alar hit the man with a looping right that caused him to stumble backwards into the donkey. The animal bared his teeth, biting his owner on the arm. The satisfied look on the animal's face almost made Alar start laughing.

Prodded on by the unexpected pain from the bite, Ortut shook his head, then stepped forward, swinging at Alar with both fists. A block, then three quick blows from the woodsman left the man lying on the ground, dazed and bleeding.

"Don't hit me again!" he panted. "I am sorry! I did not mean to hit the woman. Believe me!" He pointed towards the donkey. "I was so frustrated by that stupid beast that I lost my temper. Forgive me. I didn't know what I was doing."

Alar was torn for a moment as he looked at the man's bloody face. He hesitated, then took pity on the merchant. Alar helped Ortut to his feet, then turned to look for Avais. She had tumbled down the embankment and was lost from sight. She is probably lying in the deep weeds, he thought. I hope she isn't hurt.

"Avais," he cried. "Can you hear me? Are you all right?"

No answer came from the embankment. Alar began to worry. Was she badly injured? Had she lost consciousness?

He prepared to scramble down the embankment to look for her.

Alar was so concerned about Avais that he forgot about the man behind him. He did not hear Ortut take a quick step towards him, nor did he hear the rustling sound made by the donkey's harness as a club was pulled from it. Ortut slammed the club into the back of Alar's head before the woodsman had taken two steps in Avais' direction. Alar crumpled to the ground, his eyes rolled back, then shut. Ortut spit at the prostrate figure of the woodsman, then reached into his coat and withdrew a short, curved sword. He stooped over the young man, raising the sword above his head.

"Good bye, road trash," he said as he plunged the sword downward.

Seconds before the sword connected with Alar, a black and shiny object flew through the air, glinting in the sun as it tumbled. The wind that whistled off its open mouth must have distracted Ortut, as he turned to look at it, then pitched forward as it struck him flush on the face. The merchant tumbled down the slope, still gripping his sword.

Alar opened his eyes, trying to focus through the fogs of unconsciousness that danced before his eyes. The woodsman watched the merchant tumble end over end as he fell down the embankment. Blood seemed to fly everywhere as the man rolled down the slope.

Alar's unsteady gaze shifted to the figure of Avais, crouched cat-like in the weeds at the embankment's base. Her hand, raised in a throwing position above her shoulders, was glowing softly. He was not sure, but it seemed she spoke a word, then rubbed her hands together, extinguishing the glow. She looked up at him with a worried look, then hurried up the slope.

Alar heard cursing behind him, then lost consciousness again.

Alar regained consciousness and was immediately aware of two distinctly different sounds. His eyes focused on Avais' beautiful face, framed by an azure sky. He lay in her lap, looking up at her as she spoke to him.

"Thank the gods you are alive. I would never forgive myself if what I did had caused your death." Her voice was like soothing music. The other sound he heard threatened to drown out everything else. Alar's ears strained to hear her over the barrage of baritone curse words that filled the air.

"Damn migratory bastards. Unwashed, violent, ass beating, scum sucking, back stabbing sons of bitches. Lord help any of his kind that dare show their faces in this area again."

Alar reached up, squeezed Avais' hands in appreciation, then struggled to a sitting position. He turned in the direction of the verbal outburst and saw Marcus throwing a world-class temper tantrum.

"Those damn nomads are nothing but trouble," he said as he stomped around like an overgrown child. "Riffraff, that's what they are. Can't stay in one place.

Too much trouble that way. They must wander from town to town, leaving trouble in their wake."

"I've got to admit that my day would have been better if I hadn't met Ortut," Alar replied as he rubbed the knot on the back of his head. Hitting a particularly sore spot, he grimaced, then smiled. "Don't be upset for me," he said. "I'll survive. It would have been nicer if he had hit me in some other spot though, my head has been getting quite a workout recently."

"I'm not worried about you," boomed Marcus. "Your head is far too hard for anything less than a catapult to hurt." He smiled and winked very slightly at Avais. "I'm upset about this," he sobbed as he pointed to the shards of black glass that littered the ground. "I was minding my own business, enjoying a stroll in the fine evening air. I had a bottle of my best medicinal whiskey. Saved the damn stuff for a special occasion. Since our run in with the Orc's, I felt it best to drink it. As you know, I'm still recovering from my battle injuries." He sighed. "I uncorked it, but before I could take even a sip, I saw that you were once again in trouble. Sometimes I don't know why I bother bailing you out, you always seem to find another way to imperil yourself. Anyway, you were about to become a human shish kabob, and seeing that I could never hope to reach you in time, I threw my still untasted, and FULL bottle at the brute. Got him right on the forehead to. He tumbled down the slope, and by the looks of the hillside, landed on his sword. He's probably dead, you are safe, and I remain thirsty. There is no justice in the world!"

Avais had unhitched the donkey who was gazing up at her with adoring eyes. She started to rummage through the merchant's wagon, looking for something to use to clean the animal's wounds. She opened a box and burst out laughing.

"How cruel you are!" said Marcus. "I have lost my medicine and will have a devil of a time replacing it. Imagine, laughing at the misfortune of others. I thought better of you." Marcus pouted, looking much like a child who has lost his candy.

"Don't worry, Marcus," she said between laughs. "You may stop your grieving, for Ortut seems to have been carrying alcohol amongst his supplies! This box contains whiskey, but I am sure you could find some medicinal use for it. If you do, there is enough here for you to open up your own hospital!"

Marcus walked over to the box and examined its contents. Twelve hand blown glass bottles rested in straw packing. He opened one and smelled the cork. "Smells like a fine vintage," he said. He looked in the bottle, nodding approvingly at the dark amber fluid inside. He took a swig. "Ahh, this batch is fit for patient use!"

Marcus broadly swept his arm in the donkey's direction. "Madam, administer to this patient. Alar, come with me. We shall check on the condition of the previous owner of the whiskey. If he was nice enough to donate this box to us, it's the least we can do."

Alar and Marcus picked their way down the blood stained embankment and were soon out of a direct line of sight. Avais looked at the donkey who was still bleeding. His hide was tattered, his head hung low.

"Poor creature," she whispered. "Don't worry, I will help you."

She rummaged through her bag and pulled out a large book. The imprint of a bird graced its clean leather cover. With practiced fingers, she leafed through it. She began chanting, all the while making elaborate hand motions. A shimmering ball of energy was soon balanced on her outstretched palm. She inhaled deeply, then blew some of her life energies into the glowing spell. It flared briefly, radiating a deep pink color. She pulled a hair from her head and dropped it into the uncatalyzed spell. The hair hit the awaiting energies, converting them into a useful spell. She rubbed the crackling energy packet onto the donkey's back. The animal seemed to understand that it was not going to be harmed and did not shy away. The energy dissipated in a flash, leaving smooth intact hide where seconds before, deep welts had lain.

The animal immediately perked up, which was fortunate as Avais was in the process of slumping against him. She had donated some of her life energies to the donkey when she healed it, but had weakened herself in the process. She felt faint and clung to the animal for support. With an obvious effort, she pulled the cork out of one of the bottles and wearily poured the contents onto the donkey's back.

Alar and Marcus came trudging up the slope carrying the body of the merchant. He was dead, having nearly eviscerated himself when he fell upon his sword.

"Ortut was killed in the fall," shouted Alar as he climbed the hill. "Any loss of life is tragic, but I must say the bastard certainly deserved it."

Alar looked up and noticed that Avais was slumping against the dripping donkey. She was pale and drenched with sweat.

"Avais, what is wrong?" he yelled. Alar dropped his half of the merchant's body and sprinted towards the wagon. Upon reaching her, he took Avais by the shoulders and led her away from the donkey. He sat her down and fanned fresh air towards her.

Though she was weakened by the spell casting, she knew that she couldn't tell this to Alar. His fear of magic would surely drive him away from her.

She spoke weakly, the words an obvious effort. "The fumes from that medicine nearly overcame me. I can't imagine how Marcus can drink it."

Alar gave her a concerned look, then looked at the donkey. True to her story, it was dripping with alcoholic smelling liquid. Its coat was now smooth. No trace of the previous open wounds remained. He walked over to the animal, running his fingers across its back.

He slowly turned in Avais' direction and gazed at her suspiciously. As he spoke, his voice had just a hint of hardness to it. "You have to be careful when you use that stuff. It can be strong and dangerous. I usually try to avoid it."

Their eyes met briefly before Alar turned away.

Marcus dragged Ortut's body up the hill. Upon reaching the road, he dropped it and turned towards Alar and Avais. The scene he saw was not a happy one. Alar was grinding his fist into his hand while sadly shaking his head. He had turned his back to Avais who was sitting in the grass, looking pale and ill. The only happy one in the group was the donkey who looked wet, but was otherwise just fine.

"Uh oh, looks like they're fighting. Ah, young love. One moment it's hot, the next it's cold. Looks like it's time to rescue Alar again," he muttered to himself.

"What is wrong with you Alar?" the big man boomed. "One moment I'm saving your life, the next I'm forgotten. I bet you probably won't even help me bury Orbut's body.

Alar slowly turned towards Marcus. His face, usually full of joy, now showed anger and doubt.

"His name was Ortut," he snapped.

"Whatever," replied Marcus as he casually looked around. "Why the glum face?"

"I'm worried. Something isn't right here. Avais stayed with the donkey while we were recovering Ortut's body. In the five minutes that we were gone, she managed to not only stop the bleeding, but to remove the scars as well. It's hard to believe that this is the same animal who was almost beaten to death minutes ago. It could not have happened naturally. I know that magic has been used here!"

Marcus walked over to the animal and examined its coat. There was liquid dripping off its flanks. He touched it, then smelled his hands. Nodding, he turned towards Avais and looked her over. My, she looked pitiful, he thought. She was slouching morosely in the grass, looking physically drained. Her eyes reddened as she tried to hold back the tears that welled within them. Marcus reached towards her and helped her to her feet. He noticed the tattoo of the flying bird on her forearm. Now it all made sense to him. He gave Avais a slight nod as he steadied her.

"Avais, you look terrible. What's the matter?"

Avais shrugged her shoulders while she made a pouting face in Alar's direction.

When he was convinced that she wouldn't fall, Marcus turned his attention back to the donkey. The animal was straining in its harness to move towards Ortut's body. From the look of its barred teeth, it wanted another bite of him.

"The donkey sure looks fine," he said as he unhitched the animal. "As a matter of fact, I feel pretty good myself. Come to think of it, I feel totally refreshed. I feel wonderful!" he shouted.

He began dancing around like a child, surprising Alar with his whoops and yells. "God, I haven't felt this good in twenty years."

He danced over to the wagon and grabbed one of the bottles. He stopped dancing long enough to examine it closely. He nodded while thoughtfully pondering the label.

"Just as I thought."

He opened the bottle and made an exaggerated display of throwing the cork away from himself. Marcus held the bottle as one would hold a month-old fish. He poured a bit of the fluid on a bug that was crawling in the road. The insect, being nearly drowned in the liquid, began to writhe and spin about.

"Ah ha!" exclaimed Marcus. "Clearly magic. Hope the girl didn't get too much on her," he mumbled, making sure his stage whisper was loud enough for Alar to hear. "I drank some of this a few moments ago. God help me. I feel its effect growing on me even as we speak."

Alar stormed over and grabbed his friend.

"You say that this liquid is contaminated by magic? No wonder the animal healed so quickly. My God, it has affected my poor Avais. To think, I thought she had cast some type of spell on the donkey. Avais, please forgive me!" he begged.

Avais smiled weakly and gladly accepted the hug that Alar offered. While in his arms, she caught Marcus' eye. The big man was once again smiling broadly. He gave her a look that spoke volumes as he touched his temple with his index finger and slowly shook his head. Avais had to shut her eyes to block out Marcus, least she start laughing.

Alar kissed Avais with renewed passion.

"I will never doubt you again."

He squeezed her, then shuddered as he looked from the wagon to the merchant's body. "There is no telling what kind of evil magic this wagon is carrying. It is time to do the right thing."

Before Marcus could say anything, Alar grabbed the merchant's sword and smashed the entire case of bottles. Marcus winced with each blow that the bottles received. He stared through sad eyes as the contents of the broken bottles soaked the straw, then the rest of the wagon.

Alar dragged the body towards the cart. He and Marcus hefted the corpse upon it. Alar spoke a few words, wishing the man peace in the afterlife. He then struck a flint against the man's sword, throwing sparks onto the alcohol soaked straw. In seconds, the wagon was ablaze. Within minutes, nothing remained of merchant Ortut's funeral pyre.

Alar put his arm around Avais and gently steered her towards the road.

"Come," he said. "It is getting dark, we must be heading back towards town."

The donkey immediately fell into step behind the couple. Marcus took one last look at the smoldering remains of the merchant's cart, sighed and followed his friends.

I'm still thirsty, he silently lamented. What I have to give up to keep that young fool happy. An 'Air Child' and a magic hater, what a combination!

The remains of the cart gave out a forlorn yellow glow as it's embers settled. The light shined deeply into the woods, awakening the giant spider. It's stood, kicked the shriveled body of the Orc aside, then slowly headed toward the light.

CH 24

The sun hung low in the crimson sky when the three arrived at Alar's cottage.

"Why don't you two come in?" asked Alar. "It will be dark soon. I've got plenty of wood, and a fine fireplace to burn it in."

Avais pondered the proposition for a moment, then gave Alar a nod. Marcus, standing out of her line of sight, shot a knowing glance at Alar.

"I must be going now kids," he said. "Try to meet me at the pub tonight... if you have the strength!" He laughed heartily, then headed towards his home, pulling the somewhat reluctant donkey behind him.

His words faded into the distance. "Calm down little beast. I will feed you and put you in a barn that will seem like a palace. If you are good, I may even share some of my fine medicine with you..."

Alar opened the door, then turned towards Avais.

"Come in," he said.

She hesitated.

"Don't worry. I was a gentleman back at the cave. I don't plan on being any less of one now. Besides, I really have no choice, my head hurts too much for me to misbehave. The spot where Ortut clubbed me feels like it is big as an apple. If I had any sense, I would have worn a helmet this week!"

Avais beamed a radiant smile at him and chuckled. "I don't know. Men do have a remarkable capacity for rapid healing. I'd wager it takes more than a bump on the head to put you out of commission. Can I can trust you? If you were I, would you go into a stranger's house, especially one who sneaks around when you are bathing?"

Alar smiled. "If I were you, I think that I would trust me. Oh course, trying to guess what a woman is thinking is the first step to madness!"

She laughed again. "Let me guess, Marcus taught you that."

"It was one his first lessons to me. Someone had to teach me about women. Hey, don't be too hard on me," he laughed. "I barely passed the course!"

"Not likely!"

Alar flashed his best disarming smile at her. "Come inside," he demanded. "I'm getting cold arguing with you."

She did and he lowered the wooden plank into the latch, locking the door behind her.

Alar's cottage was a typical villager's dwelling. It was a wooden structure, constructed from roughhewn logs. Straw and moss insulated the spaces between the logs. The house's interior was softened by the woven mats that covered the walls. The inside was neat and looked comfortable, but was by no means fancy. The furniture was plain and functional. The only appointment to the house that was ornate, was a spectacularly carved wooden chair located in front of the fireplace.

Alar placed kindling and logs in the fireplace. A crackling fire was soon burning, driving the chill from the night air. Avais sat down in the carved chair and relaxed. She admired the chair's ornate patterns, rubbing her fingers across the unicorn head that capped the chair's left arm. She shut her eyes and let her palms rest on the wood.

"The wood of this chair feels of your presence. I'll bet you made it," she said.

"Yes, I did. I built the frame years ago. It was plain, but did its job. I started to carve it one winter when the weather was particularly bad. I guess I just missed the feel of working with the wood. Now I carve when the weather is too foul to work outside, or when the mood strikes me. Carving relaxes me, you could say the chair has become a hobby of mine."

She ran her finger over one of the chair's arms. Birds in flight weaved their way across it. The other arm was adorned with flying dragons. The hand rests of both arms were unicorns, their long manes blowing in some imaginary wind.

"Alar, how did you decide what to carve?"

"I used to sit in the chair and shut my eyes. The images that came to me were the models for the chair's carving. When I first started to work on the chair, I had no idea that it would end up looking like this."

"I think it's beautiful," she said. "I feel as if I am sitting here in your dreams. The images here are what your heart longs for when you shut your eyes."

She shut her eyes, but continued to caress the wood. Alar gazed at her. In the glow of the fire's light, she was more beautiful than any woman he had ever seen. She stroked the wood in a very sensual manner. The image his heart longed for had little to do with flying.

Avais opened her eyes and caught Alar staring at her. He looked down and flushed embarrassedly.

Avais stood up and looked Alar straight in the eyes.

"What kind of man are you?   Have you no manners?" she asked in mock indignation.   Alar's shoulders sagged at the tone of her voice.

"You invite me in here, then stare at me." Watching Alar squirm, Avais slowly broke into a broad grin. "Staring is quite rude, especially when you guests are hungry. Do you plan on feeding me, or are you going to watch as I slowly die of starvation?"

Awkwardness dissipated from the air as Alar looked up and smiled. He left her in front of the fire while he prepared dinner in the kitchen. Alar filled the table with breads and cheeses, then opened and poured a bottle of wine.

"Alar's Restaurant is open for business," he yelled. "Come get a seat before they are all taken."

She joined him at the sturdy wooden table and inspected the fare. "This suits me well," she smiled.

Avais raised a glass of wine and looked deeply into Alar's eyes.

"Permit me to propose a toast.   To Alar's Restaurant, may its chef long prosper."

"To its guests," he replied, "may they all be as lovely as this one is!"

They clicked glasses, then sipped the wine. It was delicious, and the bottle soon lay empty on the table.

"Avais, where are you staying? There is no inn in town, and I don't know of anyone here who is renting out rooms."

"I have not been in the area for long. Since Dragon Springs is new to me, I have been staying outdoors, sleeping mostly in the waterfall cave. I enjoy living outdoors, it is no hardship for me."

Alar turned and looked at the window behind him. A sliver of moon shone in the dark sky.

"It would be far too dangerous for you to try to get back to the cave at this time of night." He paused, smiling slightly, "you may stay here if you wish."

"That might be more dangerous than trying to climb the ravine in the dark," she replied. Though her voice was steady, her eyes twinkled as she answered him.

Alar tore a thick chunk of bread and covered it with cheese. Avais did likewise, relishing the fresh taste of the food. They talked. The empty bottle of wine was pushed aside. A second bottle soon appeared and was upended.

"Tell me the truth, why are you here?" asked Alar. "Traveling over the mountains and sleeping in caves is a difficult lifestyle. Something important must be driving you."

As Avais drank, her face acquired a warm, slightly flushed color. Her accent deepened as the wine softened her voice.

"Yes, I am here on an important mission. Great danger lurks in the Dragon Spine mountains. My people have sent me to try to protect the village from an ancient evil."

Alar stared at her with an astonished look. "What danger threatens us?"

She shook her head, avoiding his gaze. "I say too much."

"You're drunk," he concluded. "You are a wonderful woman, and quite brave, I know that from the way you saved Ortut's donkey. There may be a great danger about to threaten the realm, but how could you single handedly protect us from it? Surely, you can't drive away an invading army, or banish a herd of attacking dragons? The wine must be speaking for you."

She did not answer him, but her gaze never wavered.

He smiled nervously and took her hand. With a slight wine induced slur he pronounced with theatrical bravado, "Do not fear, I will help you with your quest, fine warrior woman. Let me be your squire. I will follow you into battle and banish evil from where ever it lurks."

"I accept your offer," she coolly replied. Her voice lacked any hint of humor. "I have spent most of my life training to help others. I am needed here. If you are serious about assisting me, I would be glad to have you at my side, for it was said that I would be aided in my task. If you are humoring me, be forewarned, this is not a joke."

Alar was a bit taken aback by her sudden seriousness. Leave it to me, he thought. The most beautiful woman I have ever seen is sharing a meal with me at my house. Instead of words of romance, we are talking of quixotic adventures.

"Avais, I will help you in any way that I can. Did I not rush to your aid in the 'Adventure of the Beaten Donkey?' It is a good thing that I was there. Were it not for me, you and Marcus would not have had anyone to rescue!"

She laughed. With relief, Alar poured her another glass of wine.

"I warn you Alar, the women of my family are known for their wine drinking ability. Unless you own a vineyard, do not plan on getting me drunk!"

His reply was warm and friendly. "Didn't I tell you that my father is the village wine maker? Why do you think Marcus is so nice to me?"

"I sense a challenge being offered."

"Oh, do you?"

They drank and talked for hours.

Alar poured the last drop of wine into Avais' glass. The empty bottle clinked against the others piled by the fireplace. Alar clicked his glass against Avais'. He put his arms around her and spoke. His speech was slightly slurred as he gazed drunkenly into her eyes.

"The protector of our realm has won the challenge. That is the last bottle I own. What do I owe you for winning this most well fought contest?"

Avais turned slightly, escaping Alar's grasp. She giggled, then replied, "I believe a dance with you might go a long way towards repaying your debt. We were supposed to meet Marcus at the pub, remember? Why don't we go there now?"

Alar reluctantly agreed. Avais steadied Alar as the two weaved towards the pub.

When they arrived at the pub, a party was in full swing. Musicians had cleared the tables from one end of the room and were energetically playing their instruments. Locals played fiddles, lutes and drums. While the men pulled a lively beat out of their instruments, the crowd clapped their hands in time with the music. The center of the room was filled with dancing villagers.

Alar and Avais pushed their way into the noisy pub. Avais clung to Alar as he worked deeper into the crowd. They reached the dancing area and caught a glimpse of Marcus. He was in the middle of the floor, swinging a short brunette woman wildly around. The woman's deeply tanned skin beautifully accented the brilliant white teeth that flashed with her frequent smiles. Her long curly hair flew about as she danced. She hiked up her skirt and spun with Marcus, her shoeless feet gracefully gliding across the floor. Marcus moved in time with her. Despite his energetic gyrations, he managed to keep a flagon of ale balanced in his free hand. Couples whirled around them, following the torrid pace that the music set.

"That is Marcus' wife, Barona," yelled Alar, his voice barely reaching Avais over the din of the music. "Let's join them!"

Alar pulled Avais onto the floor. He took both her hands and began to move with the music. The fog from the wine seemed to lift as he began to dance.

Alar was an excellent dancer. He was surprised to see how well Avais followed his every move. To the crowd, it must have looked like they had been dancing together for years. He spun and dipped her in perfect time with the music. Her red hair flowed behind her like the tail of a comet as Alar swung her close to the floor. They gazed deeply into each other's eyes as they danced.

The band played faster and faster, challenging the dancers to keep up. Alar and Avais' dancing was natural and comfortable, as if they had been partners for years. They picked up the pace with ease, matching the band's efforts.

The music played faster and faster. One by one, other couples dropped out. Soon only four dancers remained on the floor. Marcus and his wife whirled at one end of the floor while Alar and Avais danced at the other. The music reached a feverish pitch as patrons in the bar began to wager on whom would last the longest.

Alar's feet seemed to fly as he wheeled around the dance floor. His speed and strength were such that Avais was lifted off the floor and swung around by him. She seemed light, almost weightless to Alar. She soared around him, her hair and dress rippling in the wind their speed created.

Sweat dripped from Marcus' brow as he tried to keep up with Alar and Avais. His ale went flying as he whirled about. The liquid soaked the floor, causing him to lose his footing. He fell, landing squarely on his bottom. As he fell, he pulled Barona down with him. She landed in his lap, laughing convulsively.

"I quit, I quit!" he yelled between labored gasps. "There is too much weight on me to continue!"

Barona punched at his panting belly. "The only weight on you is right here!" she yelled.

Alar and Avais swung by. He spun her one last time, then bent her over in a great dip. Her head hung inches above the floor as she balanced in his outstretched arm. The crowd spontaneously burst into applause. The weary band put down their instruments and joined in the ovation.

Alar looked deeply into Avais' eyes. He pulled her to her feet and drew her near. They held each other tightly, then kissed long and hard. The crowd's applause grew louder.

Neither heard the clapping from the crowd, or the raucous comments of the laborers at the bar. They were in a world that only had room for two.

After the kiss, they talked briefly with Marcus and the others, then left in each other's arms and walked towards Alar's cottage.

Avais clung tightly to Alar as they worked their way back towards his house. Something told her that he was the One.

Her mind drifted back to the days before she left her home forests of Enolar. She had been called before the Magical Elder, Jalen. He was an ancient, but kindly man, dressed in a silver robe that seemed to sparkle in the dark light of his library. Dusty books and scrolls filled the room from floor to ceiling. His gentle manner was not enough to put her at ease, for his voice was filled with tension.

"We have great need of you, my child," he had said. "Catharvus, an evil from our distant past has awakened. He is a magician of great power who has strayed from the path we have chosen. Life means little to him. If he escapes his mountain prison, he will destroy all those that stand in his way. The realm is in great danger. We need your help to defeat him."

"Why me?" Avais had asked. "I am the youngest of our sect. I do not have the knowledge and experience that you possess. I fear that I may fail. Why don't you send one of the others?"

"We are old men Avais. Our powers have dimmed with the passage of time. You are young and strong. I have seen you fly. You alone can survive the journey over the mountains. There is not enough time for us to make the trip around the mountain chain, it is far too long of a journey. By the time we reach Dragon Springs, there will be nothing left to save."

She nodded, her dark eyes wide with apprehension.

"We have consulted all of our writings on this matter. Speed is of the essence. Each day of delay increases the risk that Catharvus will escape. Once he is able to leave the mountain, there will be no way to stop him."

Avais nodded. As she listened, she fingered the edges of her robe nervously. The old man spoke again.

"There is another reason that you must be the one to cross the mountains. It is written that none of us will be able to defeat Catharvus alone. There is a man, the 'unknown child' who is destined to join in the battle against Catharvus. He may help us, or he may defeat us, but one thing is quite clear, we will have no chance at all without him. I fear he will not join the cause if he meets one of the elders first."

"I must be the one to enlist the aid of the 'unknown child'?"

Jalen nodded solemnly.

"How will I find him?"

"That, I do not know."

"Then, how will I recognize him?"

"You will know that it is him," Jalen replied. "He will be aided by a friend whose heart is as pure as his. You will know them when you see them."

"But...," she stammered.

"That is all that I can tell you, my child," said Jalen, as he led her to the door. "We will leave in the morning. Since we fly around the mountains, and you will fly over them, I fear that all will be decided before we arrive."

Avais had left for Dragon Springs that day. She had flown over the mountains, her heart pounding in her chest as she fought against the thin air, and the winds that swirled around the cloud shrouded peaks. Avais had seen Alar almost immediately upon arriving. Now she walked arm in arm with him.

There was little doubt in her mind that Alar was the One. There was just something about him that told her that he was the man the prophecy spoke of.

She felt that she was with the 'unknown child.' That made her happy.

She was with Alar. That made her happy too.

The couple soon arrived at Alar's home. They walked in together, still holding each other tightly. There was an almost palpable silence. While they had been effortlessly talking for hours, they now struggled to find words strong enough to interrupt the mood.

Avais began to hum the tune the pub musicians had been playing. She hummed it slowly, her voice caressing each note. Alar joined her, their voices blending melodiously.

He took her hands and began to dance. They circled the room, eyes locked on each other. Slowly, he drew her towards him. His muscles tightened as she pressed against him. She was soft and warm. The feel of her body, combined with the delightful aroma of her perfume, aroused a passionate fire within him.

They danced more closely. As if following a cue, both stopped humming the music. Their eyes remained locked as their dancing slowed, then stopped. They clung tightly to each other, the glowing embers of the fire throwing a thousand delicate shadows over their faces.

Alar kissed her. Avais' lips warmed and moistened at his touch.

As they kissed, Alar caressed her back with nimble fingers. She reached up and ran her fingers through his long, curly hair. Her caress was feathery and warm.

When she touches my skin, it tingles as if the tail of a comet floated down from the heavens and landed upon me, thought Alar.

He followed her lead, stroking her hair and kissing her. Alar let his lips drift downward, showering her throat with kisses. His tongue traced tiny circles across her neck. A soft moan escaped her lips. Alar's passion burned in him like a flame. He swept her into his arms and walked into the bedroom. She clung to him, her head spinning more than it had during their whirling dance. Their lips met again.

Alar gently laid Avais upon the bed, still kissing her passionately. She drew him close. Their clothes seemed to melt away in the flickering light of the room's single candle.

Avais ran her fingers across Alar's back, her nails scraping tantalizingly against his skin. Her touch was fiery enough to make Alar struggle for control.

They made gentle love. The two held each other so closely that they seemed of one body. Alar's every movement was matched by her's. Soon their bodies intertwined like the roots of two rose bushes growing in the same pot.

Their passion grew more intense. Avais pulled away from Alar's kiss, her eyes clenched tightly shut. Tremors wracked her body as pleasure overcame her. The arching of her back triggered unstoppable forces in Alar.

Both shuddered fitfully as waves of pleasure overcame them. Again, and again they pulled each other tight. They simultaneously tensed one last time, then collapsed into each other's arms.

They clung to one another. All thoughts of the world were banished as they savored each other's presence. So peaceful was their sleep, they almost didn't hear the screams that erupted from the pub as the giant spider crashed through the back wall and charged towards Marcus.

Marcus relaxed at his table. The sound of animated voices filled the air.

"Did you see those two dance?" asked one fellow.

"Did you see the look in their eyes?" replied another.

"Did you see how fast they left here. I'll bet no clothes cover them now," interjected Marcus, his thoughts as always, settling immediately on life's more basic subjects. The high alcohol content of his blood did little for his ability to restrain his always runaway tongue. His wife, Barona, punched him on the arm, admonishing him to mind his manners.

With a look of mock fear in his eyes, Marcus changed the subject. "I have known Alar since he was a child. I have seen many women come and go in his life. The look that he shared with the redhead was one that I haven't seen before on him." Unable to restrain himself, he continued. "The poor kid, he doesn't know what he's in for."

"Settling down will do him good," snapped his wife, unwittingly taking the bait that the big man was dangling before her. "How long can he run from love?"

"As long as he stays slim and fit," answered Marcus. He patted his ample midsection before continuing. "Had I not lost my form, I might still be playing the field."

"Had I not lost my mind, I might not have married you," replied Barona, warming to the upcoming verbal battle. She gently patted the mug of ale nestled in her husband's hands. "If I were not around to keep an eye on you, you would spend more time sleeping in a field than playing it."

"Not true, not true!" Marcus' face filled with a look of mock astonishment. "I never drink more than a fair ration."

One of the men at the table answered with a laugh. "You never drink more than the fair ration for an army!"

"Unfair," cried Marcus. "Two attacking one. I will not play under such unequal conditions. It reminds me of the time that..."

Marcus' wife cut in. She knew her husband well. He had an almost supernatural ability to change the subject of a conversation. She decided that this time, she would not let him.

"He should stay with one woman. The time they spend together will only increase the love they will feel for one another. With time, he will feel the happiness that you and I do."

Marcus looked at her affectionately. Fire was brewing in her eyes. He decided that saying "what happiness" would get him in far more trouble than the joke was worth. She was a woman of great beauty, both physically and intellectually. Her sharp tongue delighted Marcus as much as her looks did. Arguing with her was to be considered a proper sport, but now probably was not the best time to be testing the limits.

He took her hands in his, preparing to utter the proper romantic words that might undo the damage that he had just done.

A shuddering crash filled the air, drowning out the words that Marcus was speaking. Thatching fell from the ceiling as the back wall of the pub collapsed. Support beams staggered drunkenly before crashing to the ground. A black hairy shape, large and covered with debris, bounced into the room on thick jointed legs. It shook the boards and dirt from itself, revealing the form of a huge, slavering insect.

The spider scanned the faces of the astonished bar patrons, locating Marcus at his table. The table was situated against a wall, the only exit from the bar was yards to his right. The spider leaped with astonishing swiftness to a spot that would cut off Marcus' escape route. It then started to approach him with slow stalking steps, its leisurely pace in sharp contrast with its previous speed. It had always enjoyed a kill, especially if the prey was trapped. Given its frustrations with Catharvus' spell, a pleasurable hunt was what it needed.

One of the woodsmen, a strapping fellow of over two hundred pounds, stood from his table and faced the spider.

"Leave now!" he yelled, grabbing a stray board and banging it against a table for emphasis. The spider stopped in front of him, eyeing the board with contempt. It casually flicked a leg in his direction, striking him in the chest. The man flew back, crashing into a table halfway across the room. He moaned in pain for a moment, then slipped into unconsciousness.

The beast again began to advance. Screams filled the air as patrons scrambled in all directions seeking escape. Those that could, fled the bar through the door or the hole that stood where the back wall used to be.

Marcus jumped to his feet, pulling Barona with him. She grabbed an empty bottle from a table and threw it at the spider's head. The beast shook the shards of glass from its face, then began advancing again.

Marcus shielded his wife with his body and tried to slip along the wall. The spider scampered after him, cutting off his access to the door. Marcus then ran in the opposite direction, trying to circle the spider and reach the hole in the back wall. The spider cut him off again.

Marcus looked around, spying a window in the wall a few yards behind him. Though he was too large for him to fit through, his wife probably could use it to escape. He whispered to her as the spider slowly advanced.

When the spider was no more than ten feet in front of them, Marcus grabbed a chair and hurled it into the spider's body. The spider advanced, crushing the chair underneath its legs. It stumbled momentarily, then kicked the chair aside. While the animal was untangling itself from the chair's wreckage, Marcus seized the opportunity to escape.

He grabbed Barona and threw her towards the window. She crashed into the window sending glass flying everywhere. Ignoring the shards of glass stabbing into her arms, she pulled herself through the opening.

With his wife out of danger, Marcus turned to face the spider. He grabbed a table and charged the monster, using the table like a giant shield. The spider was only now freeing itself from the chair and was not fully braced for the big man's impact. The beast was not used to lesser creatures putting up resistance. Most became paralyzed with fear, making them an easy kill. The spider lowered its head, then took the impact of the table without flinching.

The table split in two and fell from Marcus' hands. He jumped and rolled, barely escaping the retaliatory pounce of the spider. Marcus looked around for weapons. There wasn't a sword or ax to be found. He scrambled to the fireplace and grabbed a poker.

The spider pounced upon him, knocking him to the ground. As the snapping jaws descended towards him, he slammed the poker into the spider's face. The creature backed away, momentarily stunned by the blow. Marcus ran for the door. He was almost out of the pub when he felt a stabbing pain in his left shoulder. The spider had caught up with him and had sunk its mandibles deeply into Marcus' flesh. The spider tightened its grip, then dragged Marcus back into the pub.

Marcus struggled desperately. The feeling was rapidly leaving his shoulder as the spider pumped venom into his flesh. He flailed away behind him with the poker, trying to loosen the beast's grip on his shoulder. The spider took the blows as if Marcus was hitting it with a piece of paper. Marcus felt his legs grow weak. As he fell to the ground, his eyes began to blur.

Marcus saw movement out of the corner of his eye, then felt the grip on his shoulder loosen. He struggled, squirming and thrashing about. Summoning the last of his reserves, he twisted his body violently, pulling himself out of the spider's grasp.

Marcus turned around to face the spider. The venom had numbed his entire left side, and he was feeling woozy from blood loss. The sight he saw caused an adrenaline surge that knocked the fatigue from his body.

His wife was clinging to the spider's back, gouging at its eyes with a piece of broken glass. She must have jumped on the animal from the window, distracting it enough to permit Marcus to wiggle free.

The spider roared in pain from the woman's assaults. It began to spin, trying to shake Barona from its back. The glass flew from her hand as she clutched at the animal's shell. The creature spun faster and faster, causing Barona to slide back, as her grip on the monster's shell loosened. The animal clicked its bloody mandibles in anticipation.

Marcus grabbed a chair with his good arm, lowered his head, and charged at the spider. He swung the chair with all his might, hitting the beast flush across the face. Wood splinters showered the area as the chair exploded into a thousand tiny pieces.

The impact caused the spider to stagger. Barona seized the opportunity and leapt to the ground. She ran towards the door, yelling at her husband to follow her. Marcus tried to follow her, but the venom was affecting his coordination. His legs were stiff, his movements slow and clumsy.

The spider was in an insane rage now. It roared from the wounds across its face and side. Purple blood leaking from the gashes that Barona had made, dripped onto the floor.

The spider sprung at Marcus and slammed him to the ground. With its front legs, it held him down. The spider's weight was crushing the life out of Marcus. Ribs popped as he fought for air. He turned his head towards Barona who had run back into the room and forced out words through the waves of pain that engulfed him.

"I love you, my wife," he gasped. "Run away! Save yourself! Please leave while you have the chance."

"Shut up you drunken fool!" she yelled as she threw herself against the spider. She pounded against the animal's shell with her bare hands.

The spider reached up with a back leg and flicked Barona away like a speck of lint. She flew across the room, crashing into the rubble of the collapsed wall.

Marcus' vision faded to black as the spider buried its mandibles in his chest. His body spasmed, then went limp as the beast shook him about. When it was sure that no life remained in the man's body, the spider dropped it and charged towards Barona.

Barona looked up at the monster. Her husband's blood dripped from the mandibles that snapped in front of her. She tried to get up, but when she put weight on her leg, it collapsed from under her. The leg lay twisted at an unnatural angle, jagged edges of broken bone poked through the flesh in two places.

She closed her eyes, bracing herself for the inevitability of her upcoming death. Sadness did not fill her. She would join her husband in the afterlife. Her pain would be brief.

The spider stared at the woman crumpled on the floor. It waited for her to open her eyes. It wanted to see the waves of terror wash over her face before it killed her.

Barona waited for what seemed like ages, but felt nothing. A roar erupted in front of her. It was so powerful that her hair rustled from the breath that propelled the scream. She raised an eyelid, daring a peek at the nightmare her world had become.

The spider was backing away from her! It turned around, facing an adversary that she could not see. One of its hind legs lay on the floor. Blood oozed from the wound where the limb had been severed from its body.

The spider lunged at its attacker. It was slowed by the loss of the limb and missed. It lunged again, but again struck only air. With each lunge, it was being drawn further away from Barona. She tried again to stand, but her leg wouldn't support her. Pulling herself along with her arms, she crawled towards her husband's body.

Once she reached him, she cradled his head in her hands and cried. The battle roared on in front of her. The spider charged forward, snapping at an opponent who dodged behind the bar to escape it. As the spider limped forward, a figure climbed on the bar, then dove across the room and wheeled to meet the animal. Barona looked up and recognized her rescuer. It was Alar.

Alar, barefoot and bare chested, swung an ax at the spider. He had connected with the spider earlier when the beast was preoccupied with stalking Barona. The blow had severed its hind leg. Now that the beast was not distracted, Alar was having much more difficulty with it. The spider charged forward, crowding Alar so that he couldn't take a good swing with the ax.

Alar backed away, desperately trying to get enough room to attack. He jumped on a table, then leapt towards a light fixture suspended from the ceiling by a chain. Ignoring the burning candles, he grabbed the fixture and swung across the room. He landed on his feet behind the spider, drew back his ax and slammed the blade into the spider's carapace. The blade momentarily stuck, but pulled out when the animal spun to face Alar.

Blood poured from the gash in the monster's shell, but it didn't turn away. The spider recognized Alar, and the 'Obey Spell's' effects kicked in. Instead of being slowed by the wound, the spider, driven by the spell, roared with anger, and attacked with renewed vigor. It roared, then lunged forward. The monster snapped at Alar, ignoring the windup that the man was taking with the ax. Alar swung at the spider, confident that if he could connect with the animal's throat, he would be able to kill it.

His ax whistled towards the spider who sidestepped the blow and snapped its mandibles shut on the handle. The two-inch thick shaft snapped like a twig, its blade skittering across the floor.

Alar was now unarmed. He poked at the spider with the stub of the ax's handle. The spider, undaunted by the stick, advanced steadily towards him. Alar backed away, but hit the wall behind him.

The spider charged forward, pinning him against the wall. Alar rained blows on the spider, but to no avail. It reached up with its front legs and forced Alar to the ground. Alar watched as the jaws opened then clicked a few times in front of his throat. Marcus' blood dripped from them into his face. Barona screamed in the distance. The jaws opened once more, then moved forward towards his neck.

Alar's eyes stared at the approaching death. Blue light glinted off the saliva dripping from the spider's jaws. Suddenly, the room was rocked with an explosion as showers of sparks rained down on Alar. The spider tumbled end over end and landed on its back after slamming into the far wall of the pub. It clawed its way upright, then limped out the hole in the wall, and escaped into the forest.

Alar looked around the room for some explanation. He saw Avais running towards him.

"My darling, are you all right?" she asked, her voice filled with worry.

Alar nodded, too stunned to talk. Avais turned towards Barona and Marcus. Marcus lay limp in her arms. His skin was a mottled blue, his eyes stared lifelessly at his wife. She was crying softly, her tears spilling onto Marcus' blood stained beard.

She kissed him on the lips whispering between kisses.

"My love. I must not be separated from you, my love. Give some of the beast's poison to me so that I may stay with you forever. I do not want to live without you."

Avais walked over to Barona and put her arms around her. She spoke comforting words while staring deeply into her eyes. She pulled her away from Marcus' body and lifted her in one of the bar's few remaining chairs.

"This is the doing of one of my kind. It must be undone. I will help you," she said in a distant voice so soft it was almost a whisper. Avais' accent deepened as her thoughts turned inwards. "Alar, comfort Barona. Do not let her stand on her leg until I can fix it."

Alar nodded to her. She stared blankly at Marcus as tears welled in his eyes.

Avais recited a healing spell and joined the broken bones in Barona's legs. The crowd that was forming gasped in astonishment. Avais then took off her robe and covered Barona with it. Standing naked over Marcus, her eyes seemed to glaze over. She began to chant in a strange tongue. Alar noted that the tattoo on her arm seemed to glow as she moved her hands about in a serpentine manner. She drew out energies from her own body, compressing them into a glowing ball. Avais held the shimmering cloud for a moment in her hand, then brought it to her lips. She inhaled, then shut her eyes and place her lips against Marcus'. Ignoring their cold, rubbery texture, she pressed against them, then exhaled. Marcus' chest rose as her breath drove the magical energies into his body.

Avais slumped down. Despite his shock, Alar noticed how pale and weak she suddenly looked. Her hair hung over Marcus' face obscuring it from view. A shuddering gasp came from below her face. Marcus' legs twitched twice, then lay still.

Suddenly the big man's voice boomed out. "Don't get me wrong. I loved it, but if you kiss me again, make sure Barona isn't looking! You know how jealous she can be. She'll kill me!"

Barona gasped, then ran over to her husband. She kissed him repeatedly as tears of joy streamed down her face.

Avais slowly put her robe on, then turned towards Alar. His face was pale, almost as pale as her's. She reached for his hand but he pulled it away from her. As she moved towards him, he backed away in fear. Alar turned his back to her and went to help Marcus and Barona.

Avais, her eyes moist, picked up her pack and slowly walked out the door into the night.

The sun rose, driving away both the shadows and the terrors of the night. The entire village congregated at the pub as if a town meeting had been called. Together they worked to rebuild the wreckage of what was once the keystone of their social life. The healer tended to the injured, fixing cuts and bruises that had occurred during the escape from the pub.

Alar was conspicuous by his absence.

The story of Avais' heroics kept the villagers entertained as they worked. The people talked excitedly about the return of the Air Children to the area. Most of the villagers agreed that she must have been summoned by the blue moon eclipse, though nobody knew why.

With the town's combined effort, the pub was rebuilt. By late afternoon, the back wall had been repaired, the window above it fixed. Those not working on the reconstruction cut wood and constructed new tables and chairs, or cleaned up the bloody debris that was strewn throughout the pub.

As the sun blazed brilliant shades of rose and lavender on the horizon, the people took seats. It was time for drinks and thanks-giving. Marcus stood on a table and with the help of a friend hoisted the severed spider's leg into the air and lashed it over the front door.

He admired his work and boomed out a pompous proclamation.

"Ladies and gentlemen. A celebration is in order. Let me..."

"Quick, get him a drink!" whispered his wife. "If he gets going, it will take half the night to shut him up!"

Marcus ignored the interruption and continued.

"I want to take this opportunity to thank all the people of Dragon Springs. Working together, we have rebuilt our pub. It is only fitting that the pub receive a new name to match its new walls.

"My fellow townsmen, let us raise our glasses to celebrate the opening of the 'Bug's Leg Pub!'"

The air was filled with upraised glasses. The people toasted each other as well as the pub's new name. Hard work and togetherness were easing the horror of the night before.

Once the formalities were done, the drinking began in earnest. Other than the hairy leg mounted above the door, the night was no different from any other pub night, except of course for the cache of weapons piled near the bar. The townsmen would be prepared should the monster return.

After a few drinks, Marcus whispered something to his wife, took an extra flagon of ale with him, and left the bar.

He weaved his way through the village until he came to Alar's house. He knocked on the unlocked door, and after hearing no reply, let himself in.

Alar was seated in his carved chair staring into the fireplace. The fire had just about burnt itself out, leaving nothing but dying embers in the hearth. His eyes were bloodshot, he looked as if he had been up since the spider attack of last night. He clutched a white feather that Avais must have left behind. He absentmindedly stroked it as he thought.

"I brought you a drink," Marcus said softly. He offered the mug to Alar who did not even turn to acknowledge his presence. "Are you sure you don't want some ale? From the looks of you, it might do you some good."

Alar continued to stare at the dying fire. He didn't give Marcus any indication that he knew he was there.

Marcus was undaunted.

"Drink, or I'll get a funnel and force it down your throat!" He moved towards Alar, pushing the mug into his hands. "My friend, drink! The ale is going down your throat one way or another."

Marcus' presence finally broke Alar's reverie. He blinked his bloodshot eyes and looked up at his friend.

"I'm sorry. I didn't hear you at first."

Marcus smiled knowingly.

"Either your hearing is failing you, or you are troubled. I think that you are far too young to be going deaf. Want to talk about what troubles you?"

"No, not really," Alar answered, probably more harshly than he had intended.

Marcus frowned while raising his bushy brows.

"Well, I suppose I could beat it out of you. No, that would be the wrong thing to do to a man who tried to save my life yesterday... Alar, you are my friend. Talk to me. I want to help you if I can."

Alar began slowly.

"I don't know... Its Avais."

Marcus nodded understandingly.

"It's not monster attacks or celestial foreboding," the big man said. "It's a problem with a woman. I knew that nothing simple would get you so upset."

Alar didn't laugh. "It's just that I thought she was perfect," he sobbed. I loved everything about her. Then I find out that she was nothing that she appeared to be. She is a sorcerer, a witch. I thought that I loved her. How could I have been such a fool?"

"Alar, the fact that Avais knows how to practice magic does not make her any less of a woman. Her beauty, her kindness and her intelligence are no different. She is just a person who has learned to modify the natural forces, just as you, a wood carver, modified a tree's wood into that beautiful chair."

Alar shook his head while rapping his fist against the chair's arm.

"Why didn't she tell me she was a sorceress? Why did she have to play me for the fool?"

"Maybe she tried to tell you. Sometimes we hear only what we want to hear." He noticed that Alar seemed to be listening to him. "Alar, why do you fear magic so? It is an art and a lifestyle no different from any other. Its practitioners are men and women just like ourselves. Under the robes are bodies that are made of flesh and blood."

Alar smiled weakly.

"Alar, did you not enjoy Avais' company? I've never seen you so happy."

Alar nodded affirmatively.

"Then, don't be a fool boy. Love may come along only once in a lifetime. You are destroying yourself and probably Avais as well, for reasons based on superstition, fear and misunderstanding."

He continued, but noticed Alar's tightly clenched jaw.

"How can you hate someone you loved only yesterday? You are talking about a woman who gave me back my life! Were it not for her, Barona would be wearing black and visiting me in the cemetery, instead of waiting for me in the pub. Open your mind to fresh ideas! How can the man I helped raise be so thick headed?"

Alar did not answer him. He slowly looked away from Marcus and stared into the ale that Marcus had given him. Heavy silence filled the air.

When it was clear that Alar had nothing further to say, Marcus sadly shook his head, turned away and walked to the door. He looked back at Alar who was once again staring into the fireplace.

"You are a fool!" he said softly as he closed the door.

Marcus walked back towards the pub, his heart heavy with Alar's torment. He looked back at his friend's house. The door remained shut. A cold wind kicked up, causing him to shiver. He hurried towards the warmth of the pub.

Alar slumped deeper into his chair and watched the embers until they barely glowed. He threw the feather into the fireplace, noting the writhing contortions it went through before the heat consumed it. The hearth went cold. He sat in the darkness, staring at nothing, as the night passed on.

The morning broke revealing a spectacular day. The air was crisp and heavily scented with the smell of flowering vines. The beauty of the day did little to resolve Avais' sadness.

She sat at the entrance of the hidden waterfall cave and stared at the valley below. Dew sparkled like jewels on the vines surrounding her. Far below, the river glistened as it coursed through the craggy rocks that surrounded it. The beauty of the scene before her could not overcome the emptiness that she felt. She had only known Alar for a short while, yet he had aroused feelings in her that she had never experienced before. She missed his smile, his gentleness, his touch. The fact that magic was the wedge that had driven them apart only made her feel worse since that was the real reason she had been sent to meet him.

She felt like a total failure.

A pair of doves flew by the cave opening. One of the birds noticed Avais sitting amongst the vines. It banked towards her and was soon followed by its mate. The birds fluttered in front of Avais long enough for her to see that they did not bear the markings of magical transformation, but in fact were real birds.

She smiled at them and said, "Come my friends, I could use the company."

The birds alighted on her hand and began to coo. She scratched the head of one of the birds who ruffled its feathers approvingly.

"Children of the wind, you look so happy together. You soar, unfettered by worries or earthly bounds. How I envy you! I will never know the joy that you two feel, for the man I love hates me for what I am."

The bird on her hand gazed knowingly into Avais' eyes. It stroked her thumb by rubbing its head and neck against her. Soft cooing accompanied its efforts.

"Thank you kind friend," she replied. A wistful expression came to her face. "Your invitation is most comforting, but I am afraid that now is not the time for me to fly off with you. Though nothing would make me happier, I must not leave. I have a great task to do whose importance far out shadows my minor problems. You see, I must find a way to return the ancient one to his long slumber. He aims to bring death and destruction to this valley. Only I can prevent the great tragedy that will surely come if I fail. I know that Alar is the key to the defeat of Catharvus, yet he shuns me as if I am the evil one. I don't know what to do."

She closed her eyes in an effort to stem the flood of tears that threatened to fall.

Both birds looked at her. They seemed to share her sadness. She continued to stroke them, the action soothing her as much as it did them.

"You must be hungry," she said. "Let's go into the cave and get you a treat. Come with me."

Avais carried the birds into the cave. They clung to her as she navigated her way through the tangle of vines that fell from the ceiling. Inside, she opened her pack and took out some seeds. The birds ate as she sat on a rock looking at them.

"I have done no harm to Alar," Avais lamented. "I have saved his life many times since I first saw him in the forest. You know, for a hero, he sure needs a lot of rescuing!"

Both birds stopped eating. The larger of the two, a male named Pax, firmly gripped Avais' thumb, then pivoted until he was hanging upside down from it. He let go with his feet, squawking as he fell towards the floor. At the last possible moment, he spread his wings and soared back to Avais' shoulder.

Avais smiled.

"You saw him fall from this cliff. Yes, he was a sight as he tumbled towards the rocks. He doesn't fly too well," she laughed.

The birds renewed their attack on Avais' seeds.

"The prophecy says that a woodsman will be chosen. He is to have both the ability to defeat the evil sorcerer or to help him escape. I am sure that Alar is the one the elders spoke of. From the moment I saw him, I knew that he was the One. He has grabbed my heart. Why can't I touch his?"

Tears welled in Avais' eyes. The birds stopped eating and tried to comfort her. They jumped into her hands and Avais held them to her cheeks. The birds cooed softly. Despite their ministrations, she cried more and more. Great sobs wracked her body as tears ran down her cheeks dampening the feathers of the doves.

She was so overwrought with grief that she did not notice the rustling that came from the vines as something forced its way past them and entered the cave.

Catharvus gazed into the orb at the sleeping spider. The animal lay in the woods, unmoving. It twitched a few times, then wearily rose.

Good, thought Catharvus, it still lives.

"It is about time you arose," he spoke as he stared at the wavering image in the orb. "You have been asleep for more than a day. I trust that you are feeling well, I have a job for you."

The spider felt far from well. It ached from its many injuries. Part of its brain cried out to ignore the voice that tormented it. The obey spell remained, but had it weakened? The spider would try to rebel against the sorcerer.

Catharvus' voice echoed painfully in the spider's head.

"I know you want revenge on the human who severed your leg. I have followed him with the orb. He now waits for you in a mountain cave. The orb will send you the image of where the cave is. Go to him. Kill him. Bring his body back to me."

The spider ignored the instructions and turned towards the deep woods. Angry waves of pain exploded in its head as the sorcerer yelled into the orb. The spider attempted to ignore Catharvus' orders and continue towards the woods. The agony in its head increased until the exploding bolts of lightning became totally intolerable. Death would be preferable to the torture it was suffering. Unable to resist any more, the spider shuddered, then found itself turning towards the ravine. The torment only relented after the shaking monster left the forest and began to climb the rock face towards the cave.

The birds in Avais' hands squawked in fear. Avais, heeding their warning, wheeled around. The vines at the cave's mouth were moving as something tried to force its way past them. With one unbroken motion, she threw the doves into the air and began to summon a fighting spell. She knew that she would not have enough time to ready a ranged attack, but hoped that a contact type spell could be ready in time.

Her hands glowed with crackling electrical energy as she prepared to meet the shape that was emerging from the vines. Her heart raced as she braced herself for battle. Catharvus was an evil enemy. Who knows what abomination the old sorcerer had sent her way? The doves screeched as they wheeled about the narrow confines of the cave.

Avais lowered herself into a fighting stance. She locked her arms in front of her and half closed her eyes in anticipation of the flash that would occur when the magical energies discharged. Her spell would cause a localized conversion of magical energy into heat. Such a contact explosion could severely injure or kill an adversary. By crouching, she meant to strike up into the face of the intruder as it reached for her. She wondered if the creature would even have face.

Alar burst through the vines and ducked to avoid the circling doves. The sun outside shone directly into Avais' face through the parted vines. With the halo of light behind Alar, and his face covered in shadow, Avais couldn't recognize the figure that stood before her. She wasn't even sure if it was human.

The intruding figure stood up, then spread its arms widely and advanced towards Avais. She backed up slightly, bracing herself for contact.

Alar was surprised at the way Avais cringed before him. He had a thousand things he wanted to tell her. He wanted to apologize to her, to tell her that he couldn't live without her. He would change his ways. He could learn to appreciate her magic as a gift instead of looking at it as the future cause of his death.

Most of all, he wanted to hold her again.

Avais braced for contact with her attacker. She knew that with her first touch, there would be an explosion. Her hands were magically protected, but the intruder was not. The flash of releasing energy would create great heat as flesh catalyzed it. Her attacker's skin would blister and peel as the magical heat burned it. Since she was aiming for the face, he would probably be blinded. While the intruder rolled about the floor in pain, she would have time to collect her things and escape.

As she stepped forward to set off the spell in Alar's face, Avais was startled by the doves. Feathery wings batted against her mouth and cheeks. Frantic cooing filled the air.

Surprised, she opened her eyes widely. One of the doves was hovering before her, doing everything in its power to distract her. Its cooing took on a more frantic tone as she tried to duck away from it so that she could get a better bead on her attacker. Seconds later, the other dove joined in. It landed on her arm, tightly gripping her sleeve.

Avais' heart skipped a beat as the intruder spoke. Her disbelieving ears barely heard the soft voice say, "Even the birds get between us, I am the unluckiest man alive."

She recognized Alar's voice immediately. She clasped her shaking hands together dissipating the spell.

With the birds now calmly riding her shoulders, she replied in a voice choking with emotion, "Alar, I wouldn't bet on that!"

Alar and Avais stared silently at each other.

Alar noticed the tears still clinging to Avais' cheeks. He knew that he was the reason she had been crying. Beneath the robes of a sorceress was a very real woman, one whom he had greatly upset.

Alar walked to her.

"I'm sorry, my love," he whispered. "I have learned my lesson. I promise that I will change. I will never hurt you again, that I swear. If it means that magic will be my death, so be it. I do not value life if it is a life without you."

He took her in his arms, holding her tightly against him. The tension in her body melted away as she buried her face in his chest and sobbed.

Alar's eyes began to mist. Gently, he steered Avais over to the rocks by the waterfall and sat her down on one. He stroked her hair and kissed her, his lips brushing away the falling tears.

The doves watched them keenly. Flying to the rocks next to them, they noticed how occupied the humans seemed. With no chance of getting attention from Avais, they began to bathe and play at the water's edge.

Alar sat next to Avais and gave her a gentle squeeze.

"I spent the entire night thinking about us," he said. "Though I still fear that magic will be the death of me, I love you too much to not be with you. Avoiding you would not remove magic from the world. It would only prevent me from sharing the joy of your company. I would be spending my life alone in misery, separated from the woman I love by my own doing. I will not do that to myself."

Avais looked up and smiled weakly. She took his offered hand and squeezed it. The skin of his palms was rough from years spent working in the woods. How could it be that his fingers were so soft?

"Alar, I love you too. I tried to conceal my magic from you. That was wrong. What was I to do? I didn't want to lose you, yet you wouldn't accept the things about me that I cannot change. It is difficult to be punished when the only crime that I committed is to be what I am."

Alar put his finger to her lips. "Shhh... You did nothing wrong. My actions were driven by emotions that I do not fully understand. By hiding your magical talents from me, you gave me a chance to get to know the real you. I realize now that the person that you are is far more important than the clothes you wear."

He tried to kiss her, but she pulled away. He tried again, this time their lips lingered in a long embrace. Avais chuckled slightly, then with a quick motion, pushed Alar backwards. He gasped as she slipped from his arms and he tumbled backwards into the waterfall's pool. Avais stood, arching her back in glee as Alar came sputtering to the pool's surface.

"That was for throwing me out of the pub after I had saved your life!" Avais smiled coyly as she looked down at Alar.

Alar noted that immersion in the water of the pool did nothing to extinguish his desire for her. He lunged forward, grabbing her foot. Despite her squeals of protest, he dragged her into the pool.

They made love in the showering spray at the base of the waterfall, then crawled onto a smooth spot on the rocks. Body heat kept them warm as they held each other closely.

Alar whispered, "I love you." She looked deeply into his eyes and told him that she loved him too.

Sleep overtook them. As they dozed, the doves eyed them fondly.

Alar awoke as Avais arose and started to dress. What a vision she was! Alar shuddered inside at the thought of how close he had come to losing her. He vowed to be more open minded, no matter how strange future situations might appear. He would never again look at the magical arts with a mind clouded by hatred and fear.

Avais slipped into her clothes and held her hands out to the doves. They flew to her, she held them close. The birds nestled in her arms like kittens, cooing contentedly. When she cooed back to them, they listened.

Alar stood up and stretched. He walked to Avais and watched her caress the birds.

"It amazes me how tame they are with you," he said. "One would think that you had raised them from the egg, they trust you so."

Avais smiled broadly and rubbed her cheek against the cooing dove. It did not struggle, but nibbled gently on her face. The tickle of the bird's beak made her laugh.

"They are my friends. The birds know that I mean them no harm. All animals like to be petted and held. If I remember, you are no different!"

"True," laughed Alar, "but I am a creature of the land. I am sturdy. Contact does not frighten me. Birds, by their very nature are different. They are fragile. A bird lives only as long as it can flee from its enemies. When a dove is held in the hand of man, it usually is about to be eaten."

Avais answered, her accent a combination of understandable words following a cooing cadence.

"These birds know that I would not hurt them. Once they overcome their fear, they love nothing more than the contact of a friend." She held out one of the birds. "This is Pax. He wants to meet you!"

Alar reached tentatively for the bird. It was the bigger of the two and possessed a beak that could probably deliver a painful nip. Pax hopped onto his hand and stared intently at him.

Alar returned the bird's gaze, cocking his head as the bird did. He gingerly touched the bird's head. The animal did not flinch, nor did it try to bite him. Soon, Alar was absentmindedly rubbing the animal's head and neck while he talked to Avais. Pax fluffed up his neck feathers as Alar found a particularly pleasurable spot.

"Avais, the birds love you. There seems to be a special bond between you and them. Even your tattoo has a bird on it. Can you tell me more about your link to birds?"

"The bird is the symbol of my sect," Avais answered. "The 'Air Children' have learned much from them. Birds are animals that have learned to harness the forces of nature. The wind that blows in our face lifts the bird's wings, allowing it to soar in the sky. Our magic works in much the same way. By harnessing the natural energies, we are able to produce magical changes. My people have studied birds and nature for generations. We have learned much from our friends. The bond that has developed between us is one of both admiration and respect. The birds treat us as brothers."

While Alar pondered her words, he stopped petting the dove. Pax was not pleased at Alar's pause for thought. He rolled in Alar's hand until he lay on his back, feet sticking up. The dove grabbed Alar's finger with his feet then gently bit his thumb.

Pax's antics distracted Alar from his thoughts. He was soon engaged in a wrestling match with the dove. Pax was obviously enjoying himself. He gripped the man's fingers while sparring wholeheartedly with his thumb. Fearsome squeaks emanated from his mouth as he wrestled with Alar.

Alar chuckled, then burst into laughter.

Avais scolded him. "Don't laugh at him, you will hurt his feelings!"

Seemingly on cue, the bird gave up its struggle, flipped itself over and flew to Avais. He cooed softly, then began to preen. Avais helped him, stroking his rumpled ego as she smoothed his feathers. She talked softly to the bird; it answered with series of coos and chirps.

Avais beamed a smile in Alar's direction as she fought to suppress a laugh.

"Pax says that you fly worse than he wrestles!"

"What do you mean?" replied the slightly stunned Alar.

"He saw you when you fell from the cliff wall below this cave. He thinks that your tumbling was a pretty poor excuse for flying. Pax says that if I had not cast a Feather Fall spell on you, the rocks below would look like an egg had rolled out of a dragon's nest!"

Avais laughed, but stopped abruptly when she saw the look on Alar's face.

"I have always wanted to fly," he said. "While I was falling, I made peace with myself, and I know this seems silly, but I actually enjoyed the weightless feeling of the fall." He thought for a moment, his brow creasing as he tried to make sense of all that had happened to him. "I was very high. The fall would have killed me. It seems that I must thank you again for saving me."

Alar started to say something, then stopped. He stared at his feet. When he looked up, he asked, "Were you the one hidden in the forest when Marcus and I were attacked by Orcs? Did your magic save me?"

"I was, and it did," replied Avais. "Though I knew little about you, I could not bear to let those evil creatures hurt you. You are a kind and gentle person. I saw that when you went out of your way to save the bird's nest. Such goodness deserves goodness in kind."

"Were you about to use magic when the merchant tried to stab me? Did your magic heal the donkey?"

"The answer to both your questions is yes. My magic was responsible. Wouldn't you have done the same if the roles were reversed?"

"I guess that I would," admitted Alar. He looked at Avais with a new found feeling of admiration. As he stared into Avais' dark eyes, Alar said, "You know, you are a very special woman. Thank you again for being there when I needed you."

As Alar reached over to kiss Avais, Pax squawked again.

Alar winked at him. "Sorry sport. You know, for a little guy, you sure have a strong grip. If you were my size, you would be able to crush a boulder!"

Avais translated Alar's words into a series of coos and squeaks. The bird seemed placated by his words and flew back to him, landing on his shoulder.

Alar continued. "You know, Mr. Pax, you do wrestle better than I fly. Man was not meant to fly, though I wish it wasn't so. You will never know how much I envy your ability to soar through the sky, to see the landscape pass by in distant miniatures. I would trade my wrestling ability for your wings in a heartbeat."

Avais spoke softly, "You can."

Alar looked unsteadily at her. He seemed torn by internal turmoil. Finally, he spoke.

"With magic, I can fly?"

"Yes. The 'Air Children' have learned to harness the natural energies to change ourselves into other forms. I can use magic to turn into a dove. In that form, I was able to fly past you, unnoticed. You were watching the opening, waiting for a human to walk out.

You never expected me to leave the cave in the form of a
bird.

"I remember," Alar answered. "I saw a dove
enter the cave while I was eating my lunch. I also saw
one leave it while I was waited for you. I had no idea
that such a transformation was possible. Now that I
know what you can do, some of the mysteries are
disappearing. You were able to fly out of the cave and
down to the river's edge in seconds. That is how you
were there to save me. If you travel as a bird, you could
cover great distances, and not look road weary. It is all
beginning to make sense now!"

"That is right. In my bird transformed state, I
can fly and do whatever a bird can. I think the thoughts
of a human, but I have the body of a bird. You can
harness these powers too, Alar. I have observed you
closely. You possess the temperament and grace to be
able to control the energies that abound around you."

Alar looked stunned. "You mean that I could
create magic myself. You would not be throwing a spell
on me? I would be casting it myself?"

"Not only would you cast it, but you would
control it. Think of it Alar, you could make yourself fly.
We could fly together!"

Alar's heart raced. A distant part of his mind screamed for him to get away. Running would take him out of the chain of events that was immersing him in magic. What if this was the magical death he had dreamed about? Before the feelings got the better of him, he caught himself. He had promised to look at things with an open mind, here was a chance to explore the world that the woman he loved lived in. It was also a chance to explore the parts of him that he both longed for and feared the most.

He took a deep breath, then forced hesitant words from his mouth.

"Avais, I love you. I trust you with my life. Teach me what I must know."

Avais got her pack and sat by Alar. She opened it and withdrew a large book. The pages of the book were trimmed in gold, the lettering was ornate, the flowing script the work of a skilled calligrapher. The book had the image of a flying bird engraved on its leather cover.

"Look closely, my love," she said, "and I will show you how my magic works."

Avais opened the book to the page that contained the 'Feather Fall' spell. Alar noticed the stylized figure of a feather drifting slowly down to earth that graced the top part of the page. She showed him that each spell was made up of three parts. The first, neatly printed under the elaborately drawn title, was the spell's preamble.

"Reading this part makes the magical energies visible to the naked eye. They flow around us at all times, but are normally unfocused. Once you have made them visible, you can concentrate and focus their energies to do your bidding. There are many types of Earth energies that we can manipulate. Different preambles bring up different kinds of energy. Each one is slightly different in its color and the way it can be manipulated. The spell instructions will be very specific in the preamble. Call up the wrong type of energy, and you have a recipe for disaster!"

Alar gulped nervously. He laced his hands and took a deep breath.

"I think I understand, Avais. Show me more."

Avais reached over and gave Alar's hand a squeeze. "Don't worry, it is not as difficult as it sounds," she said reassuringly.

Avais then pointed to the middle section of the page. The text there described hand motions. Small pictures of hands helped illustrate the concepts that the words spelled out.

"Once you can see the energy waves, performing these motions will concentrate them for you. You will produce a packet of energy that awaits only the addition of the appropriate catalyst to complete the magical spell. The catalyst is described in the bottom section. All spells have catalyst requirements. If you do not add a catalyst, the concentrated energies will unravel and the spell will fizzle out."

"What if you add the wrong catalyst?"

"If you add the wrong substance, the spell will misfire, anything could happen. Most of the time, the catalyst that you add makes sense, but sometimes the object that is needed will surprise you. I have seen some magical disasters happen from misfired spells. Trust me, catalyst research is an area of magic that is best avoided!"

"Don't worry," Alar muttered under his breath.

Avais ignored him and continued.

"Watch closely," she said as she began to chant the words from the top section of the page. Alar was amazed to see pink lines of energy become visible throughout the room. The energy forces zipped from wall to wall, then shot through the rocks themselves, and out of the cave. With each word from Avais, the lines of power glowed more deeply.

"Observe how I manipulate the energy," she said as her hands corralled the energy lines. Avais deflected, redirected and compressed the energy until it formed a glowing pink packet. She held this in her hand and presented it to Alar.

"This is the uncatalyzed spell. Touch it. Don't be afraid, it won't hurt you."

Alar gingerly reached out and poked at the glowing mass with one finger. He was surprised at the way it felt. It seemed solid to the touch, yet throbbed and undulated before his eyes.

"Would it be safe for me to hold it?"

"Yes," she replied. "The energy will not be released without a catalyst. The catalyst for this spell is, appropriately enough a feather."

Alar took the energy packet and turned it over in his hands. It had form, yet no weight, a most unusual sensation! It was like holding his hand against the wind.

Alar studied the energy packet closely. He poked at it and tossed it from hand to hand. He tried squeezing it. It was spongy and resilient, rapidly returning to its original shape. As he stared at it, its edges became fuzzy. It blinked twice, then unraveled before his eyes.

"What did I do?" he asked frantically.

"Nothing my love. The compressed spell energies have a time limit to them. If the catalyst is not rapidly added to them, they unravel. This applies to all of the spell that I know. They cannot be stored or given away. This is unfortunate as it can be very difficult to cast them properly in an emergency."

"I'll bet it is."

"Now Alar, let's try again. I will need your help. Pick up a rock and hold it at about chest height."

Alar picked up a pink and black granite stone about eight inches in diameter.

"Now drop it," she commanded.

The stone fell to the floor, bouncing twice before cracking nearly in half.

Pax immediately began squawking. Avais tried to suppress it, but burst out into laughter.

"What did he say?" demanded Alar.

Between gasps of laughter, Avais answered, "The stone flies about as well as you do!"

Alar glared at the dove.

"Roasted dove is one of Marcus' specialties," he snickered. "Care to come over for dinner?"

"Boys, boys!" interrupted Avais. "Now shut up and watch." She began to recast the 'Feather Fall' spell. When she had the formed energy packet in hand, she told Alar to pick up the rock again.

"Now watch as I catalyze the magical energies."

She reached into her cloak and pulled out a small feather. Carefully, she placed it onto the glowing mass in her hands. The was a sharp flash of light, followed by a muffled pop. The spell had changed into a whirling rainbow cloud of sparkling colors.

She said, "Now I am going to throw the activated spell against the rock you are holding."

Alar backed up a step, then stood rigidly. Avais noticed the beads of sweat form on his forehead. She lightly tossed the spell at the rock in Alar's hand. It streaked away from her like a comet and enveloped the rock. The energies danced over the surface of the rock, causing it to shimmer and undulate like a mirage. Alar inched the rock forward until he held it pinched between two fingers like a piece of rotten fruit.

"Relax! You have already had this spell thrown against you, remember? That is why I picked it! Now drop the rock, will you, you look like you are afraid it will burn your fingers off!"

Alar gratefully let go of the rock. Instead of falling like it had a few moments before, the stone drifted lazily downward. It fluttered in widening circles until it settled lightly on the cave's floor.

"Wow!" exclaimed Alar, his excitement causing his voice to crack. "That was wonderful! Tell me, is that the spell you use to fly?"

"No, it isn't. The 'Feather Fall' spell could let you drift downward from a cliff, but it won't let you fly.

I wanted to start you out on that spell because you knew its effects first hand. To fly, we use a Transformation spell. Remember I told you of my sect's close links with the birds?"

Alar nodded.

"Well, when we use the Transform spell, we are changed into bird form. In that form, flight is natural to us. Here, let me show you the spell in the book."

Avais turned the book to the first page. She showed Alar the steps as she read the preamble, then gracefully molded the raw energies into a heart shaped, purple energy packet. The compacted magical energies sizzled and popped in Avais' hand.

"Is the catalyst for this spell a feather too?" asked Alar.

"No, though that would be a good guess. The catalyst is the tattoo on my forearm. All the 'Air Children' have the same tattoo. The inks that form it are magical. When the concentrated spell packet comes in contact with the tattoo, the energy is released, changing my shape into that of a dove."

"Does the spell wear off on its own?" he asked."

"No," she laughed, "it doesn't wear off. If it did, I wouldn't use it. Time limitation on a spell like this would be a disaster. Imagine what would happen if you were to change back into a human while flying a hundred feet above the ground!

When we change into bird form, the tattoo reforms on our chest feathers. When the tattoo is touched to the embossed seal on the front of the spell book, the energy leaves our bodies, returning us to our human form. The 'Transform' spell does not have a time limit. A person will remain in bird form until he touches the 'Air Children' seal."

Avais held up the energy packet, closed the spell book, then slipped out of her cloak. She kissed him, then yelled, "Watch me fly!" as she stepped away from him. She touched the spell energy packet to her tattoo activating the spell.

A blinding flash of light occurred as the energy reacted with the tattoo. When the spots disappeared from Alar's eyes, he noticed a white dove in the place that Avais had previously occupied.

He could not contain his gasp of surprise at seeing her gone. Though she had gone through the spell step by step, the results it produced still shocked him.

Avais took off and was immediately joined by the other doves. They circled the room, their wing beats echoing off the stone walls of the cave. Alar looked closely and noticed the differences between Avais and the birds. She was a pristine white that contrasted with the brownish shade of the natural doves. The discoloration on her breast feathers did look like her tattoo, now that he knew what to look for.

Avais and the birds circled the room, picking up speed as they went. They spun and looped around Alar. He had never felt so left out. Alar sat his land locked body down on the rocks and watched them play. His heart longed for their freedom. As he watched them circle, he felt the last tattered shreds of doubt fade away. His mind was made up. He wanted to join them!

Avais broke formation and landed on his shoulder. She reached over and rubbed her neck against his. The feathers that covered her were downy soft. He gently stroked her back, then kissed her on the beak.

"I love you," he said. "Return to me so that I can join you in flight."

She fluttered to the book, then pushed her breast feathers against its cover. Alar noted the sizzling sound that the energies made as they flowed out of her body and into the book's cover. As the shimmering energies left her, she grew before his eyes. Feathers were replaced by flesh in seconds. The entire transformation was over in a moment.

Fully restored, she turned towards Alar and asked, "Are you ready?"

He kissed her passionately, then held her tightly. "I can't wait," he replied.

Avais stared deeply into Alar's eyes.

"For the first part of the conversion, you must take your shirt off," she said. He did, and she rested warm hands on his shoulder as he sat down on the rocks next to her.

"To transform you to bird form, you must first wear the mark. It will be applied magically. No pain is involved, yet I must warn you, once it graces your skin, it can never be removed."

Alar briefly struggled with his emotions, then held out his arm. "I am ready. If the tattoo is permanent, so be it. How can a lifelong reminder of you be anything but good?"

Avais' eyes misted slightly. She kissed him. The kiss was long and passionate. As Alar's hands began to wander up her bare back, she gently pulled away.

"It is time."

Avais opened the book and recited the spell's preamble. Alar watched as yellow energy lines formed in the air around him. He followed every hand motion that Avais performed, watching her hands and the book's pictures simultaneously. She molded the magical forces into a coin sized packet, then gently placed it on Alar's inner forearm. It stuck to him, tickling the skin much as crawling ants would. Nothing else happened.

Alar was disappointed, it showed on his features.

"Don't worry my love," reassured Avais. "For this spell, I am the catalyst."

She turned her arm so that her tattoo was juxtaposed with the energy packet glowing on Alar's arm.

She again looked at him.

"Do it," he whispered.

They interlocked fingers, pushing their inner arms together. When the spell energies touched her tattoo, they activated. Alar felt a warmth enter his arm and suffuse through his body. As the sensation spread throughout him, he was struck by the feeling of intense tranquility that followed it. For the first time, he felt complete. It was as if a part of him that had long been missing had suddenly returned.

Alar became acutely aware of Avais' touch. Her fingers felt warm and soft. He felt closer to her, almost as if part of her now resided within him.

He looked at his arm and admired the new tattoo. The image of a bird, gracefully flying through the air, was identical to Avais'. He touched it. There was no pain.

He felt Avais' eyes on him.

"You are the newest member of my sect," she said. "You are now an Air Child. By carrying our mark, you can use the spell book to harness the Earth's natural powers."

"I feel at ease with myself," he answered, "but I certainly don't feel like a powerful magician."

"That's because you're not!" She laughed softly at him. "Mastery of the magical arts takes years. I have been training for most of my life, and at times I feel like I have just scratched the surface."

"Great," he grumbled. "I am no closer to flying than I was before."

"Don't worry, I will teach you. Somehow, I feel that you will learn quickly. Besides, if you are to be my squire for my greatest trial, you must know magic. I cannot succeed without you."

Alar looked surprised, then remembered his drunken promise to her.

"Avais, you need not flatter me. I am only a poor woodsman who dreams of flying. How could I possibly make a difference in your quest?"

"Alar, I tried to tell you of this earlier. This valley is in great danger. An ancient sorcerer, Catharvus, was once a member of our sect. He became corrupted with evil power and had to be imprisoned. He has been locked away in a dreamless sleep for generations. As you may know, he has awakened."

Alar nodded as he thought about the strange events of the last few days.

Avais continued. "Prophecy states that a stranger will be summoned to battle him. He may either defeat him, or set him free, but there is no hope of defeating Catharvus without him. I am sure that you are the one that the elders speak of."

Alar was shaken by this revelation. He felt a chill come over him as beads of sweat formed on his forehead. His mind flashed back to his nightmare. He could almost smell the scent of death in the air. The magical assault was starting. He could hear the buzzing of the energies as spells flew through the air. His skin started to burn, his life was slipping away from him. He must run, must do anything to escape. He had to get away!

A gentle hand on his shoulder brought him back to reality. Avais wiped the sweat from his brow.

"Don't worry. I know you can do it."

"I am not sure that I am cut out to be a hero," he said. "If I remember correctly, you seem to be doing all the rescuing."

"Your time will come, Alar."

Alar became quiet. He stared at his tattoo, a worried look clouded his features.

She touched him lightly on the face. He smiled as her touch relaxed him.

"Care to try on those wings, my hero?"

The spider climbed the ravine, drawn by Alar's scent. It was wracked by pain, but due to the sorcerer's spell, could not rest. The stump of its severed leg throbbed. The shell on one side of its body was cracked and scorched from Avais' missile. It staggered due to weakness caused by loss of blood.

From his cell in the mountain, Catharvus pushed the spider forward. He gazed into the crystal ball, whispering instructions to his monster. It heard his instructions and was powerless to disobey.

The spider climbed the steep rock face. It longed for death to set it free from its enslavement. Someone or something had to die. Exactly who died did not matter. The death of the woodsman or its own death would have the same effect. Killing Alar would satisfy the mage, letting the spider rest. Its own death would hopefully do the same thing, though with master wizards, one could not be certain. It trudged forward.

As it climbed, the scent of humans intensified.

"Hurry, you useless bug!" the voice of the mage screamed in its brain. "Hurry! They will die of old age if you move any slower!"

Powerless to disobey, the spider climbed onward. It saw the mouth of a cave on the ravine wall above it. With mindless determination, it stared at the opening and marched towards it.

The familiar scent of the young woodsman grew in strength as the spider approached the cave. Despite its fatigue, a sense of anticipation began to form. The spider began to salivate as it climbed. Pain faded away as thoughts of revenge and escape began to dance around in its mind.

This time it would surprise its prey. It would pounce on the woodsman, kill him, then drain all the juices from his body. The mage would release the spider from its bondage, and it could finally rest.

I have learned from my mistakes, it thought, I will not fail again.

Alar read the preamble of the transformation spell with Avais' help. The words, exotic and foreign to him, came haltingly. Avais nodded approvingly as yellow energy beams became visible in the cave. With painful slowness, Alar tried to gather the forces into a packet. The lines of magical energy were fast moving and difficult to stabilize. His shaking hands did little to make the task easier. After many futile attempts, Alar was ready to quit. Grabbing fish from the river while blindfolded would be an easier task!

Pax squawked and rolled his eyes. Avais shot him a scolding glance.

Avais saw creases of frustration form on Alar's face. She told him of her first attempts at harnessing the magical energies. It had taken her forever. She placed a steadying hand on Alar's shoulder and encouraged him to continue.

Her touch relaxed him. He read the words again. Alar followed the book's instructions and reached for the glowing yellow energy beams. He slowly corralled them, then pressed the crackling lines together, noting how their colors changed as they congealed. With a feeling of immense pride, he cupped the glowing purple packet in his hands.

"You did wonderfully!" Avais gushed, as she prepared a spell of her own. Her fingers molded the energy into a packet identical to Alar's in seconds. "Remember to stay near the cave when you fly. We cannot transform back to human form without the book, and I am going to leave it here. I normally throw a miniaturization spell on the book and take it with me, but let's keep things simple for now. The feeling of flight is intoxicating. The first time I flew, I got myself totally lost. If my mentor had not followed me, I would probably still be trying to find my way back to the book."

Dutifully warned, Alar prepared to transform. He clenched his eyes tightly shut, took a deep breath, then timidly touched the spell energies against his tattoo.

Alar felt like he had just been struck by lightning. His flesh crawled as the tattoo unleashed magical energies throughout his body. His mind was assaulted by waves of vertigo. He clenched his eyes tightly shut, trying to ignore the sensations that rushed through him. He felt himself changing and shrinking, his form becoming more streamlined. His skin prickled as feathers grew on limbs that were previously bare.

When the vertigo resolved, Alar opened his eyes and looked around. The roof of the cave seemed to tower above him. The waterfall looked huge. Avais' spell book lay on the rocks next to him, its cover was bigger than his whole body! Avais had transformed into a white dove and was looking at him approvingly.

He heard a soft cooing next to him. No human words were spoken, yet he could understand that the noise came from Avais. The mental image, "Are you all right, my love?" formed in his mind.

He answered, "I think so," but no words came out. Instead of hearing his voice, all he heard was a rather harsh squawking. He tried again. The sounds were the same.

The natural doves flew to him. Alar noted that they were almost as tall as he was. Pax started to coo. Alar again formed a mental image of what the bird was saying.

"Will you look at him," Pax said. "Leave it to the 'Tumbler' to transform into something like that."

"Pretty attractive if you ask me," replied the bird's mate. Pax clucked disapprovingly at her.

Avais said, "Alar, look at yourself. Come to the water's edge. You will be able to see your new body in its reflection."

Avais flew to the rocks at the pool's edge. The natural doves joined her. Alar, not yet fully trusting his new form, walked to the chattering birds. He noted that his stride was short and rolling. He dared a peek towards his feet and was taken aback by their pink, scaly appearance.

He climbed the rocks and peered into the water. He gasped and staggered backwards. He looked again. The rippling image that stared at him was that of a small green parrot. It was green with blue wing tips and orange legs. Compared to the graceful doves, it was heavily muscled. As a parrot, he had a formidable looking beak that housed a black tongue. His head was a shiny and black.

"Is that me?" he gasped, the words again coming out as harsh squawks.

"This is your Air Child form," replied Avais, her white feathers rustling slightly as she spoke. "As in your human form, you have strong chest muscles. It looks like you will be a very strong flier, Alar. Why don't you test your wings against the air?"

Alar gripped the rocks with his claws. He fought back a shudder as he felt his new talons scrape against the stone. Gingerly, he spread his wings, admiring the way their colors shone in the light that reflected off the pool.

Alar hesitantly flapped his wings once, noted no untoward effects, then tried again. All seemed well. He began to beat his wings in earnest, delighting in the feeling of lift that they produced. Dust flew from the cave's floor, swept up by the wind he was producing. He laughed. The parrot like squawks that came out no longer bothered him. Alar let go with his claws and rose into the air.

With great strokes of his wings, he circled the cave. There was no hesitancy in his flight, this all felt so natural! Avais and the doves strained to keep up with him.

"To the open sky!" he yelled.

Avais and the doves took off after him.

Alar swooped out of the cave's mouth and banked up sharply. He rode the air currents rising off the cliff's face, his eyes fixed upwards toward the heavens.

Avais and her friends strained to keep up with their soaring friend. "Do not lose us," she yelled. "You are stronger that we are. You fly faster than we can."

Alar slowed down slightly, letting the doves join in formation with him. He banked and turned, exhilarating at the feeling of weightlessness. The sun shone warm on his back. The air smelled crisp and fresh. He dove, the doves followed in hot pursuit.

Alar looked down. The river was but a shimmering ribbon below him. Trees looked like green puffs of cotton. Alar circled his village. The eyes of his bird friends were upon him as he glided high above his home.

None of them thought to look back towards the cliffs. If they had, they would have seen the spider emerge from behind the boulder that had previously shielded it from their view. They would have seen it lumber up the cliff face and enter the cave. Once in the cave, it turned, folded its legs under itself, then patiently waited for their return.

Catharvus peered intently into his orb. He watched the parrot and three doves fly from the cave. He saw the Air Child marks on the chests of the parrot and dove. He smiled broadly.

"This is almost too good to be true," he cackled. "Avais must have recruited my woodsman into the sect. I see no harness on either of them. They have not shrunken the spell book and taken it with them. Since they transformed in the cave, the book must still be there."

He spoke into the orb. "Hear me well, my spider friend. The humans have left the cave in bird form. They must return to the cave to transform back into human form. I want you to immerse yourself in the pool at the back of the cave. Wait for the humans to arrive. When they do, spring on them and tear them to pieces."

Alar banked sharply, enjoying the feel of the wind against his chest. He pulled out of the turn and flew alongside Avais. How beautiful she looked as she soared in the heavens!

Pax flew towards Alar. "Tumbler," he cried over the howling of the wind, "let's see if you fly better than you fall. Try to catch me!"

The dove then folded its wings, tipping forward into a vertical dive. Alar copied its posture and followed. The two birds streaked downward. Avais and the other dove kept an eye on the males, but followed at a more leisurely pace.

Alar thrilled at the roar of the wind in his ears. The beauty of the ground rushing up at him like a spiraling kaleidoscope almost took his breath away. The dove kept itself locked in the dive, hurtling ever closer towards the ground. Alar stared at the birds' tail feathers and followed at breakneck speed. Since he weighed more, he was slowly pulling even with Pax.

Twenty-five feet above the trees tops, and only seconds before impact with them, the dove lost its nerve, and pulled out of the dive.

"I can fly better than you can!" whooped Alar as he streaked past the fluttering dove.

"Be careful!" yelled Avais, "you are getting too low. Come back here now!"

Alar was about to pull out of the dive when he swerved to avoid a flash of yellow that approached from the corner of his eye. He lost control of his dive, spinning as he tore downward towards the forest canopy. With the screams of Avais ringing in his ears, he plunged towards the tree tops.

Avais realized that there would not be enough time for her lover to pull out of the dive before he hit the trees. She yelled to him, her cooing an anguished whisper in the winds. In her current form, she was incapable of harnessing the magical energies. There was nothing that she could do to save him.

Alar, intoxicated on the feeling of speed, did not realize how much danger he was in. He thought that a simple adjustment of a wing angle should get him flying straight again. He tried, but over-corrected, worsening the spin. Avais' screams of warning came at the same time that he realized he was now too close to the tree canopy to pull away. His mind raced as he tried to think of a way to escape.

"Idiot!" he said under his breath. "I wait an entire lifetime to taste the thrill of flying, then crash myself into the forest on my first flight."

He squinted his eyes and braced for impact as he hurtled into the tree tops. In desperation, he dodged around the first branch he encountered. He spread his wings to try to lower his speed. With wings aching from the strain of his deceleration, he stared intently into the approaching mass of foliage. He thought he saw sparkling light shining through a slight gap between the branches. With all his strength, he threw himself toward it.

He almost made it.

Alar's fall was too fast. He couldn't navigate the gap in the trees and glanced off one of the branches. He lost all control and began to tumble in midair. Spinning end over end, he lost sight of the rapidly approaching ground. He braced himself for the impact that would surely kill him. Nothing could save him now.

Alar crashed onto his back, his claws futilely grabbing at the air above him. The impact stunned him. His eyes fogged up, his vision became blurry. He choked as his lungs fought for air. The little parrot's gasps brought only a harsh burning to his chest.

He struggled, but found his limbs moving in slow motion. Alar felt himself growing weaker, his wings seemed to tangle with each movement. He stared upwards. He wanted to catch one last glimpse of Avais before life left him.

A dark shadow swept out of the corner of his eye and covered him in black.

Marcus sat with his back against a tree. He was thoroughly enjoying himself.

He had needed to get away. The events of the last few days had been nerve wracking to say the least! Between the rumblings in the mountain, the adventure with the Orcs, the turbulent love affair between Alar and the red headed sorceress, and the spider attack, he was exhausted. Barona's nagging, and the unwanted attention of his neighbors had taken up virtually every moment of his spare time. He felt that he needed some time alone to rest and collect his thoughts. Since a bottle was an ideal vessel to help collect objects, he had brought one along with him.

Marcus took a great swig from the bottle and stared at the scene before him. How beautiful this spot was! The forest pond that lay before him was covered by water lilies that were just coming into bloom. Their thick leaves blanketed the pond's surface, leaving only small areas uncovered. The light that escaped through the canopy of the forest's trees lit up these gaps like liquid jewels.

Marcus took his boots off. He took another swig from the bottle, relishing both the brew's flavor and its fiery burn. He felt his muscles loosen as the alcohol and the peaceful scenery pushed his worries further into the distance.

After a few more pulls from the bottle, he looked around again. The crisp smell of the water plants was pleasantly contrasted by the sweet aroma of the orchids that bloomed high in the trees.

His eyes fluttered closed as he drifted asleep.

He was awaked by an approaching ruckus. The screaming of birds filled the air. He squinted as he looked upwards towards the source of the noise. Far up in the sky, he saw two birds diving at breakneck speed. One was a dove, the other a bird that he didn't immediately recognize. They hurtled towards him like two out-of-control lightning bolts. The dove spread its wings and pulled out of its dive at the last moment. The greenish bird was not so lucky. It seemed distracted by a passing shadow and veered suddenly in the air. It glanced off a tree branch, then tumbled out of control.

Marcus followed the bird's course as it crashed into the waters of the pond. He got up, walked over to where it had hit the water, and looked down. The bird lay on its back, slowly sinking into the pond's depths.

From above him, Marcus heard the frantic screeching of a strangely marked dove. The brownish discoloration on its breast heaved as it fluttered above him. It seemed to be calling out to him.

Marcus looked up at the dove. He then took a long look at the half empty spirits bottle still clutched in his hand. He shook his head murmuring, "This stuff must really be getting to me."

He tossed the bottle into the pond, turned his back on the madness behind him, and walked towards the village.

As the darkness increased, Alar felt life slipping away from him. He had lost all strength. He couldn't breathe. His wings lay useless at his sides, tangled in clumps of water weeds. His eyes drifted shut. Images of Avais' smile lingered in his brain.

As he was about to leave her, to surrender to the feelings of overwhelming emptiness, he felt something clamping down on his leg. There was no pain, he was too far gone for that, instead he felt a vague, unpleasant pressure coming from the area above his claws.

The pressure disappeared for a second, long enough for him to doubt that it had really been there, then returned, this time stronger. Seconds later, Alar was unceremoniously jerked upwards by his feet. As he dangled upside-down, great rivulets of water fell from his body. He sensed he was moving. Through it all, he kept his eyes tightly shut. His oxygen starved brain was too shocked to process thoughts rationally, instead, it ignored the chaos outside.

Alar hung upside down, sputtering and coughing as the water drained from his lungs. He felt himself being lowered onto a firm, dry surface. He heard Avais' voice ringing in his ears.

"Speak to me, my love! Oh please, speak to me!"

Never had Alar heard anything sound so wonderful.

He opened his eyes, expecting to see her. Somehow, she had rescued him from the pond. What he saw, was definitely not Avais. Instead, he found himself staring into an eye that was as large as a plum. It was deep brown, curious, and hovered no more than a few inches away.

He panicked, beating his wings desperately to escape.

"Hit me with those stubby little wings again, and I'll put you back into the pond," a deep, yet gentle voice boomed.

From behind the giant eye, Alar heard the voice of Pax.

"Tumbler, you still fly worse than I wrestle! Calm down will you! We are trying to help."

Alar coughed the last of the water from his lungs, took a deep breath, then looked around. The large eye continued to stare at him. Close inspection revealed that it was attached to the face of a tawny yellow horse. The horse somehow looked familiar though Alar couldn't place where he had seen it before.

The horse whinnied, accented words formed in Alar's mind.

"Lie still, my soggy friend. Do not beat your wings against me. You have already done enough damage to yourself for one day."

Alar tested his voice. His parrot squawks sounded weak, but were recognizable.

"How is it that I can understand you?"

"That is easy, wet bird. I am a creature of the air, just as you are." It flapped its wings for emphasis. "We all can understand each other. From the looks of you, you probably could communicate with the fish and turtles as well."

Alar ignored his rescuer's humor and looked at the horse. Folded daintily behind its back were golden wings. It was a flying horse!

Alar looked very closely at it. The horse had a flowing coat, a long spiraling horn on its forehead, and gossamer wings. It continued to look familiar to him.

"Do I know you?" he asked.

"I believe so," laughed the horse. "I am Windracer. We met many years ago. You were in your other form then. If I remember correctly, you grabbed me and dragged me out of a thicket. My mother, who had placed me there for safe keeping, became so mad, she almost killed you."

"It comes back to me now," chuckled Alar. Despite his near drowning, the memories were embarrassing enough to make him laugh. "You were the colt I met in the woods. We have both done a lot of growing since then. At the time, I thought that you were trapped in the thicket. I was only trying to help."

"I understand," Windracer replied. "My mother must have figured it out too, otherwise, you wouldn't be here today."

"You saved me from the pond, I owe..."

"I had no choice," interrupted the horse. "First, you almost hit me as you dove downward. In avoiding me, you lost control and crashed into the pond. Your friend Avais yelled and screamed so much, I figured that rescuing you was the only way that I could get some peace."

Alar crawled to his feet. He was shaken, but apparently intact. With each breath, he noticed more strength returning.

"Avais, where are you?"

Windracer backed up so that Avais could get by. She fluttered to Alar and looked at him. He was soggy.

The feathers on his back were wet and matted together. Strands of aquatic vegetation still clung to him.

She touched her beak to his. Even in this state, he was the most beautiful thing she had ever seen.

"Be more careful next time," she scolded. "How can you save the realm if you can't even keep yourself out of trouble? Let's get you cleaned up."

Alar had to put up with the preening and scolding of Avais as well a large dose of good spirited banter from Windracer and the other birds. He soon felt well enough to try to fly.

Alar spread his wings and beat them vigorously. He was pleased to feel his feet leave the ground. He would be able to fly again.

Avais watched him prepare to fly. "We go straight to the cave this time. Agreed?" she asked. "We have had enough adventures for one day!"

Alar nodded at her. "Yes, no detours. We fly back to the cave. It will be safer there."

Catharvus, gazing intently into his orb, laughed out loud.

Alar and his friends took off together and flew towards the cave. Alar chatted with Windracer as they flew. Since both Alar and the horse were strong flyers, they gradually pulled away from the other birds. About half way to the cave, Windracer broke ranks and banked upwards.

"Safe flight, my friends," he yelled as he pulled into the open sky. Windracer put on a burst of speed, continued his climb, and soon faded into the clouds near the mountain top.

Alar, was a fast flyer. He was more muscular than the doves and a nervous energy drove him onwards. Because of this, he had a sizable lead when he arrived at the cave. Though he didn't know why, a great uneasiness had overcome him. The yearning to transform into his human form was steadily increasing.

Alar dove through the thicket of vines and landed in the cave. He walked towards the spell book which still lay where he and Avais had left it. The book lay on the rocks near the waterfall's pool. Its pages glowed faintly in the dim light of the cave.

Alar did not see the spider lurking in the waters of the pool. He was preoccupied by the strangeness of his new world. How different this body felt. Instead of crunching the small stones beneath his feet, his nails lightly scratched them. As he walked, he left tiny bird tracks in the dirt. He hopped on the rock that the spell book lay upon. His hop was effortless, even though the distance was greater than twice his height.

The spider waited impatiently. The monster's eyes narrowed, its jaws were only a few feet from Alar. It began to salivate, the spit dripping from its mandibles into the pond water. The waterfall's spray made more than enough noise to cover up the sounds the spider made as it waded through the shallow pool.

Alar grabbed the book's cover with his beak and pulled. He had to strain to lift the cover to close the book. I kind of miss my big body when it comes to lifting things, he thought. Being big does have advantages.

He turned himself so that his tattoo would line up with the drawing on the book's cover; in doing so, he turned his back to the spider.

In a distant cave, Catharvus watched the orb and chuckled to himself. He smiled an evil grin as he pulled the orb closer to his face.

The spider was ready to grab the bird when its muscles froze. Its orders were clear, kill the humans when they returned to the cave. The bird, at least in its current form, was not a human. The spider pondered its dilemma while the odd colored parrot fiddled with the spell book.

Alar's heart pounded in his chest. Why am I so nervous, he thought? There is no danger here. Maybe it's the strain of being in this magically altered body. I must be time to change back to my human form. I'm sure I will feel better then.

Alar touched his chest against the book's cover. His marked feathers met the magic seal and catalyzed the reaction. Magical energies left his body and flowed into the book. Alar again felt a sensation of overwhelming vertigo. His senses spun, causing him to clamp his eyes tightly shut. His body increased in size. Strong arms grew in the place of wings. His face reformed. Alar's normal sinewy frame replaced the bird's lighter structure.

Alar opened his eyes and immediately felt better. Back to normal, he thought. He stepped down from the rock and reached for his clothes. The spider pounced forward, spreading its mandibles widely. As the spider slammed its jaws shut, Alar was struck in the face, lost his balance, and fell stunned to the cave's floor.

Avais struggled to keep up with Alar. He was a much faster flyer than she was and had rapidly left the doves and her behind.

He is doing it again, she thought. That man has more looks than brains.

"Windracer, keep an eye on him!" she yelled. Her tiny voice was swept away by the blowing winds. "Come on guys," she shouted at the doves, "fly faster. We must catch up with Alar."

Avais flew like she had never flown before, but Alar and the horse pulled away, leaving her to follow in their turbulent wake. Alar's form shrunk to a dot silhouetted against the ravine in the distance.

After Alar had bid Windracer goodbye, Avais watched the horse bank upwards, leaving Alar alone in the sky. Feelings of dread welled up in her. Though her muscles ached, she pressed on.

"Wait Alar, don't go in there alone!" she yelled.

He didn't hear her. With a flick of his tail, he dove towards the vine choked entrance of the cave, and was lost from sight.

"Hurry my friends," Avais cried to the doves. "I don't know why, but I have suddenly been filled with a great fear. We must get to the cave, for I feel that Alar might be in trouble."

"We are with you," cried Pax, his voice a mixture of concern and irritation. "It looks like the Tumbler needs us again."

They flew onward, straining for extra speed. Avais navigated the opening of the cave and hovered to let her eyes adjust to the dim light inside. What she saw made the blood freeze in her veins.

Alar was transformed into his human form and had started to dress. He stood on a rock by the waterfall's edge, his back to the water. He was naked from the waist down, but was slipping his shirt over his head. Since the fabric covered his eyes, he did not see the giant form looming behind him. The spider, partially submerged in the pool's waters, rushed at Alar. Glistening mandibles the size of garden shears opened behind his neck.

Avais screamed, but her bird transformed voice did not carry over the din of the falling water. She realized that she wouldn't have time to transform. She screamed again, this time out of both fear and frustration.

With strength born of desperation, she flew towards Alar, her wings digging deeply into the cave's still air.   Avais banked toward her love as black mandibles encircled his shirt covered head.

Avais dove towards Alar. In seconds, he would be a decapitated corpse. The monster's jaws began to shut. Without slowing down, Avais slammed into the side of Alar's face. The impact almost killed her. Stunned, she fluttered limply to the ground.

Alar's face was covered by the shirt when Avais struck him. He was startled by the impact, lost his balance, and tumbled off the rock. A click echoed above him as razor sharp jaws snapped shut on emptiness.

It took Alar only a moment to pull his shirt all the way on. He sprung to his feet and looked around. He was shocked to see the nightmare of black flesh advancing towards him.

Avais, still stunned from the collision, lay on the ground with wings twitching. The spider stood behind her, its eyes locked on Alar. As he began to back away from the monster, it advanced towards him. If the spider moved only a few more paces, Avais would be crushed beneath its feet.

Alar grew desperate.   He saw the two doves cowering in the corner of the cave.

"Help me!" he shouted. "Help me save Avais!"

They heard him and understood. The birds took off and circled the spider, screaming as they flew. The distraction they provided slowed the spider enough to give Alar a chance. He saw the spell book, lying on a rock near the spider's legs.

Alar lunged forward and grabbed the spell book. The spider snapped at him, its jaws clicking shut inches from his throat, its giant, hair legs missing Avais by inches. He dodged away from the the monster's jaws, still clutching the tome. Alar charged towards the spider, fending off its jaws with the book. He snapped a kick to the spider's throat. Alar's blow did little more that enrage the giant insect. It roared, then charged at him. Alar waited until the very last second, then dropped to the ground at the spider's feet. He used his body to shield Avais while he covered his head with the spell book.

As the spider charged, screaming like an approaching tornado, the doves wheeled about in front of its face. It snapped at Pax, shearing off a few of his tail feathers. The falling feathers fluttered in front of the spider's face, grabbing it's attention for an instant. Distracted, the spider passed over Alar without stepping on him. It wheeled around, accidentally striking him with the side of one of its legs. The force of the impact threw Alar across the cave. He clutched Avais and the spell book in his hands as he tumbled through the air.

My God, he thought. When I land, I will crush Avais!

He threw the dove away from his body and braced for impact with the cave's rocky floor. He hoped that the landing wouldn't leave him too injured to fight on. To his pleasant surprise, the embrace of warm water surrounding him was all he felt. The spider had kicked him across the cave, into the far corner of the waterfall's pool.

The spider roared in frustration. It jaws reached down and grabbed at the pile of possessions Alar and Avais had left at its end of the cave. The animal took Alar's ax and snapped its handle like kindling wood. It shredded Avais' back pack and threw its contents aside. The crystal orb shattered into a thousand gleaming fragments when the beast threw it against the caves rocky floor.

While the spider tore at his possessions, Alar scrambled out of the pond. He looked at the soggy spell book, but knew that he wouldn't be able to get a spell off before the spider was upon him. He grabbed for his pants and faced the spider. It tossed the last of Avais' pack aside and advanced towards him with eyes radiating a combination of hatred and hunger.

From another cave, Catharvus looked on. His face was so close to the orb that his breath fogged its surface.

Alar's left hand held the spell book like a shield. He laughed to himself as in desperation he began to spin his pants with his right hand. Perhaps, as a bola, they might make a serviceable weapon. He snapped the pants at the spider who sliced the fabric with each snap. The animal advanced, its jaws menacing. Alar backed away, trying to keep as much distance between himself and the monster as possible.

The spider charged, forcing him against the wall. Alar scooted away, trying to keep clear of the animal's jaws. He felt the scrape of vines against his legs.

He was at the cave's entrance. Alar knew that he could never navigate the steep sections of the cliff while trying to fight off the spider. He had retreated as much as he could. Now was the time for his last stand.

The spider advanced through the spinning pant legs, ignoring the kicks that Alar threw in its direction. It flexed its jaws, sending a spray of venom flying.

The animal lunged at Alar, its mandibles aimed at his throat. Alar felt the ground crumble beneath his feet as the rock that he stood on began to succumb to the combined weight of man and spider. He tried to block the spider's attack with the book, but the animal's jaws snapped shut on the lower third of it. The razor-sharp mandibles pierced the book's cover and locked. The spider shook its head like a dog, trying to pull away Alar's shield.

Alar clung to the book. He felt his feet lift off the rock as the spider tossed him about like a torn sail in a storm wind. Avais and the doves flew around the monster's head, pecking at its eyes. This close to the kill, the spider was not about to be distracted. It battered Alar against the rocks of the cave's opening.

Alar's stubbornly clung to the book. The animal whipped its head again, slamming him against the floor. Again, he heard the sound of cracking stone. Alar managed to regain his footing and dug his bare feet into the rocks. He pulled on the spell book with all of his strength.

The tug-of-war between Alar and two tons of raging spider was too much for the book. A ripping sound filled the air. Everything in the cave seemed to freeze as the tortured pages of the book gave way to the tearing forces.

The sudden lack of tension caught Alar by surprise. He struggled to keep his balance, but began to fall backwards. Avais cried out. Clutching the torn spell book to his chest with one arm, Alar flailed at the air with the other.   His toes gripped the rocks as he desperately tried to regain his balance. The ledge crumbled beneath his feet, pitching him backwards into the void.

Avais abandoned her attack on the spider, and dove after her falling lover. With wings tucked to her sides, she hurtled after him. When she overtook him, she buried her claws into the fabric of his shirt.

"I will not let you die!" she sobbed, as she fluttered her wings desperately.

Her tiny wings could not support Alar's weight. They fell faster.

A storm was rolling in. The sky around them darkened as the towering banks of thunderclouds blotted out the sun. As the world below was bathed in shadow, an overpowering feeling of hopelessness settled on Avais. She realized that this time, she wouldn't be able to save Alar. They fell faster, the wind tearing at them like an angry hand. The tears that welled in Avais' eyes were whisked away and swallowed by the falling rains that followed them downward.

Alar felt Avais' claws pierce his shirt and scratch against him. He tried to brush her away.

"Let go, my love," he yelled. "There is no sense in both of us dying. You have wings. Use them! Fly away from me."

The continued flutter of wings was her only reply.

"Let go of me! One of us must live! If both of us die, the forces of evil will rule unopposed!"

Avais ignored him.

The ground approached at dizzying speed. The rocks which only moments before had looked like grains of sand, shown now as jagged boulders. The river, curling amongst the rocky ravine walls, lay too far away to break Alar's fall.

Alar glanced downward. The rocks were no more than fifty feet below. He clenched his eyes tightly shut, no longer able to watch his approaching death.

"I will love you for all eternity!" he yelled as he reached back and swatted Avais off his shirt. She tumbled away, barely able to regain control. As she banked away, she let out an anguished wail.

Alar tried to make peace with himself. His mind wandered as he experienced the weightlessness that would be his final flight.

His reverie was interrupted by a loud ripping sound. Alar pitched forward, his shirt drawing tight against his throat. The sudden deceleration that followed, along with the pressure around his neck, made him dizzy. He stole a quick peak downward, the ground's headlong rush towards him was slowing.

Alar twisted, struggling to look behind him. He was rewarded for his effort by a sharp pain at the base of his skull. He tried again, but could see nothing before the pain became too severe.

Alar drifted downward. A few feet above the rocks, he heard a loud rip, then fell to the ground. He fought for balance, but tumbled backwards when his feet lost their footing on the mossy rocks.

Alar lay on his back in the gravel at the river's edge. Rain poured down upon him. His legs straddled a barrel sized boulder, his hands still clutched the spell book to his chest. The tattered remnants of Alar's pants fluttered downward, landing in a puddle behind him.

He felt the coldness of the rocks against his bare behind. This must be a good sign, he thought, I doubt the afterworld is cold. He tried to wiggle his toes. They seemed to follow his commands.

He looked around. Standing before him was Windracer, a piece of Alar's collar was impaled on the horse's horn. Windracer pawed at it, then shook his head wildly.

"Get it off me!" he snorted, "Get it off. God this clothing stuff is disgusting. I can't imagine going through life wearing such a shabby coat."

One more shake of his head sent the cloth flying into the river.

Windracer looked down at Alar. The woodsman was staring at him through shock clouded eyes. Windracer stared back, then lowered his gaze to the man's bare lower half.

"What an unusual place for a horn," whinnied the horse.

Alar followed the horse's gaze, then pulled his knees together when he realized what the horse was looking at.

"Avais," Windracer whinnied in a stage whisper, "don't you think an enlarge spell would be helpful?"

Avais landed on Windracer's head and scolded him for making fun of Alar. She clenched her beak together trying not to laugh, but gave into it as she watched Alar struggle to put on his mangled pants, all the while trying to hide behind the spell book. The spider had sliced his trousers into a very provocative pair of shorts, and the figure that Alar cut while trying to jump into them was nearly indescribable.

Avais' giggles proved infectious, and soon both she and Windracer were roaring with laughter.

Alar shot them a withering glance as he tied the drawstring. "What happened?" he asked, his voice still quivering with shock.

"Rescued you again," Windracer replied matter-of-factly. The horse used his horn to overturn a rock and started nibbling on the moss that was exposed.

"I..., I don't understand," stammered Alar.

Windracer whinnied, his eyes rolling upwards. Alar wasn't sure what was worse, being mocked by a horse, or having bits of half eaten moss sprayed upon you.

With a look of strained patience, Windracer continued. "I was about to cross the Dragon Spine mountains, and head towards the King's palace. They say his roses are in bloom this time of year. I love roses, they are so tasty! Anyway, as I approached the peaks, a big storm seemed to be building. I like roses, but they are not worth flying through thunderclouds for, so I turned back. As I headed towards the valley, I saw Alar pop out of the mountain cave. You know, you still can't fly worth a damn."

Windracer munched on another bite of moss while his audience listened in the rain.

"I saw that you were falling towards the rocks. I didn't want you to mess up one of my favorite snacking spots, so I flew down to help. I was going to hook your belt like my mom did, but your pants were off."

At this point, Windracer gave Avais an amused look. "Does he always cause this much trouble?" he murmured under his breath. He shook his head, spraying Alar with water from his wet mane, then continued his story.

"After seeing no belt, I briefly toyed with other ways of catching you, but they seemed too distasteful. Finally, I speared your shirt collar and brought you down."

"Your horn was pressing against my neck," said Alar. "That's why I couldn't turn my head. Thanks for being there when I needed you. You are a good friend, even if you are a little hard on my wardrobe."

"You owe me," Windracer said, as he winked. "What in the name of the wind gods happened to you guys, anyway?"

Alar looked about him. They were a sorry looking bunch. His clothes hung in tatters. Pax was missing half of his tail. Avais' feathers were rumpled and stained with purple blood.

Alar told Windracer of the spider attack. When he got to the part about the spider tearing the spell book, Avais gasped and flew to him.

"The book! The book! Let me see the book!" she pleaded.

Alar turned the book over and set it in front of her. The book had been ripped clean through. Only tattered edges remained of the book's lower third. The leather cover fared no better. Most of the 'Air Child' seal had been torn away.

Avais shrieked, then pushed her chest against what was left of the seal. Nothing happened. She tried again. Her attempts became frantic as panic overcame her. Alar, afraid that she would hurt herself, gently took her into his hands. She began to tremble.

"Avais, my love, what is wrong?"

"I am trapped," she sobbed. "It is gone."

"What is gone?"

"The seal. When the book's cover was damaged, the seal of the 'Air Children' was destroyed. It is the catalyst that is needed to transform me back to human form. Without it, I will remain a bird forever."

The spider was caught by surprise when the spell book ripped. It lost its footing and stumbled backwards. After it regained its balance, the spider took a halfhearted swipe at the doves. The birds evaded the attack, then flew after the falling woodsman. The spider shuffled to the edge of the cave to watch Alar die.

The monster's joy was short lived. It recoiled in horror when the woodsman was rescued by the winged horse only yards above the jagged rocks. It moaned in fear as it thought of the sorcerer's wrath. As panic seized it, the spider bolted out of the cave.

Before it had gone more than a dozen paces, a voice roared in its head.

"Stop now, you imbecile!"

The spider ignored Catharvus. It shook its head, then began to climb down the rock face.

Vile words exploded in its brain. "Halt, you sniveling bug," yelled Catharvus. The command boomed and echoed in the animal's brain. It was so loud, it caused the spider to stumble and fall. With waves of searing pain buffeting its mind, the spider tried to get up and run.

"Try that again, and you will die!" the voice rang out. The spider stumbled onward. "Very well, you eater of flies, sample my rage."

The sorcerer picked up an iron wand from the cave's floor. Catharvus tapped the wand against the crystal orb, causing it to vibrate. The soft clinking sound was magnified by the spell. Thunderclaps of noise exploded in the animal's head. Its eyes bulged outward as pressure from the sound pushed at the inside of its skull. Blood began to pour from its nostrils. It rolled over, convulsing in pain. Catharvus tapped the orb four more times. The spider writhed in agony. The sorcerer paused to watch the spider who lay panting in the dirt. Catharvus smiled, then slammed the wand against the orb. Rust showered off the wand as it struck the crystal surface. The spider shrieked, then lost its hold on consciousness as its shell vibrated, and cracked. The black body twitched and fell limp on the ledge.

The spider's convulsions almost shattered the fragile outcropping of rock. Pebbles were knocked loose and fell nine thousand feet into the ravine below. Alar and his friends looked up, but the spider's form was lost in the mists of the approaching storm clouds.

The spider lay motionless for some time. Slowly, painfully, its eyes fluttered open. Its world was a blur as hundreds of wounds cried out for attention at once.

The smug voice of Catharvus shattered the welcome silence.

"Bug, you will listen to me now. Get up! Do not dawdle!"

Each step was like torture for the injured animal. The spider hesitated as the pain nearly overcame it.

"Must I remind you again?" Catharvus sneered as he rubbed the wand against the orb. The faint screeching was enough to prod the animal on. It gathered its strength and hauled itself to its feet.

"Climb back to the cave. Good spider, I can see that you are finally listening to reason. Look around you," Catharvus ordered. "I have the orb. I can see what you see. We must learn more about the two that threaten me."

The spider poked through the remnants of Avais' pack and Alar's clothes, pausing as it looked at each item. Catharvus staring at the orb from his cave, directed the monster in its search. After not finding anything useful for its master, the spider's gaze fell on the tattered edges of the torn spell book.

"Stop!" yelled Catharvus. "What do we have here? It seems that you are not so inept after all. You have destroyed Avais' spell book. Turn it over, I wish to examine it."

The spider groaned as it reached for the torn pages. It pinched them between its mandibles and flipped them over.

"Oh my," said Catharvus. "You have done well. The seal of the 'Air Children' has been torn from the book. Avais will not be able to return to human form without it. She will remain as much a prisoner of the 'Air Child' sect as I am. In her transformed state, she threatens me no more than a sparrow would. My understanding of this imprisonment spell grows daily. Soon I will be able to solve the accursed riddle of the chain. Both Avais and I know that she does not have enough time to journey over the mountains to Elonar to have her transformation spell released."

The spider swayed weakly in the cave. It continued to bleed, its blood leaving great purple blotches on the floor. The fire had left its eyes. It felt deader now, than it had before Catharvus revived it.

"Take the pages and bring them to me," Catharvus ordered. "I do not want Avais or her woodsman friend to retrieve the spell book fragments."

The spider limped out of the cave and headed towards Catharvus' prison. Its blood smeared the walls as it made its way along the rock face.

The falling rain formed dimples in the viscous purple blobs, but did not wash them away.

Alar watched the storm roll in. A jagged flash of lightening split the sky, then almost on cue, the bloated storm clouds dumped rain on the valley.

Avais was sobbing in his hands, ignoring the rain that moistened her feathers. He gently tucked her into what was left of his shirt, then sprinted for cover.

A short way upstream, the river took a sharp bend. Years of conflict between the river and the confining ravine walls had left the river victorious. The current had undercut the bank, leaving a rock overhang at the water's edge.

Alar stopped at the opening and looked back at his friends. The doves were being buffeted about by the storm's wind. They struggled to stay in one place, beating the air frantically with their wings.

"Go you two," Alar commanded. "This area is too open for you. Fly back to your roosts in the forest before the winds worsen."

"I will see you again," yelled Pax, as he and his mate flew into the safety of the trees. "Take care of Avais for me!"

Alar ducked as he entered the cave-like shelter. Windracer trotted over to the overhand and stuck his head in.   "It looks kind of tight in there for me," he said. He turned towards Alar. "I must be going now, I have better places to wait out a storm than here. Take care of yourself. Avais needs you. Remember, we will fly together again someday."

Windracer lunged into the air and soared overhead. The beauty of the animal in flight inspired a sharp pang of jealousy in Alar. How he would love to fly with him again. Alar sighed dejectedly. He knew that if he transformed into a bird, he would be trapped like Avais. Without the seal, there would be no way to change back to human form.

Rain pounded savagely outside. The inside of the shelter was lit by flashes of lightening, then shaken by thunderclaps.   The temperature became uncomfortably chilly as the storm front moved in.

Alar sat on the sandy floor and leaned against the rock wall. Avais huddled dejectedly in his hands.

"I have failed," she said softly. The novelty of being able to understand her bird talk had worn off. Alar was painfully aware of the sadness in her voice.

He stroked her back as he held her close to him.

"No one will stop Catharvus," she sobbed. "It is only a matter of time until he figures out how to escape from his magical prison. Once he is free, he will murder all that live here. The valley will be transformed into a smoldering graveyard. There is nothing that I can do. All is lost."

Silence overtook them as each was lost in thought.

Alar's face suddenly lightened.

"Why can't you cast spells in bird form?" he asked. "It seems to me that magic would be equally powerful no matter who, or what, summoned it."

"It cannot be done," she sobbed.

"Why not? I have no trouble understanding your speech."

"The trouble is not with my speech, it is with these," she said, flapping her wings slowly.

"I don't understand. "What do your wings have to do with magic?"

Avais sighed. "I can summon the magical energies with my speech, but these wings cannot mold the energy into a usable form."

Alar nodded in understanding. His eyes widened as a thought came to him. "I have hands!" he blurted out.

Avais looked up at him and blinked away her tears. She started to say something, but Alar cut her off.

"Avais, maybe he can be stopped. I have sworn to help you, and help you I shall. Though you are trapped in bird form, I am not. I know that I am not well schooled in the magical arts, but I have received the mark of the 'Air Children.' I can learn to throw the spells. Together, we will defeat Catharvus."

"That is an incredibly brave thing for you to say. I know how you fear death by magic. The thought of a mage apprentice marching into Catharvus' lair makes your dreams look frighteningly prophetic. I love you too much to let you sacrifice yourself."

"I won't sacrifice myself," Alar insisted. "I can learn the spells. Teach me."

Avais said nothing as she fought with her emotions. She shuddered, then nodded. "It is getting cold in here, she said. "A 'Magical Fire' spell wouldn't be a bad idea right now. Why don't you get the spell book and find the right page?"

Alar thumbed through the mangled book until he found the spell she sought. The heading of the page showed a campfire glowing an eerie green.

"Here it is," Alar said as his hand absentmindedly stroked the page's torn edge.

Avais hopped on his shoulder. Her claws tickled his skin as they poked through his shirt's fabric.

"That's the right one," she said. "Read the preamble, but be very careful with the pronunciation."

Alar struggled through the passage, his tongue having trouble with the strange words. Green beams of energy became dimly visible. As soon as he stopped speaking, they faded away.

"Speak the words louder," she suggested, "and put more emphasis on the second syllable of each word, I think you accent is throwing things off."

He tried again. The beams reformed, and this time they continued to glow after his recitation ended.

"Alar, you have done well. Now try to compress the beams. Follow the hand motions exactly as they appear in the book. If you do it right, the energy packet will form a perfect cube. I only wish that I could do it for you.

Alar felt like he was the master at some strange puppet show. His hand stiffly tried to corral the energy, but the bolts deflected off him, and rocketed across the cave's walls and out its entrance. Despite the air's chill, beads of sweat began to form on his forehead.

Avais' voice was soothing in his ear. "Relax. Calm down. You'll get the hang of it."

Alar took a deep breath and prepared to try again. To his dismay, the beams faded away.

"What happened?" he cried, as he slammed his hands together in frustration.

"The preamble's effect only lasts a few moments. Don't worry, you can read it again."

Alar nodded, but thought of trying to do battle with a great magician while struggling to harness these energy forces. He could barely do it while sitting in a cave, what would he do if he was fighting for his life? He shuddered. Avais watched him, but said nothing.

Alar again read the preamble. This time the beams glowed brilliantly. He followed the book's directions exactly and soon had a glowing green cube resting in his palms. It looked like a strange colored lightning bolt, frozen into the shape of an ice cube.

Avais fluttered to his lap. She examined the spell packet. Her head tilted to one side as she stared at it. Alar had to bite his lip as her bird-like posture unleashed a flood of emotion in him.

"It is perfect," she said. "Now you have to apply the catalyst."

Alar looked at the book. The catalyst section was missing! The spider had torn it away when it had ripped the book. The lower third contained not only the Air Children's seal, but all of the book's catalysts.

"Our hairy friend seems to have borrowed the catalyst information," Alar whispered. "Do you remember what it is?"

"Yes, I remember this one, but I don't remember all of them. This spell needs a twig or a bit of parchment to catalyze the energy. It is easy to remember, even a magical fire needs fuel. Unfortunately, not all catalysts are so obvious."

Alar found a small twig by the water's edge.

"Does it matter if its wet?"

"No, the magic takes care of the water. Put the packet down, then drop the twig on it. Be careful to get your hands out of the way. The effect is like pouring oil on a hot ember."

Alar dug a small depression in the sand and put the spell energies in it. He carefully dropped the twig onto the cube. Nothing happened. He frowned as the stick just sat there. He was about to kick sand over the whole affair when he saw a faint glimmer on the twig's bark. In seconds, it was glowing brightly. A loud pop filled the cave as the catalyst finally took. A melon sized ball of green light filled the hole. It pulsated slowly, throwing a gentle warmth throughout the cave.

Alar held his hands in front of the magical flames. "That feels nice! It isn't giving off any smoke either, in a cave that sure helps!"

"No ashes to clean up afterwards," Avais added.

They relaxed in the fire's glow.

Alar stared at the spell book. He ran his finger along the torn edge.

"We will have to go back to the cave," he said.

"But the spider may still be there. It will see us coming. I don't think you can defeat it in such a small area, there is no room to maneuver."

"We have to try to retrieve the book's missing pages," he said. "There may be enough of the seal left to transform you back into human form. Even if there isn't, we need to know the catalyst information to be able to fight Catharvus."

"I can't argue with you," she said, "but it will be dangerous. Let's talk about it after the storm passes."

They sat by the fire, each lost in his own thoughts. Avais fluffed her feathers as she snuggled against Alar's neck.

"I love you," she whispered, as she fell asleep.

Alar spent most of the night studying the remains of the spell book. As the light from the fire began to fade, sleep finally overtook him.

The spider stumbled into Catharvus' prison. It stopped in the middle of the cave and looked at the sorcerer, awaiting further orders. Catharvus cast a scornful eye at the beast. It looked pitiful. A large crack in its carapace still oozed blood. Clots clung to the edges of the wound,while dried purple smeared the rest of its shell. The flesh surrounding the stump of its severed leg festered with infection. The spider swayed slightly as it waited to be told what to do. It carried the tattered pages of the spell book in its jaws.

Catharvus strode over to the spider. The chain dragged along behind him, kicking up small clouds of dust.

"Release the pages to me," he commanded as he reached for the wad of paper.

Catharvus examined the torn paper. He burst into a smile. Good, he thought. The seal is here. Avais will remain trapped in the form of a bird. She shall no longer trouble me!

He summoned the magical energies, shaped them, then dropped the cube they formed on the cave's floor. He placed the torn pages on the cube, catalyzing the spell. A blinding green light was given off as magical flame began to consume the pages. He covered his eyes with the shard of leather that had once been part of the book's cover, its seal glowed rebelliously in the fire's light.

Catharvus chuckled to himself as he watched the spell book burn.

The spider sought to avert its gaze from the bright light, but stumbled when it turned its head. The animal was so weakened by its wounds that it couldn't move without falling.

Catharvus watched the spider. It was shivering though the cave was warm with the energies thrown off by the burning pages.

"You are ill, my friend," he said, his voice softening with pity. "You have served me well. Because of your efforts, the sorceress is trapped in a form where she cannot trouble me. I think that now would be the right time to release you from your servitude and take away your pain."

On some dim level, the spider understood. Peace would finally come to it.

The sorcerer conjured a spell. The packet of energy glowed in his hand as he strode towards the spider. Deftly, he placed the spell on the spider's side.

It pulsated with a glowing blue light that matched the weak beats of the spider's heart.

The sorcerer reached down and took a grain of sand from the caves floor. He flicked the catalyst towards the blue glow. A huge flash of light was released as the spell was activated. The spider moaned as powerful forces raced through its body.

The energies that were affecting the spider, were not those of a healing spell. Its eyes stared, uncomprehending at Catharvus' spell book. The heading on the page it was open to said, 'Shrink.'

The spider began to shrink, its body contorting like a deflating balloon. Within seconds, it lay on the floor, its body no bigger than a coin. The spider tried to stand, but immediately fell. Its injuries had persisted.

Catharvus looked down at the spider. He towered above it like a giant.

"Do not worry, my child. You have served me faithfully. I will take care of your pain."

Catharvus reached for the spider, scooping its shuddering body into his hand. He worked the magical energies with his free hand, producing a healing packet. He looked at the spider, paused, then extinguished the glowing spell.

He dropped the spider to the floor and crushed it beneath his boot heal. He twisted his foot, grinding the carcass into the dust.

"There," he laughed, "your pain is gone."

Catharvus turned towards the burning spell pages. They had curled into tiny shavings as the magical fire fed upon their energy. As he watched, they disappeared entirely. He took the seal of the Air Children and turned it over once in his hands.

"Trash," he muttered to himself, as he threw it onto the magical fire. The flames flared again, then consumed the cover.

Miles away, Avais awakened from a fitful sleep and shivered. She nestled closer to Alar's body and stared into the darkness.

Soft rays of pink light filtered through the opening of the shelter where Alar and Avais had spent the night. Birds began to chirp in the woods outside. The morning sun drove the chill from the air.

Alar forced his eyes open as his mind grudgingly brushed away the fogs of sleep. Avais still clung to him. She was trembling.

"What is wrong my love," he asked' as he rubbed his sleepy eyes.

"Something horrible has just happened," she whispered. "I am very afraid."

The fear in her voice drove the last remnants of sleep from him.

"Tell me about what frightens you."

"I'm not sure. Something is wrong. I feel weakened, far more than yesterday's battle can explain. A great loneliness has overcome me. It is as if a part of me has died."

"Could this be from the magic of Catharvus?"

"I don't think so. The sense of loss is unlike any magic that I have known. It pains me so."

Alar held her tiny body close to his. He was warm and strong. His voice acted like a soothing potion on her. The rays of the morning sun shone in on them. She closed her eyes. Gradually the trembling stopped. When she awoke, the world outside was brightly lit.

Alar looked up from the spell book. "Welcome back to the world of the living," he said. "I was wondering when you were going to wake up."

Avais' feathers fluttered as she stretched her wings.

"Forgive me it is not like me to sleep so late."

Avais hopped off Alar and peered at the outside world. The day was beautiful! She felt worries fade away as she watched the bright sun glisten off the river, throwing dancing sparkles of light on the ravine walls. The woods on the other side of the river smelled of greenness and fresh rain.

Avais turned towards Alar. The rest had done her well. The sense of foreboding and loss had disappeared with the night's darkness. She felt suddenly playful.

"Are you going to sit there and stall all day?" she asked, her voice breaking as she tried to suppress a giggle. "I know reading the spell book is interesting, but you've probably got it memorized by now. Let's get going, I need to try to get to the cover of my spell book."

Alar flashed her a crooked smile.

"Yes, exalted leader," he said as he snapped to attention. "I am ready to follow my feathery commander into the field."

"Shut up or I'll peck your eyes out!"

Alar shut the spell book and followed her out of the cave.

"Be careful, little bird," he warned.

"You should tell me about being careful? Ha! I could have put old Catharvus to bed twice by now if I wasn't tied up rescuing you!"

"Your words are true, but be careful anyway. I love you!"

Alar craned his neck upwards as he watched Avais fly up the side of the ravine. As she approached the mouth of the cave, she circled around it, trying to peer inside its vine shrouded entrance. A moment later, she disappeared from view as she plunged into it.

Alar watched the opening, hoping to see her come out. For what seemed like ages, she remained in the cave. Finally, when he was sure that he couldn't take the strain a second longer, she reappeared.

She dropped down the cliff face like a falcon in a dive. She remained in bird form, but did not appear to be carrying any part of the spell book. Within minutes, she landed beside him.

She was obviously disappointed that her form was unchanged. Alar was too.

"There is nothing useful left in the cave," she chirped. "The cover of the spell book and all of my things are gone. I fear that Catharvus now holds them."

She looked at Alar. The bright sunlight played off the muscles of his abdomen, making the ripples stand out. She felt herself relax.

"How do you feel about the magic?" she asked.

"I must have spent half the night reading, yet it seems a blur to me. I never realized there was so much to learn."

"Alar, you must realize that the art of magic is an unmrasterable one. No one can remember all the spells. We use spell books to remind us of the small details. Did you know that my spell book only contains general

spells? The advanced stuff is written down elsewhere.
The books of a master would fill an archive."

Avais hopped to the river's edge and bathed in
the shallow waters that swirled near the bank. Alar
washed his face as she preened herself dry.

"Let's get going," he said. "There is nothing else
we can do here."

She flew to his shoulder and clung there as he
crossed the river at a shallow spot. Alar looked back at
the cave, then at the rocks below where he had almost
met his death. He shuddered, then stepped into the
woods.

Gloominess seemed to descend upon them. Alar
tried to break up the dark mood.

"Shall we stop for some seed first, or do we take
the enemy on an empty stomach?" he joked.

Avais gave him a spunky look. "I meant what I
said when I threatened to peck your eyes out!"

Alar smiled, then said, "I meant what I said. I
am starving. Let's find some food!"

Alar foraged for berries while Avais picked at
seeds she found on the forest floor. Avais had soon
eaten her fill. Alar looked at the small handful of

blueberries he had found. They wouldn't make a dent in his appetite!

Avais followed his gaze to the berries. "It looks like being small does have some advantages!" she chirped. "It doesn't take much to fill me up."

Alar sighed. "True, you are well fed, but I haven't found enough to feed a good-sized rat."

"Let me show you a spell that can help," Avais cooed. "Open the book, I think it's on the seventy first page."

Alar sat down on a tree stump. He started to pop the berries into his mouth as he thumbed through the pages.

"Hold on there!" scolded Avais. "You need to save those for the spell."

Alar frowned. "Great, if I mess up the spell, I'll starve to death."

Avais ignored him and hopped to his lap. She looked down into the spell book. It was opened to a page that showed a bountiful table of large vegetables. The heading of the page said, "Create Food."

"That is the right page," she said. "Try the spell."

"I read it earlier, let's see if I remember it."

Alar closed his eyes and spoke the strange words. Yellow energy beams soon threw glittering light against the trunks of the forest's trees. Alar slowly herded the beams together. The packet broke apart the first time he tried the spell, but held together on his second try. When he had done it correctly, a small basket lay shimmering in his hands.

Alar looked at the pulsating spell energies. "And there you have it," he proclaimed, "lunch! Don't eat too much or you'll get as fat as Marcus."

"Calm down, show off," Avais scolded. "You still need the catalyst, remember?"

Alar looked at the torn pages of the book. "I'll need your help on this one. What must I put on this little picnic in the making, to transform it into a meal suitable for the starving squire of a magical bird?"

"Enough with the sarcasm. Just put the berries in the opening of the energy basket."

As Alar was about to drop the berries into the spell, she cautioned, "You just might want to stand back a little."

Alar shot her a puzzled glance, then stood up and left the pulsating basket on the stump. He walked a few paces, then lofted the berries towards the opening. All but one of them skittered off the spell's sides and fell to the forest floor. The berry that landed in the spell tripped the magical reaction. Sparks flew as it absorbed the energy. The berry withered and shrunk as the forces worked upon it. The spell faded, leaving a wrinkled nubbin that looked like an over-dried raisin, resting on the stump.

"Damn," yelled Alar. "I can't even do a breakfast spell correctly!"

Avais flew to a branch of a nearby pine. Her beak seemed to smile as she watched Alar stomp about in frustration. He began to root around the base of the stump, trying to find the berries that had missed the spell and fallen there. She called out to him. "Did I forget to mention that this spell had a double catalyst?"

He looked up at her and smiled weakly.

"Roasted bird would hit the spot right now," he muttered.

"I'll pretend I didn't hear that. You need to wet the berry to complete the spell. Again, you might want to step back a little."

Alar walked to the river's edge, pulled off his tattered shirt and dunked it into the water. He walked back to the stump and held his wet shirt above the wrinkled fruit. He squeezed the shirt, causing water to fall towards the berries. Alar didn't bother to jump back.

The first drop of water that hit the berry catalyzed the spell. A thunderous pop sounded as a volcano of yellow light was released from the wrinkled fruit. The berry expanded instantly. In seconds, it was the size of a boulder. As the fruit grew in size, it slammed into Alar's waist. The peel ripped, showering him with thick, blue juice as it knocked him down. The berry quivered for a second on the stump, then rolled off. It hit the ground next to the prone Alar, and burst.

Avais laughed so hard she almost fell out of the tree. Alar lay in a puddle of blue jelly. Sheets of blue skin covered his bare chest. He looked like he had been swimming on the inside of a fruit pie. He coughed out a mouthful of berry juice, spouting like a strangely colored whale. After fuming for a second, he too began to laugh.

"Don't play with your food," Avais gasped, between fits of laughter.

Alar sat up, peeled a wad of fruit out of his hair, then brought it to his lips.

"Delicious," he said, as the flavor of the fruit hit him. "It may be large as a pig, and just as messy, but it tastes just like a real berry."

"That's because it is," Avais laughed. "You have altered its size, but not its make up."

The trees to the right of Alar rustled as something large forced its way through them. Avais squawked as she took to flight. Alar sprung to his feet, but slipped on the peel of the giant berry. He fell backwards, sinking deeply into the mush that lay at the base of the stump. He heard a grunt and heavy breathing as something stopped in front of him. The pulp that covered his face was blinding him. He struggled to his feet and swung wildly at the figure that loomed before him.

Vice-like hands grabbed his wrists.

"You're either the smallest blue-skinned Ogre I've ever seen, or my friend Alar has been attacked by a giant dessert," boomed a familiar voice.

Alar twisted his hands free, then clawed at the mess that covered his face. Standing before him was Marcus, a monstrous smile split his face. Without hesitating for a moment, he reached for Alar's hair, then pulled a bit of pulp from it. He popped it into his mouth and smacked his lips as he ate it.

"I knew those legs were too scrawny for you to be an Ogre!" he laughed. "Since when were you reincarnated as a berry?"

"It's a long story," sighed Alar.

"Then tell me about it," chuckled Marcus. "On second thought, wash off in the river first. You're starting to draw ants!"

Bahaom sung to himself as he hiked up the mountain trail. As usual, he was off key. As usual, that didn't bother him. He knew that his wife would have scolded him for his lack of tone, but the beauty of his surroundings filled him with such joy, he just couldn't help but sing.

He sat on a rock and looked back at the path that had led him there. His voice trailed off as he saw the wisps of clouds below him. Bahaom had climbed the field of loose boulders that lined the ravine, then scrambled up the ravine walls like a scrawny mountain goat. He was so high, the valley's river and the surrounding forest of trees looked like props for a child's game.

"I have climbed to the heaven!" he shouted to a passing bird. His voice echoed softly in the distance. The smell of the mountain air caused a giant grin to form on his face. He began to sing again.

Bahaom had reason to be proud. He was seeing sights that none of his kind had ever seen. He was a member of the Gormon tribe, and the little people of the Eastern realm were a ground loving race.

He looked around again.

"A Gormon on the side of a mountain? Nonsense," squeaked Bahaom in his most stuffy imitation of a village elder. "We were born under the trees, and that is where we should stay."

He smiled broadly, then began to laugh. His high-pitched voice bounced off the rocks of the ravine below and echoed back a joyous chorus.

Gormons usually stood less than three feet tall. They were most comfortable in the close confines of the woods, a location where their speed and small size was an advantage. Out in the open, they were exposed and vulnerable. No normal Gormon would even consider venturing out from the protection of the forest's canopy, not to mention climbing the side of a mountain.

Bahaom was not a normal Gormon. All his life, he had been an exception. His unusualness was obvious from the time that he was a child. He was fair skinned and blond, unlike the rest of his clan whose heads were covered with coarse black hair. He was thin, and compared to his friends, tall. Standing nearly four feet in height, he looked more like a human child, than an adult Gormon.

Bahaom's mother used to joke that he had inherited his adventurous spirit from the same passing demon who had left him with his fair complexion. His father, a swarthy, and exceptionally short Gormon, failed to see the humor in her gentle ribbing.

Bahaom's spirited streak had been a source of great worry for his parents. From the time he first walked, he was rebellious. He ran, when others his age could barely crawl. Not content to play on the forest floor, he astounded his friends by learning to climb trees. Despite skinned knees and sprained wrists, he did not become discouraged. Nothing, it seemed, could keep him on the ground. His unusual talents brought him prosperity, for among his clan, he alone could get to the tops of the forest's trees. Bahaom collected rare mosses and sold them for a handsome profit to the healers. Delicacies from the forest's canopy were accessible to him, and no other.

One exceptionally clear day, while swaying from the top of a very tall tree, he caught site of the Dragon Spine mountains. Their cloud shrouded peaks called to him, touching an empty spot in his soul. From that time on, he was changed. Bahaom told his friends that he wanted to explore the mountain tops. They told him not to go. He would have to leave the protection of the forest, they warned. It was too dangerous. Think of the ravenous beasts, the treacherous weather that you might encounter.

Since he had young children to care for, Bahaom worked hard to suppress his desire to conquer the mountains. He locked his thoughts of mountain climbing into a tiny corner of his brain, then built walls of denial around them. The mountains still called to him. They were like a stream, always trying to erode their way through the banks of his defenses. His mind's walls, buttressed by the responsibilities brought on by parenting, stood firm against the steady pressure.

His children matured, he slowed down. Bahaom's life settled down into one of predictable comfort. As he grew old, he became content.

One day, Bahaom's wife let him know that they would be having salad with dinner. He knew that buds of the Roc-feather tree were a favorite of hers. The day was quiet, and he was bored. He decided to surprise her and hiked to a Roc-feather tree near the forest's edge. Standing at the tree's base, he gazed upwards. The tree seemed to go on forever. At its very top, the bright yellow buds swayed in the afternoon breeze. Laelia will love them, he thought. Bahaom stretched the stiffness from his back, then started to climb. It always amazed him how comfortable he felt in the trees. In seconds, he was off the ground, in minutes, he was swaying in the uppermost branches. As he reached for the yellow buds, his breath escaped him in a short gasp.

The Dragon Spine mountains lay in the distance, their black rocks piercing the surrounding cottony clouds. His mind's defenses collapsed with such force that he almost fell from the tree. The long-buried desires came roaring back. From that moment on, he could not rest until he climbed those mountains!

After they finished dinner, he told his wife. At first, she cried. She told him that these were supposed to be their special times together. How could he think of leaving her now? They fought long into the night. The arguments that had worked years ago, now seemed to fall on deaf ears. She knew her husband well. The look in his eyes convinced her that this time, there would be no dissuading him.

"Bahaom, hear me now," she scolded. "At times it has been difficult, but I have learned to love you. We have spent half a lifetime together. Your mind is usually open, but when it has set itself, the gods themselves cannot sway it. This, I fear is one of those times. I know that you will go, but remember this, you do not go alone. I am a part of you. We are a team. My life is nothing without you. I will be waiting for you to return to me."

Bahaom packed the next morning. He kissed his wife good-bye, then hiked towards the distant peaks. At night, he slept in the forest. He marched towards his goal with the first rays of the morning sun. The foothills of the Dragon Spine mountains passed underneath his determined feet on the third day. Early on the fourth day of his journey, he reached the mountains and started his climb. Now, hours later, he sat with his back to the black stone, and the clouds at his feet. As joy overflowed within him, he serenaded the valley below with his tone-deaf song.

Bahaom stood and looked above him. To his right lay a jagged crack in the mountain's side. What treasures might lie within that crack, he thought to himself. I believe that I will have a look.

He pulled himself into the crack, blinking as his eyes adjusted to the dim light. The song died in his throat as he saw what lay before him.

Catharvus sat, still chained to the rock, like some ancient gargoyle. The old man stared at him with soul-less eyes, then slowly smiled.

"You may continue singing," the old man said pleasantly. "It has been a long time since I have heard another's voice. Your song pleases me greatly. My name is Catharvus, who are you?"

Bahaom took in the sight of the man. He looked frail and pitiful.

"They call me Bahaom. I am from the Gormon tribe."

"That I can see," said Catharvus. "Tell me little man, you look rather old to be a traveler. What are you doing so far from the forest?"

"I wanted to explore these mountains. You see, I have always liked to climb," he answered excitedly. "When I saw these peaks, I was drawn to them. My friends think that I am crazy, yet I wanted to know what it was like to see the world from up here."

Catharvus nodded knowingly. "You seem to have the air spirit," he chuckled, "how appropriate. Tell me Gormon, how did you get your friends to join you on this quest?"

"They did not," Bahaom answered. "I climb alone."

Catharvus smiled even more broadly.

"The people of my village all knew of my climb, yet none were brave enough to come with me," the little Gormon boasted. "They will have to wait for my return before they can hear of my adventures. And what a story it will be!" he exclaimed. Again, his voice was rising. The excitement that filled him threatened to make his already high voice squeak like a young boy's.

Catharvus nodded. "My new friend, forgive me, for I am being a rude host. I have not offered you refreshment, and I know that you must have worked up quite a thirst in your great adventure. Sit down," he said as he pointed to a nearby rock. "Do you like wine?".

Bahaom's eyes focused on Catharvus' gnarled hands. The gleeful way the sorcerer cracked his knuckles made the Gormon's hair stand up as he fought back a shudder.

Bahaom realized that he was staring and looked away.

"I do, but I really must be going," he stammered.

"Please don't leave yet," whined Catharvus. "It has been so long since I have had company. The time alone is agony. Stay just a little while longer."

Catharvus looked pitiful as he whimpered. Bahaom shrugged his shoulders. What harm would there be in sharing a glass of wine, he thought? His eyes nervously locked on the old man as he slowly lowered himself to the rock.

"Would you sing for me?" asked Catharvus. His tone was pleasant, but his sentences ended with a hiss as his breath rolled off his rotten teeth. "I know a few simple conjuring tricks. Let me see if I can use them to make the wine."

Catharvus saw that Bahaom was once again staring at him. He could see indecision in his expression. It almost seemed as if the little climber was about to stand and flee.

"Sing, sing," he commanded as he shuffled about the cave. Catharvus' voice wavered like an old man's. He grabbed an ancient book, flopped wearily on his rock, and again implored the Gormon to sing. Bahaom shrugged a final time, then began to sing. His tension, combined with the dusty atmosphere in the cave, forced his tone even further off the usual scales. The old man didn't seem to mind, as he smiled broadly, and tapped his foot in time with Bahaom's rhythm.

While Bahaom was singing, Catharvus flipped through the book's pages. "Here it is," he mumbled, "the spell to make the wine. Let me see if I can still do it."

Brown energy beams formed around the old man, swirling until he gathered them up into a small packet. While his hands worked furiously, the smile never left his face. He began to nod his head in time with Bahaom's song. The Gormon was singing about flying amongst the clouds. Catharvus reached into his cloak and withdrew a piece of netting. He fondled it for a moment between twisted fingers, then gently pulled it across the pulsating brown energy packet.

Catharvus looked at Bahaom. The smile fell from the old man's face as the he stared into the Gormon's blue eyes. A feeling of dread overcame the little man, causing his song to fade in his throat. He froze, undecided as Catharvus rose to full height before him.

"Your song is over," Catharvus noted coldly. "I have a new request for you."

"Wh..., what is it," stammered Bahaom.

"Sing no more," yelled Catharvus as he threw the spell at the little man.

Alar waded into the river. He scraped at the fruit pulp, relaxing as the current carried the sticky mess away. His clothes, tattered and stained, lay in a pile at the river's edge. Flies were already buzzing around them.

Alar cast his clothes a glance as he waded to shore.

"Marcus, I hope you've brought some extra clothing with you. I am not looking forward to putting on that pile of rags."

"Judging from what you did to them, they are probably not looking forward to being subjected to more abuse," he laughed. "Relax, I have an extra shirt and pair of breeches in my pack."

He looked at Alar for a second, then patted his beer belly. "They might be just a tiny bit loose on you though."

Alar chuckled as he reached for the clothes. A dove sitting in the upper branches of a tree seemed to laugh with him. Marcus stared at the bird, then turned back towards Alar. The tattoo on his arm caught the big man's eye.

"Alar, when did you get that tattoo? I have seen one like that on Avais, but I didn't know that you have ever been inked."

The big man glanced at the dove, this time noticing the brownish pattern on its chest. "There is some weird stuff going on here," he murmured.

Alar sighed. "I guess it's time to do a little explaining."

He motioned to Avais who flew towards him. She landed on his head, fluffing her feathers as she nestled in his hair.

Alar sat down, gesturing at Marcus to do the same. Avais hopped off Alar's head and picked at the berry pulp. As Marcus shook his head in disbelief, Alar explained the events of the last few days to him.

"Let me get this straight," he said as he ran his hand through his beard. "You are now one of the Air Children, Avais is trapped in the form of a dove and can no longer use magic, and the spell book is missing its most important part."

Alar nodded, his blond curls swaying as his head moved.

"The realm is in great danger from the return of an evil sorcerer," Marcus continued.

Avais nodded this time.

"Alar, you are a sorcery student with two whole days of experience, and are the only thing that stands between us and almost certain destruction at the hands of this evil madman?"

Both Alar and Avais nodded in unison, her beak bobbing in time with his curls.

Marcus looked at Alar's stained and mangled clothing. He grabbed a great gob of berry pulp and waved it at Alar.

"Did your magic create this?"

"It did," he replied.

Marcus tossed the mush against a nearby tree. It stuck to its bark, then broke loose with a sucking sound, and fell to the forest floor. Marcus' head followed the pulp as it fell.

"Great," he muttered, "our fate lies in the hands of an incomplete sorcerer."

Lightening seemed to explode around Bahaom's head as the spell activated. He was buffeted by a deafening explosion as the magical energies transformed the air around him into bars of steel. For an instant, the cage that formed hovered in the air. As the reaction became complete, the energies faded and the cage came crashing to the ground. Dust and bits of rock sprayed in all directions.

Bahaom looked around frantically. He was in the center of a six foot, cylindrical cage, its massive bars made of gleaming steel. The cage had no bottom. It rested on the cave's floor. Its great weight had cracked the stone is several places when it fell, driving the lower part of the bars into the rock.

Bahaom grabbed the cage bars and shook with all his might. There was no give in the steel. He threw himself against the bars, trying to tip the cage over. It did not budge.

Catharvus laughed heartily. "A cave troll could not escape from that cage. Don't waste your time trying."

Bahaom slammed himself into the bars again. His shoulder gave way as the impact crushed the bones within it. He gasped in pain and fell to the ground as waves of agony engulfed him.

Catharvus looked at his prey and snickered. He walked to the cage and stared at the little man crumpled on the floor.

"I... I have nothing of value," Bahaom sobbed.

"I do not believe that is so," hissed Catharvus.

"Let me go. I will bring you gold, gems, whatever you desire."

"I will take what I desire."

"What is that?"

"You shall soon see," chuckled Catharvus as he reached inside his cloak and touched the pulsating handle of his dagger.

Catharvus toyed with the dagger, rolling it in his hand as Bahaom cowered in the cage. The handle of the knife shone a brilliant red as the blade's pulsations threw ominous colors onto the cowering Gormon's face.

"I am not afraid of you!" yelled the little man, desperately trying to keep his voice from wavering.

"My, how brave you are," sneered Catharvus, as he knelt before Bahaom's prison. He tilted his head as he took in the image of the little Gormon trembling on the cage's floor before him. "If I was in your position, I would be terrified. You see, there isn't very much that you can do to protect yourself."

"What are you going to do with me?" Bahaom asked, though deep inside, he knew the answer.

Catharvus smiled.

"Whatever I want to," he snickered.

Catharvus stood, then began pacing the floor in front of the cage. The chain dragged behind him, its links tinkling softly as they rubbed against each other. The clouds of dust that the chain displaced drifted towards Bahaom's prison. The sorcerer stopped, then turned towards his captive.

"You should have nothing to worry about, little creature. A good man would never want to inflict pain on another. It would be unthinkable to hurt someone who was unable to defend himself."

Catharvus knelt down before Bahaom's prison. "My little friend, do I look like a good man?"

Bahaom tried to answer, but his voice failed him as terror squeezed at his throat like a noose.

Catharvus' voice rose as he stood and began to pace again. He turned back towards the cage. "Am I?" he yelled, showering Bahaom with saliva.

The terrified Gormon cowered on the floor of his prison.

"Answer me!" yelled Catharvus, "or I will take your life now."

"Ye..., yes," the halfling whimpered. "You are a good man."

Catharvus slowly nodded his head.

"I was.... I really was. Until those bastards chained me in this cave like an animal! They were jealous of my power. They used treachery and cowardly tricks to defeat me, then locked me in here like so much vermin! They, even now, have returned to this realm. I can sense their presence, even though many miles separate us. Their presence despoils this land, fouling every aspect of it. Even the mountain air gags me as it carries their stench to me."

Bahaom looked into the glazed eyes of his jailer. They contained no trace of humanity. Hatred filled Catharvus' gaze with the unholy fires of insanity.

"Let me help you," whispered Bahaom. "I will help you strike back at those who imprisoned you."

"Look at yourself, you pathetic half-grown imp! Do you really think that you could slay one of the Air Children? Your puny little body has not the strength to defeat them in combat, and surely, your half-wit mind could not out-think them."

Catharvus sized up his captive. "You will help me defeat them, but not in any way that either you or they would expect."

He laughed softly to himself as he turned his back to Bahaom and began chanting.

Bahaom knelt on the dusty floor of the cave and prayed. He did not ask his god for help in escaping. Deep inside he knew that wasn't possible. He fervently asked for strength, but what he prayed for wasn't for himself.

"Dear god of the forests," he prayed. "Grant strength to my darling Laelia. I have loved her all my life, and now through my own stupidity, must leave her alone. Take care of her and comfort her through these hard times that I have brought upon her."

Catharvus turned to see the halfling praying. "That will not help you now," he spat.

The sorcerer grabbed Bahaom through the cage bars. As the pygmy tried to squirm away from his grasp, Catharvus waved his dagger in front of the halfling.

"Feed well, my friend," he yelled, "but make sure life force remains in his body."

Catharvis thrust the dagger downward. The sound of sizzling flesh filled the cave as the blade, glowing like molten rock, pierced the little man's chest. He shrieked, but continued to struggle, flailing at his attacker with clenched fists. Despite the handicaps of a broken shoulder, and being half Catharvis' size, he almost pulled the dagger from Catharvus' hands.

"No!" yelled Catharvus.

The dagger momentarily glowed white and emitted an ear-splitting howl. Bahaom's body spasmed like it had been struck by lightning.

Paralyzed by the dagger, the Gormon stared angrily into Catharvus' eyes. As his strength faded, the little man ceased fighting against the blade's magic. Bahaom's body went limp. Catharvus pulled the dagger, its handle now painfully hot, from the Gormon's bloody chest. The blade left Bahaom's body just his eyes were fluttering shut.

Catharvus looked closely at the little body that lay crumpled in the cage before him. He nodded approvingly when he saw that Bahaom's chest still rose and fell. The sorcerer pulled back his sleeve, tickling himself as he ran the pulsating blade of the dagger up his arm. He pierced his arm, draining most of the blade's energy into his own body.

As always, the stealing of life energies, changed his appearance. Years seemed to disappear as his body absorbed the vital essences of another.

Catharvus feasted upon the stolen life energies of Bahaom. He let himself totally relax, and felt the dagger connect with his soul.

Images formed in his mind as his eyes drifted shut. An elven face shrieked in terror as the dagger was thrust into its chest. The ravaged body was tossed onto the floor, joining the ten other bodies that lay there. Elders, adults and children lay upon the ground, identical dagger wounds marked their chests.

The blade glowed insanely red in Catharvus' vision. He watched as it was thrust into the arm of the elf that carried the dagger. After taking the family's life energies, the elf started walking out of the primitive hut. He stopped when he heard the cry of an infant. Turning around, he noticed a tiny baby, swaddled in a crib. The blade began to vibrate in the elf's bloody hand.

He stalked over to the crib, ripped the blankets away, then held the blade above the naked baby. As he started to lower the dagger, he gasped once, then froze.

"What kind of monster have I become?" sobbed an elven accent in Catharvus' vision. "I must escape this evil. I shall throw this accursed litch blade away, and never return to it!"

The elf tried to drop the blade, but the dagger glowed an eerie green and the fingers of the elf's shaking hand seemed to lock on its handle. He frantically pulled on the blade with his other hand, but could not loosen the blade.

The sobbing elf ran frantically up the mountain path until he came to the opening of a huge underground cavern. He tried once again to drop the dagger, but could not make his hand release its grip upon it.

"There is only one escape for me," he sobbed.

The elf threw himself into the void above the cavern, crashing onto the stone floor hundreds of feet below. The blade stayed locked in his hand. His body was crushed. The injuries from the fall were lethal. Only after the elf breathed his last breath did his grip upon the evil blade's handle loosen.

Years later, the shaking of a minor earthquake caused the blade to skitter a few feet from the elven skeleton.

Catharvus shook his head as the vision left him. He shrugged his shoulders and smiled.

No longer distracted, and feeling almost high on the stolen life energies of the Gormon, Catharvus skipped across the cave and retrieved his spell book. He smiled again then began to chant. He created a pulsating energy field that spun around his outstretched hand. Waves of cold emanated from the spell when he added the pinch of graveyard dust that was the catalyst. With hand motions, he steered it towards Bahaom's crumpled form.

Catharvus was casting a Wraith Spell. The spell was a particularly cruel one. It imprisoned the victim's soul, making it the temporary servant of the caster. By stealing the soul, the spell left nothing but an empty shell where its victim's body used to be.

A blast of icy air struck Bahaom on the face, shaking him from unconsciousness. He forced his eyes open, only to immediately wish he had kept them closed. An ice-cold field of shimmering green was settling over his face. Through the waves of energy, he saw Catharvus' face leering at him. The pulsating energy of the spell morphed into something that looked like an octopus. He felt unbearable pain as it enveloped his head, then began to pull at him with a hideous sucking sound. His brain swelled, then began to explode.

With the last of his breath, Bahaom uttered his final words, "Laelia, I will always love you..."

He pitched forward as life left him.

The ice-cold body of Bahaom settled into the dust of the cave's floor. A light blue shimmering form left the body, then floated through the air towards Catharvus. The wraith, Bahaom's former soul, faced the sorcerer and waited. Waves of cold emanated from its nebulous form, causing frost to settle on his cloak.

Catharvus looked at it and smiled. "Wait there, I am not ready for you yet," he commanded.

He began a chant, his voice boomed as his hands danced a complex ballet in the air. The cage that surrounded Bahaom's corpse vaporized, only to reform as an orange ball of light. The fiery ball, following

Catharvus' directions, rose to the cave's ceiling, then crashed downwards onto the little body lying in the dust. In seconds, all that remained was the Gormon's skeleton.

Miles away, Laelia slumped into a chair and burst into tears.

Marcus helped Alar gather up his few surviving possessions. He chuckled as Alar tried to tuck his oversized shirt into the pants that he had given him. Watching his friend trying gather handfuls of material and shove it into pants that were big enough for two grown men was entertaining. The look on Alar's face when the drawstring slipped and the pants slid down to his ankles was hysterical! Alar looked down and shook his head.

"You look kind of scrawny there..., pole bean," chided Marcus. "If you were a fish, I would throw you back!"

Alar ignored him. Unwilling to let his victim escape so easily, Marcus kept up a steady stream of ribbing. Alar listened to the full scope of Marcus' opinions, his face reddening as he waited for a chance to cut in. When the big man broke into a spasm of laughter after calling Alar a poorly fed bird, Alar snapped at him.

"Can we leave now? I for one, have heard quite enough!" he cried. "If you weren't so damned fat, I wouldn't look like a minnow with a damn jellyfish draped over it!"

Marcus looked aghast, then turned on his heels and stomped onto the path that led back to the village.

"No need to get personal...," he muttered under his breath.

Avais, who had watched the two men torment each other from the relative safety of a tree, hesitated as Marcus waved towards her.

"Come here Avais," he called out. "Travel with me. You may look like a bird, but at least you have a good sense of humor!"

Avais leapt from the tree and hovered in the air above him. She landed on his outstretched hand, cooed twice, then fluttered towards Alar. She tried to land on her lover's shoulder, but struggled to keep her balance as Marcus' oversized shirt slid about on Alar's frame.

Alar smiled as he helped her onto his collar. It, like the shoulders, was three sizes too large for his lean and narrow frame.

"Sorry about the clothes," he said. "It has been many years since their owner has skipped a meal!"

Marcus raised an eyebrow as he glared at Alar.

"The beggar complains about his alms? Another word out of you, my ungrateful friend, and Alar, savior of the realm, shall be trekking through the forest wearing nothing more than berry pulp!"

Both laughed. Marcus slapped Alar on the back, possibly a little harder than he need have, then turned towards the trail that lead into the forest. The trio marched onward, spurred on by Marcus' booming voice. The stories he told filtered along the trail's many twists and turns, losing themselves in the stillness of the surrounding woods.

Alar's told Marcus about the impending danger to Dragon Springs, and how they needed to get there quickly. Marcus agreed that time was of the essence. He led Alar and Avais down a seldom used trail that cut through the deepest parts of the forest. The terrain was rough, but the path was more direct than the river trail which wound its way around the countryside as it followed the river basin.

As Alar walked with Marcus, he couldn't help but notice that the trail that they followed was narrowing. As they ventured more deeply into the forest, the going got rougher. Their progress was slowed as fallen trees littered the path, causing them to pick their way along in single file. The canopy of trees which had previously been thin, now thickened and met over their heads, throwing them into darker shadow with each stride. The deeper they hiked into the forest, the more the temperature of the air seemed to drop.

Avais, clinging closely to Alar's collar, noticed the shudder he tried to stifle. She also felt chilled, far more than the falling temperature would account for. Only Marcus seemed oblivious to the increasing gloom. He chattered on as each passing step carried them further into the woods.

"Keep vigilant, my love," Avais whispered.

She tried to peer into the surrounding forest, but saw nothing through the encircling foliage.

"There is something wrong," she said. "The sounds of the birds are absent here."

Marcus turned and stared at the chirping bird.

"What is the little chicken saying?" he asked. "As a non-tattooed human, I feel distinctly left out of this conversation."

"Avais says that the woods are unusually quiet here, that is, except for your incessant rambling!" Alar snapped.

"Rambling!" sputtered Marcus. "I am trying to share the wealth of my life's experiences with you. A treasure trove of knowledge such as this would normally fetch a king's ransom, yet I offer it to you freely. Do the two of you realize the gift I am offering? I think not!

Complaints are all I hear from you two. Sometimes I wonder why I bother..."

Avais chirped sharply in Marcus' direction.

"What did she say?" he asked.

"Hush! You sound like an old woman," translated Alar. "She says that you are making enough noise to cover the approach of an army."

"Marcus, Avais is not the only one who is uncomfortable here. I too feel a sense of foreboding. Now still your mouth a moment, I want to listen!"

Marcus huffed in mock astonishment. "If only I had a bottle to occupy my lips..." he murmured.

Avais squawked again. Alar looked at her, then at Marcus. He bit his lip, but could not keep himself from bursting into laughter.

A hurt expression clouded Marcus' features. "What did she say?"

"I won't tell you all of it," gasped Alar, "but I would think twice about calling a sorceress a chicken, if I were you!"

Marcus flashed a tight-lipped smile at the bird and bowed slightly. The three of them scanned the trail, saw nothing, then proceeded into a slight clearing.

The rocky ground of the clearing crunched below their feet. Unlike the rich forest loam, the stony soil kept the trees and underbrush at bay. The bowl-shaped area it formed was about twenty paces across, and better lit, as the tree canopy was thinner above them. Light filtered in through the tree tops, speckling the leafy floor with a myriad of colors. Deep gouges crisscrossed the rocky soil.

Marcus whistled softly as he bent down to examine one of the grooves.

"It looks like a giant's plow has been working the soil here. I wonder what unholy creature has claws big enough to do this?"

Avais burst into flight as the answer to Marcus' question came crashing into the clearing.

Three tons of heavily muscled hide bounded into the clearing, knocking down saplings as it moved. The beast, back from foraging unsuccessfully in the darkest depths of the forest, looked at the two humans, then let out a roar that caused Marcus' hat to fly off. Its unsuccessful hunt had left a great hunger gnawing in its belly. The beast sniffed at the air, filling its nostrils with the warm, meaty scent of the humans.

The huge animal stared at the closest human, Alar, and roared again. Alar's chest shook with the resonant vibrations of the creature's howl. The monster's foul breath rustled the leaves of the trees behind the woodsmen. It rose upon its hind legs, flexing its claws in Alar's direction.

Alar stared at the animal. Never before had he seen such a creature. It was vaguely bearlike, but impossibly large. His eyes were level with the beast's knee. The creature bellowed again and began to advance. Glistening fangs poked out from lips covered with matted red fur. It snapped at the air, thirty feet above Alar's head.

"What in the name of the gods is that," Alar murmured as he looked the creature up and down.

"It's a werebear," screamed Marcus. The big man drew his sword and pushed Alar behind him. "I know of them. They are deadly when hungry, and this one looks famished. Werebears are known for pulling down their prey from behind. If we both try to run away, he will surely take us down and kill us."

Marcus took a step in the werebear's direction, then crouched down into a combat stance.

"Run you fool! I think I can occupy him long enough to let you escape!"

"Nothing doing, my friend!" yelled Alar. "I leave when you do. We are in this together."

He stepped forward until he was even with Marcus and faced the rearing monster.

Marcus smiled to himself, then stepped in front of Alar, and began to wave his sword in small circles as he edged towards the werebear.

"Be gone you overgrown throw rug," he yelled at the monster. The creature dropped to all fours, roared again, then lunged forward. swiping at Marcus' sword. Though Marcus held the sword in both hands, it was knocked out of his grasp as if it were an autumn leaf blown by a stiff breeze. The werebear sniffed at the sword with nostrils as large as drinking mugs. It put its giant paw on the blade, then bit into the sword's handle.

Shaking its head like a dog with a stuffed toy, it bent the blade to and fro. The werebear, finding the weapon to be unpalatable, soon tired of mauling it. He stomped on the twisted blade, driving it deeply into the forest floor, then looked again at the woodsmen.

The monster rose to its hind legs again and bellowed. The creature's fetid breath surrounded Alar and Marcus in an eye watering cloud. It looked down at the little creatures that stood before it, then charged at them.

Avais took flight, screeching as she circled the monster's head. "Cast a befriend spell on it," she yelled.

The monster took a halfhearted swipe at the circling dove, then resumed its attack on the men.

Alar backpedaled and started chanting frantically. Energy lines began to form in the air around his hands. The bear stopped for a moment, its curiosity drawn to the chanting man. It poked at him curiously. Alar dodged the huge paw, making sure to pull the glowing spell packet with him. The creature roared and took a real swing at Alar. The wind pushed by the massive paw made his eyes water and threatened to knock the forming spell from his hands.

"Try to buy me some time," yelled Alar. "These spells take time, and I am not good at conjuring them."

Marcus nodded, then lowered his shoulder and charged at the distracted animal. He hit it hard on the leg, causing the rearing monster to lose its balance, and spin away from Alar. It turned and snapped at the man who attacked it. Marcus rolled away, just escaping the jaws that would have torn him in half if they had caught him. The beast bellowed in anger, then lunged towards Marcus.

While Marcus dodged about, trying to stay away from the snapping jaws, Alar finished the hand movements needed to form the spell. "What is the catalyst?" he yelled.

Avais called out to him, but her voice was drowned out by the roaring of the enraged bear.

"I can't hear you," he yelled. "Come closer."

Avais banked towards Alar and hovered before him.

"Pluck one of your hairs, and put it into the spell," she yelled. "That will identify you as the one that the werebear will befriend."

The monster, distracted by the screeching of the dove, abandoned its attack on Marcus, and headed towards Avais and Alar. Avais fluttered in the animal's face, then dove downward. The werebear swung at her, but missed as she saw the attack coming and banked upwards. Unfortunately, the paw's follow through struck Alar on the legs, knocking his feet out from under him. Though he was lucky to have been hit by the bear's forelimb, instead of the claws, he was thrown end over end into the air.

Alar landed with a thud on the forest floor. The monster sprinted after him. It lunged for the seemingly helpless man, but he managed to roll out of the way. As the animal turned and bore down on him again, Alar frantically grabbed at his blond locks and stuffed half a handful into the glowing spell packet. The spell transformed with the sound of a bull whip cracking as the catalyst activated it.

The werebear pawed at Alar, dragging him towards its mouth.

"Throw the spell on the beast!" yelled Avais. "It won't work until it strikes its victim!"

Alar tried to roll away from the monster. The werebear seemed to enjoy playing with its tiny prey. It cuffed him, sending him tumbling through the air. Dazed, he landed in a heap at the monster's feet. Alar looked at the bear and blinked, trying to clear his double vision. The beast opened its jaws and reached for the helpless man.

"Take me, take me," cried Marcus as he waved his arms in front of the bear. "Alar, get the hell out of there!" he yelled as he dug his fists into the animal's side.

"Throw the spell," screeched Avais.

The pounding he had taken had stunned Alar. He movements were slow and labored. He was seeing double.

Desperate to drive the attacking monster away, he picked one of the two blurry images he saw, and threw the spell at it.

He chose the wrong image.

The spell passed by the werebear's head and ricocheted through the forest, sending showers of sparks as it bounced from tree to tree.

The monster reached out with a paw and pinned Alar under it. It opened its jaws wide and prepared to rip the struggling man in half.

Before it's jaws could snap shut, the monster was pelted by a shower of pine cones. Startled, it looked at Marcus. The man was still punching at it, but had nothing in his hands. More pine cones seemed to drop from the sky onto the surprised animal. Tendrils from vines that clung to trees at the edge of the clearing released their grip on the tree's bark and writhed towards the bear's giant legs. By the hundreds, they wrapped around it's limbs.

It howled nervously and let Alar go. The beast sprung into the air trying to shake the vines off its back legs. While it was rearing up, a sapling seemed to bend itself back. The tree arched like a bow, then released itself and smacked the werebears firmly on the haunches. Within seconds this was repeated dozens of times.

The combined impacts, knocked the animal over. It howled as it rolled to its feet, still trying to shake off the clinging vines. A tree, easily forty feet tall, creaked loudly, then fell, striking the crouching werebear on the shoulder. It yelped in fear and charged towards the deep woods, jerking the encircling vines from its back paws. The sounds of falling trees followed it into the forest.

"What in the name of the gods just happened?" asked Alar as he tried to get up. He was still dazed from the blow that the werebear had given him and stumbled backwards. A branch from a nearby oak tree stretched out and broke his fall.

Avais was consumed with howls of laughter. Marcus looked at her, then at Alar who was trying to get away from a vine that insisted on brushing his clothes off.

"The way that plant is doting on you, I'd swear that you owe it money," Marcus chuckled. "I don't know how your spell accomplished it, but we were just rescued by half of the forest."

Alar freed himself from the attentive vine and walked shakily towards Marcus. Avais alit on his shoulder.

"You threw the 'befriend' spell at the bear and missed," she laughed. "The spell hit the plants behind the bear, and they came to your aid. In all my years, I haven't ever seen anything like that before."

"Alar, the catalyst for the spell was a single hair," she continued. "You threw a handful into it, that is why so many plants are trying to befriend you now. Please be more careful in the future. Catalysts are very tricky and may cause the spell to misfire badly if you don't use them exactly as they are written in the book!"

"I was a little preoccupied at the time," muttered Alar. "That monster had its paws all over me. A second more, and it would have ripped my leg off! Besides, we don't have a complete book!"

Avais rolled her eyes.

"Shall we chase after it?" asked Marcus. "If we kill it, I will skin it and have wall to wall carpeting for my entire cottage!"

Alar groaned at the big man's joke.

"I've had enough adventuring for a while! My head hurts, I can't see straight. Let's just stay here for a few minutes and rest."

Marcus nodded. He and Alar sat on one of the fallen tree trunks and ate berries that seemed to appear endlessly on a vine that nestled in Alar's lap.

Avais landed on Alar's shoulder and nestled against his neck. Alar felt the warm sunshine on his face. He exhaled deeply.

"Thank the gods that we are out of danger," he sighed.

Suddenly a terrible chill settled over the area. A blue streak of light flew past Alar's shoulder and hovered before him.

"I am sorry," a faint voice whispered. "The evil one is forcing me to do this."

Before any of them had time to react, ethereal hands reached out and grabbed Avais. Their coldness terrified her, and she began to flutter and squawk frantically. The wavering figure held Avais against its chest, then streaked away towards the mountains.

Feathers drifted to the ground as Marcus and Alar looked at each other.

"Avais is gone!" Alar yelled, his voice breaking as panic threatened to overwhelm him. "Catharvus has taken her from me! Marcus, what can we do, what can we do?"

Marcus reached down and picked up one of the feathers that had fallen from Avais during the struggle. The feather was coated with a layer of frost. He turned it over in his hand and slowly exhaled.

"This is not the work of any worldly beast," he said as he scraped at the frost with his fingernail. "Only a wraith could do this."

"I have read of such things," he continued. "A wraith is an undead soul. It is kept from dissipating by magic and is in effect the slave of the sorcerer who has captured it."

Alar clenched his eyes shut as they threatened to mist over. He pounded his fist against the ground.

"She is in great danger," he sobbed, "and I am to blame! I feel so helpless. The wraith should have taken me, not my poor Avais."

"How is that you are to blame?" asked Marcus, his voice filled with kindness. "You did not provoke the werebear, nor did you summon the wraith."

Alar's voice was barely audible. "Catharvus must have learned of the Air Children's scheme to stop him. Though I do not know why, I am instrumental in their plan."

"Catharvus has been trying to kill me since the accursed blue moon first appeared. Since he has been unable to kill or capture me, he has instead struck out at Avais. She is trapped in her Air Child transformed state. Marcus, she's totally helpless! Do you realize that she has no more power to resist him than a baby bird would?"

Marcus put a steadying arm on Alar's shoulder.

"Calm down, my friend. Things have looked this bad before, and we always managed to get by."

"I will not rest until she is safe!" Alar's jaw tightened as he spoke. "Let us climb the ravine walls, and search for him now. I will strangle him with my bare hands if he has hurt her!"

Marcus gently took him by the shoulders and squeezed.

"You know that we can't do that. Think about it. Charging up to his lair would be suicide. He wants us to rush towards him, unprepared. We would be met at the door by a magical death. No, we must surprise him, catch him unaware. Let us go back to the village. We can talk about our options and stock up on supplies. Let us find his hiding place, probe its defenses. We need to find a way to sneak up on him. The only way we can defeat him is to be patient and intelligent!"

"I guess you right," stammered Alar. "It's just that the thought of what he might do to her is driving me crazy!"

"Don't worry, we will find her. It does seem that the sorcerer wants you. Nothing else would explain the multiple attempts on your life. Avais has not been attacked at all, before today that is. As long as you are alive, there is some degree of safety for her. Let us use that to our advantage. Come, we must prepare for battle."

Miles away, Catharvus stared at the crystal ball. He saw the worried look on the faces of the woodsmen. With a slight turn of the ball, he tilted the image upwards and focused on the blue form streaking towards his cave. White feathers fluttered in its wake. One fell more rapidly than did the others. He focused the orb upon it. It was matted with blood.

The sorcerer broke into a great smile that faded only when the spell wore out and the image before him disappeared.

Avais struggled against the icy hands that gripped her. The wraith held her so tightly that she was in danger of smothering. She squirmed in the undead creature's grasp, trying to get free.

Bahaom's wraith grabbed her more tightly, smashing her into its chest. She shrieked as her tail feathers started to bend backwards. A few snapped, falling into the air behind them. The bloody stumps of Avais' feathers stung as the wraith's chill caused the blood within them to freeze.

Avais watched the ground fly beneath her. She craned her neck forward to try to see where the wraith was taking her. In the distance, she saw a hawk circling on the thermals.

"Help me! Save me!" she cried at the circling raptor. "I am one of the Air Children, and I need you desperately."

The hawk banked towards her voice. It spied the wraith and the white bird struggling to escape from its grasp. Though it was a swift flyer, it was no match for the blinding speed of the wraith. The hawk fell behind as the undead soul easily outdistanced it. The hawk screeched out its apologies to Avais and followed along as best as it could.

Avais was beginning to lose consciousness. The wraith held her so tightly that she was having trouble breathing.

"You are killing me," gasped Avais. "I can't breathe. Please don't squeeze so hard."

Bahaom cringed at the sound of her voice. He felt terrible guilt at being the instrument of Catharvus' evil. Though his free will had disappeared when the last of the life forces left his body, his soul and conscience persisted and were horrified by the ghastly deeds he was doing.

The icy hands relaxed their grip ever so slightly. Avais drew in great gulps of air, extinguishing the fire that near suffocation has lit in her chest. As strength returned to her, the little bird began to struggle again. It did no good. There was no escape.

The wraith that was once Bahaom flew up the mountain's face and into Catharvus' cave. It hovered in front of the sorcerer.

"You have done well, my off-tune friend," Catharvus chuckled. "Now give her to me."

The wraith hesitated. The sorcerer muttered something under his breath and reached for Avais. She struggled to escape as the withered brown hands grabbed at her. Catharvus snatched the struggling dove from Bahaom. He held her by the throat, taking perverse pleasure in watching her flutter helplessly.

"The Air Children will not escape me this time," he laughed.

Wrapping one hand across her back, he twisted her head until the neck was on the verge of snapping. Catharvus smiled and stared into Avais' face. He relished the look of terror that overcame her.

"They will not come if I do not live," she croaked.

He paused for a second, longing to hear the cracking noises of breaking spine bones.

His grip relaxed.

"It is true," he murmured. "You are more valuable to me alive, then dead. As long as I hold you, I can be assured that the young woodsman and his portly friend will deliver themselves unto me. It does save me the trouble of having to capture them."

Catharvus roughly twisted one of Avais' wings. She did not screech, but tears welled in her eyes.

"What an ugly thing these wings are," he sneered. "They are vile and unclean. One thing about them makes me happy, they keep you from casting magic while trapped in this disgusting form. Without your woodsman friend, you have no way of leaving here, ever!"

He shuffled to the skeleton that had once belonged to Bahaom. It now lay forlornly in the dust. With a kick, he snapped the skull off the spinal cord. He then stepped on the skeleton's lower back while pulling upwards on the ribs. The tortured bones began to give, filling the cavern with an awful grinding noise. Avais tried to be silent, but couldn't. Her muffled sobs reached Catharvus, making him smile.

The skeleton's spine snapped. Catharvus paused to look at his handiwork. He held Bahaom's rib cage in one hand, Avais in the other. The sorcerer kicked the pelvis and leg bones of the skeleton aside. He then pushed the lower part of the rib cage into the dirt of the cave's floor. As Catharvus chuckled wickedly, he shoved Avais into the top of the rib cage, through the area where Bahaom's neck used to be. While his hand covered the opening, he groped for the Gormon's skull. He grasped it triumphantly, then placed it atop the rib cage, effectively sealing Avais in.

Avais fluttered against the bones that surrounded her. With its top capped by the skull, and the bottom stuck into the cave's floor, Bahaom's rib cage had become a prison of bone.

"How appropriate," cackled Catharvus. "You are held captive within the chest of a man, while the key to my escape is equally enslaved by his heart's desire for you."

Avais clung to the ribs with her claws and stuck her rumpled head through the bones.

"I was born long after the atrocities you committed were but memories. In my heart, I felt pity for you. In a way, I still do. I now know that the actions the elders took against you were deserved. You are as evil as they said you were."

"Avais, my little prisoner, you are mistaken," he snickered as he fondled the dagger, "I am worse."

As Bahaom's wraith watched Catharvus imprison Avais, a great sadness filled it. Bahaom's spirit began to cry. Frost accumulated in the corners of its eyes as the falling tears froze. Bahaom's spirit could take it no longer. With a cry of anguish, it bolted for the mouth of the cave.

Catharvus looked up at the wraith. "Get back here now!" he commanded.

The Gormon's wraith ignored him.

"If you do not stop, you will cease to be," Catharvus yelled. "It is I alone who hold your life energies together. If I terminate the spell, you will fade away."

Bahaom's spirit continued on, unmindful of the sorcerer's threats. Its mind was filled with thoughts of Laelia. Bahaom's desire to see the world from the top of the mountain had separated him from her and caused another innocent to be ensnared by Catharvus.

This was just not right! Things could not end this way! He had to see his wife again! The need was so strong that it blocked out all else.

Bahaom's wraithly spirit streaked into the mountain air and headed towards his familiar woods. Catharvus snarled, then began to murmur the termination sequence of the Wraith spell.

With speed born of pure desperation, the spirit of the Gormon rocketed towards its home. In seconds, it had crossed the plains and entered the great forest. Bahaom dove downward towards his cottage and saw Laelia sitting upon its steps. She held her head in her hands and was crying softly.

Miles away, in the mountain cave, Catharvus neared completion of the spell. Bahaom's wraith felt his ankles begin to sting as crackling energy leaked from them into the surrounding air. He hovered before his wife.

"I may not be able to touch you my dear, but know that I am here," he said in a voice that wavered like the wind.

She looked to where she heard his voice, but saw only a shadowy glittering form.

"I will not be able to come back to you, my love," he continued.

"Somehow, I knew that," she sobbed, as the ghostly image before her faded.

"I have lost my life," Bahaom continued, his voice now the merest shadow of a whisper. "I have to say, I died doing what I loved. My only regret is that I have to leave you. I never really got to say goodbye to you, my darling."

Through falling tears, his wife watched his image flicker and fade.

"I forgive you," she whispered. "I will always love you."

Bahaom's outline had nearly totally faded. All that remained of his form was a shimmering blue cloud.

"I will never leave you again," he promised. "I will always be here with you. You will hear me in the rustle of the leaves and see me in the shadows of the trees." His voice was so faint that she wasn't sure if she heard the words, or imagined them.

She felt a warm breeze caress her face, even though the day had been windless. She looked up. Sunlight seemed to sparkle in the leaves as the wind played through them. She thought she heard the words, I love you, in their rustling.

She put her head in her hands and cried herself to sleep. The sun shone warmly through the tree tops. When she awoke, she felt renewed strength.

She knew she could go on.

"We are back at Dragon Springs," gasped Marcus. "Never have we made the trip so rapidly."

"Marcus, having the trees bow before us to open the path certainly didn't slow us down any!"

"Quite true, my inaccurate sorcerer. Now let us get ready for the battle that awaits us. What do you think we might need?"

"How about a battalion?" murmured Alar bleakly. "On second thought, they wouldn't help us against a sorcerer. I am afraid that magic is the key here. I will have to use the Air Children's magic to defeat Catharvus. I must study the spell book. There is so much I don't understand. Could you get the provisions we need, then meet me at my cottage?"

"Consider it done!" Marcus replied. "I will collect weapons, food and other necessities."

"You might want to skip the other necessities," Alar laughed as he pointed towards a bottle on Marcus' belt.

Marcus frowned. "You would have me go into battle without proper medicine? What kind of leader are you?"

Alar gave a tired grin to Marcus. "I'll see you soon," he replied with a slight laugh, then turned and walked towards his cottage.

Alar walked through the streets of his village in a daze. He barely acknowledged the worried greetings of his neighbors. His mind raced as dark thoughts filled it. How would he find Catharvus and what would he do when he found him? Which magic spells would be effective against a master magician? How could he rescue Avais and not endanger Marcus? The thought of losing both of his friends was too much to bear.

A short while later, Alar reached his home. The woodsman went inside, but first checked to see that nothing had been disturbed. He wasn't sure how far Catharvus' power reached or if he had allies, but checking for ambushes and booby traps seemed prudent. His cottage was as he had left it.

Alar sunk into his carved chair and turned the spell book over in his hands. Despite what it had been through, the scent of the waterfall cave's floral waters still clung to it. Alar shut his eyes and let his mind drift to thoughts of Avais. He ran his finger across the torn cover, letting his finger rest on the little bit of the Air

Children seal that remained. The image of the bathing Avais faded, only to be replaced by that of the frost covered feather.

Alar clenched his fists and bit down into his lip.

"I will come for you, my dear," he whispered, "I swear it!"

He threw himself into his reading. He had not moved when Marcus came to get him nearly twelve hours later.

Marcus arrived at Alar's cottage and found his friend deeply engrossed in the spell book.

"How's it going, buddy?" he asked.

"It's frightening, there is so much I do not know. Even if I had a complete spell book, I wouldn't feel confident going into battle without many years of study. Having a few days of preparation just isn't enough time, especially when you consider that I am working with one third of my book missing!"

"I understand, Alar, but it's all we've got to work with. You're not having second thoughts about going to rescue Avais, are you?"

"No, I'm not. I am just a little nervous, that's all. Have you got all of our provisions?"

"Yep, I have two fully stocked packs. There are weapons for both of us waiting outside the door. I assume that conjuring spells will keep your hands busy, but I packed a sword for you just in case."

"Yes, I'm afraid you are right about the sword. I don't think that I can create an energy pack and use a bladed weapon at the same time, but it will be reassuring to have one available, should I need it."

"Alar, how much do you know about the sorcerer who holds Avais?"

"Not much, I'm afraid. She told me he was once one of the Air Children, but something corrupted him. He gave up their ways for a life of evil. He did many terrible things and killed lots of innocent people."

"There was a great battle, he was defeated, and imprisoned somewhere in the mountains. The Air Children would never kill one of their own, so they imprisoned him in an unending slumber. Unfortunately, he has recently awakened. I think it may have had something to do with the eclipse of the blue moon."

"Now that he has been awakened, it is only a matter of time until he breaks free," he continued. "When he does, there will be a massacre. He has sworn to exterminate both the villagers and the Air Children. Avais was sent to prevent his escape. Somehow that involved recruiting me. She said that prophecy states that I would either help defeat the sorcerer, or set him free. I do not understand what that means, but given my success with magic so far, it scares me tremendously."

"What if one of my spells misfires and allows Catharvus to escape? If that happens, I would be helping to cause of the death of all the people that I love."

"All my life, I have hated magic! Why was I chosen for this task?" he sobbed. "Why does the hero have to be me?"

The big man nodded as he placed his arm around Alar's shoulders.

"Responsibility lands on both the shoulders of those that desire it and those that don't. You have been chosen. All you can do is to give it your best."

"I know, Marcus. I will try."

"Say, have you found out anything that might help us?" Alar asked.

"I spoke with some of the village elders while you were studying the spell book. No one knows where a prison cell built into the mountain might be. Other than the waterfall cave, there are no caves in this region that they know of. My best guess is that Catharvus' prison was built by the Air Children, then hidden. He has probably lain nearby, asleep, for hundreds of years. The plan worked perfectly until the blue moon eclipse caused the earthquake that awoke him."

"I think that we should go back to the waterfall cave and look for clues," suggested Alar. "That is where the spider attacked me and Avais. It was still bleeding from the wounds that it received in the pub. The beast may have left a blood trail that we could follow to Catharvus' prison."

Marcus nodded in agreement. "That is a fine idea. We should head towards the cave, but I think climbing up the rock face would leave us too exposed. Let us surprise the sorcerer if we can. Why don't we take the old logging trail and then climb up the back side of the mountain?"

"Then we can work our way down to the cave, instead of climbing up to it!" interrupted Alar. "We would be approaching from an unexpected direction. Unless he is looking up to the sky, he won't see us!"

"It is almost dawn. Are you ready to leave?" asked Alar.

"I can't think of a better time to start," the big man smiled. "Let us go!"

Alar and Marcus left the village and headed in the direction of the mountains. Before the sun had risen enough to light the sky, the two men turned off the main path and worked their way more deeply into the woods. After fighting their way through the underbrush for about an hour, they came to the old logging trail. It was abandoned and overgrown. Weeds and saplings had grown thickly in the years since the path was last traveled. In places, it was all but impassable.

"Why don't you cast one of your 'plant pal' spells here," Marcus suggested as he pointed at the overgrowth before him. "Having these weeds lie down before us would certainly beat trying to hack them down."

"I don't think that would be such a good idea, Marcus. I am so new to the use of the magical arts that I am afraid I will mess up the spell. We were really lucky when the Befriend Spell misfired. My mistake ended up saving us. I can't see that happening again."

"True," said Marcus. "Next time you try to befriend a forest, you might hit the poison ivy. I can see it now, thousands of itchy vines trying to cuddle up to you. Not a good thing!"

"Yes," chuckled Alar, "death by scratching is not how I want to go!"

"Remember, Avais was helping me cast that spell. She knows what the proper catalysts are. Using magic with a torn spell book scares me more than most of the monsters we have met."

"I don't believe you. You just don't want to part with any more of your pretty hair," Marcus chuckled as he stroked Alar's long blonde locks in an exaggerated manner.

Alar and Marcus worked their way along the trail until it became so overgrown that it disappeared. The woodsmen were hacking their way through a forest of head-high saplings when they reached a narrow path.

Alar knelt down and examined the trampled plants that lined it.

"This trail is new," he exclaimed. "These plants are broken, but have not yet died."

"The old logging trail went straight towards the mountains," Marcus said as he looked around. "This one seems to run parallel to them. It definitely isn't the trail we used to use, but it may take us to where we want to go. In any event, using a trail sure beats hacking a path all the way to the Dragon Spines. If I need to cut down one more weed, my sword shall be too dull to use in combat!"

Alar pulled himself up the trunk of a nearby tree.

"Marcus, the trail seems to curl towards the mountains in both directions. Which way should we go? The trees are so thick here, it is hard to see where each fork leads."

"I don't know. It has been ages since I have come this way. Let me scout out the left end of the trail. If it leads towards the cave, I will come back and get you. If it turns out that it goes the wrong way, we can both take the other trail."

"How about I scout the right end of the trail while you check out the left end? suggested Alar."

"That's silly," Marcus insisted. "We will both have to backtrack to join up and knowing our luck, only one end of the trail will go in the right direction. No, you stay here. Read more of that spell book, it may be the key to our victory. I won't be long."

Before Alar could argue, Marcus spun on his heels, and headed down the trail.

Alar sighed. When Marcus had set his mind to something, it was easier to move him physically, than to get him to change it. He sat down by the side of the trail then pulled the spell book from his pack. Alar thumbed through the table of contents and picked out some spells that he thought might be helpful in helping them remain undetected. He studied them intently, silently mouthing the words to each spell's preamble while practicing the hand motions. After he had done this, Alar turned the page to the Magic Missile spell. This one is important, he thought. It is what Avais used against the Orc. I wonder if it would work againt Catharvus?

He mouthed the words a little more loudly. Energy lines began to glow all about him. He followed the hand motions listed in the book and corralled the beams into a fist sized packet.

"Now what might the catalyst be?" he muttered to himself.

Alar's pondering was interrupted by a rattling sound in the distance. It came from the opposite end of the trail, so he knew it couldn't be Marcus. Alar stood up and looked for the source of the sound. He saw nothing. The rattling became louder, accompanied now by the pounding of footsteps. Alar fingered the glowing Magic Missile energy packet nervously.

Suddenly a huge skeleton, dressed in rusty armor, rounded the corner. Catharvus' orb had pinpointed it's grave and the Raise the Dead spell had disturbed the eternal rest of the giant warrior. The undead skull swiveled towards Alar. Empty eye sockets stared in his direction.

If I kill this intruder, I may be able to rest again, it thought. The skeleton drew a notched and pitted longsword from its scabbard and charged.

Alar sized up the monster. It was the undead skeleton of a giant. Standing at least fifteen feet tall, it wielded a sword that was longer than the woodsman's body.

Alar jumped to his feet and backpedaled furiously. The skeleton, its strides easily double his, gained on him with each step. As the monster got within striking range, Alar remembered the Magic Missile spell. What is the catalyst, he thought? Damn, what can it be?

The skeleton swung its sword at him. Alar dodged backwards. The sword passed within a foot of his face. Bits of rust and dirt flew from the blade and got in his eyes. Alar turned to run, but with his eyes watering, stumbled on an exposed root. He fell to the trail floor. The skeleton straddled him, pinning him down with one huge foot, then raised its sword.

Alar reached around desperately for a catalyst. He grabbed a handful of leaves from the trail and stuffed them into the Magic Missile spell packet. He cringed when he heard the spell make a sputtering noise.

Alar knew that the spell had been improperly catalyzed. When Avais had killed the Orc, he has heard a sharp explosion, not the wet sputtering noise that now emanated from his hand.

A pebble would have transformed the raw energies into a usable explosion, but unfortunately, that information was written on the third of the spell book that Catharvus' spider had taken from him. The leaves and dirt that Alar put into the spell reacted with the energy, and instead of focusing it into a projectile, caused it to expand uncontrollably. As the skeleton thrust its sword downward at him, Alar, in an act of desperation, threw the misfiring spell at it.

Alar watched with widened eyes as the wad of leaves grew massively in size. By the time the spell hit the skeleton, the leaf clump was the size of a haystack. The impact of the spell caused the skeleton to stumble backwards. It could not stop the swing of its sword and buried it to the hilt in the mass of leaves. Leaf litter and soil flew in all directions.

Alar rolled out of the way as the falling leaf clump pulled the sword and the skeleton that wielded it down to the ground. The skeleton rose to its knees and twisted its sword, straining to pull it from the smoldering pile of leaves. Alar jumped to his feet, drew his sword and faced the monster. He swung at it with all his strength, hitting the skeleton's armor breastplate. Rust exploded from the breastplate as new steel met old. Alar's right arm was jolted by the impact; it felt as though he had hit a boulder with his sword. The impact jarred the weapon from his hand, the still reverberating blade fell uselessly to the forest floor at the monster's feet. The undead beast was unfazed by the blow. It hissed and with one final pull freed its sword from the huge clump of leaves. The monster twisted, then swung the sword again.

Alar screamed as the filthy steel whizzed by his face. Chunks of loam flew off the sword, striking him on the cheek. As the skeleton drew its sword back for another swing, Alar turned on his heels and ran. The skeleton paused for a second then took off after him. With each stride, Alar could hear the rattling of its breastplate grow louder. The monster took another swipe at him, this time the sword missed by only inches.

Alar yelled like a man possessed. He sprinted with all the speed he could muster. His lungs burned as he gasped for air. As Alar passed a bend in the trail, he felt his heart pound in his chest until he feared it would burst. A loud clang rang through the air, followed by something that sounded like a thunder clap echoing off the marble walls of a temple. Alar kept running.

"Stop," he heard a familiar voice yell. "Aren't you going to help clean up?"

Alar slowed to a trot, gasping for breath. The sound of deep laughter reached his ears. He turned around. Behind him lay a huge pile of bones and standing atop them was Marcus. He roared with laughter again.

"Thank you," Alar sputtered between gasps. "What did you do to stop the beast?"

"Simple," replied Marcus as he peeled a clump of leaves off the skeleton's helmet. "When I saw how dirty the thing was, I wasn't about to fight it. By the way, was that your magic?"

Alar nodded.

"I'm impressed! You charm the trees, and trash the monsters!" laughed Marcus.

"Anyway, you came running down the trail shrieking like a terrified child. I stepped off the trail behind that tree and waited. As the skeleton passed by, I stuck out my sword and tripped the beast. Poor thing went to pieces when it fell."

"Thanks," said Alar, his breath only now coming back to him. "I owe you one. By the way, does the trail go through?"

"Yes, I think it does."

Marcus jumped off the jumbled pile of bones. He knelt down and lifted the monster's sword. As the big man held it up, a chunk of moldy leaves fell off the sword and landed on his boots.

"Yech," he grunted as he dropped the skeleton's weapon, and looked at his filthy shoes.

He turned towards Alar and wrinkled his brow. "My friend, can I ask you a favor?"

"Sure," Alar replied warily.

"Find a cleaner spell next time!"

Marcus led Alar down the trail, away from the monster's bones. They stopped in a clearing about a mile later and sat down.

"I need food!" boomed Marcus. "I will be useless as a fighting machine, if you continue to starve me!"

"Ok, ok. Just keep your voice down. We are trying to be stealthful here!"

As the woodsmen opened their packs and prepared to eat, Marcus turned to Alar. "Before you threw trash all over that poor skeleton, did you find any spell that might be useful in our battle against the sorcerer?"

"Well, I don't know. The spells are hard to control without the proper catalyst. I am almost afraid to try another one. If I use a sword, at least it won't misfire upon at me."

"I don't know about you and blades. The last time you drew it, your sword ended up under a skeleton's feet. What were you trying to do, cut its toes off?"

Alar gave him a scowl, then went back to unpacking his food.

"I'm serious about the spells," continued Marcus. "Have you found any promising ones yet?"

"Well, one that looked like it might work in the sorcerer's cave was the Stinking Cloud spell. The book makes it look like it throws a cloud of toxic fumes. Maybe we could disable the sorcerer with it. The air circulation in a cave can't be good."

"That sounds promising, but only if you can figure out what the catalyst is," Marcus replied. "If you can get the spell to work, you could throw it before we charge into the cave. Maybe while Catharvus is distracted by the fumes, I can dash in and free Avais. Once she is out of the cave, we can try to block its opening by causing a rock fall."

Alar agreed that it sounded like a good plan. As they ate, the two men discussed further strategy.

"It is too bad that you can't get that missile spell to work," Marcus said. "That one would really be helpful. Why don't you try it again? No one is attacking us now, you might just get it right!"

Alar winced. "I don't know..."

"Do it!" Marcus insisted. "While you work on it, I will climb up one of these trees, and try to get a sighting on the cave."

"Sounds more dangerous for you than me," joked Alar. "The worst thing that can happen to me is that use the wrong catalyst and blow myself up. You, on the other hand, are so fat that the tree is likely to snap in two, and dump you onto the ground!"

"Most unfair, beanpole!" Marcus chuckled. "You have upset my delicate feelings. I am upset, no, I am crushed! I must drown my sorrows!"

Chuckling to himself, Marcus reached into his pack, and pulled out a bottle of ale. He uncorked it and sat next to Alar.

Alar shot him an amused glance and shook his head. He opened the spell book to the Magic Missile spell and started chanting. When he had produced the energy packet, he looked at Marcus.

"Got any great ideas about what might work as a catalyst?"

Marcus stood up and shook his head.

"I don't know. Let me think about it."

Marcus stood up and began pacing.

"It must be something strong and dangerous. How about the extract of arguing woman's tongue?" he joked.

He took a long pull on his bottle, then bowed theatrically, probably a bit more theatrically than he intended to.

As the big man finished his bow, and snapped to attention, a few drops of ale splashed out the bottle, and landed on Alar's outstretched arm.

"Noooo!!!" screamed Alar, as almost in slow motion, one drop of Marcus' drink ran down his forearm towards the pulsating energy packet that he still clutched in his hand. The drop of ale dripped into the packet, catalyzing the spell. A loud burping sound filled the air as the rapidly expanding spell jumped out of Alar's hand and hit Marcus in the face.

Marcus sputtered in shock, spitting what was left of his mouthful of ale into the growing Magic Missile spell.

The extra ale caused the spell to grow faster. Within seconds, it expanded into a 10-foot bubbly mass that completely enveloped Marcus. He thrashed around frantically, but his fists bounced off the ale infused walls of the spell.

The giant bubble began to rise. Alar watched helplessly as Marcus was carried up into the sky by the undulating spell energies. The bubble continued to ascend until it stopped just above the tree tops where it hovered and spun.

Marcus howled like man possessed. "Help me! Help me!" He yelled.

Alar picked up a pointed stick and threw it at the undulating bubble. A frothing roar filled the air as the bubble deflated, spraying ale in all directions.

Marcus yelled, as the undulating floor of the spell disappeared from below him. He fell downward, grabbing onto a tree branch to break his fall. He clung to his handhold for a minute, seemingly staring off into the distance, then shimmied down the tree trunk.

When he was back on the ground, he turned towards Alar and said, "Yep, we are on the right trail, I saw the waterfall cave. Now stop your staring and let's get going!"

With that, he spun on his heels and headed down the trail, leaving Alar open-mouthed behind him.

Alar and Marcus followed the skeleton's trail up into the mountains. Keeping as low as possible, they dodged from rock to rock until they were at lookout point. From here, they followed a little used logging path to a small mountain that abutted the ravine. Their position was above and behind the waterfall cave's. From where they stood, the view was spectacular.

"Look at our village," Marcus whispered, as he pointed to the tiny cottages in the distance. "The world looks so different from here. All is calm and peaceful. Everything is beautiful."

"You should see what it looks like when you are flying," sighed Alar. "The air is so crisp and pure it makes your eyes water. You soar without effort. Flicking a wing is all you need to do to circle the valley. The world spins before you like a child's ball."

Alar lowered his voice. He looked at Marcus and reached out for his shoulder.

"Marcus, my friend. I know the spell to transfer the Air Children's tattoo. I watched Avais do it to me, I know the correct catalyst. The Air Children could really use your help. You know how reluctant I am to be the only user of magic during such an important time. I could give you the ability to cast spells. You could fly..."

"Oh no you don't!" interrupted Marcus. "Stop right there. I don't want to hear any more! Your flying stories make me jealous. Even the few moments I hovered above the trees in that awful beer bubble were spectacular, but don't think for a moment that I would trust you to transform me into an Air Child."

"Imagine this. You have just turned me into a bird. Knowing how your spells misfire, I would be lucky if you didn't transform me into a catfish!"

"Let's give you the benefit of the doubt, you actually get the spell to work. You would probably turn me into a turkey. Poor Marcus would still be land locked, but he would have to trade these fine whiskers for red turkey neck jowls. My biggest battle would be to escape Barona's cooking fires.

He started to strut around in an exaggerated manner. "Gobble, gobble, gobble! No way, Alar! You will stay this group's only sorcerer."

"I would not turn you into a turkey," laughed Alar. "Besides, the kind of bird you transform into is decided by your makeup, not your wishes. You would probably turn into an ostrich; big, strong, likes to eat, not too smart..."

Alar ducked as Marcus took a playful swing at him. They both dissolved into laughter and sat down beside a large rock.

"Enough screwing around," Marcus said. "Let's go into that cave and find some clues!"

They scampered down the rock face to a ledge above the waterfall cave, then grabbed ahold of the vines that grew there. They looked at each other, nodded then lowered themselves down the vines and swung into the cave's opening. Alar suppressed a shudder when his feet brushed against the broken ledge that he had fallen off a few days ago.

They entered the cave with swords drawn. Once their eyes adjusted to the light, they saw that there was no trace of the spider. They slid their weapons back into their scabbards.

Alar's head sunk when he saw what remained of Avais' possessions.

"My God, look at what the spider did to her things."

Alar picked at the fragments of her foretelling orb. The crystal slivers sparkled at him like morning dew in the cave's subdued light. Avais' iron wand was twisted into a useless knot. He exhaled slowly as he turned it over in his hands.

"Such power. Imagine what it could do to a defenseless little bird..."

"She is fine," Marcus said firmly. "They just didn't want anyone to use her tools of magic."

He pulled the twisted wand from Alar's hands and prayed his words were true.

The woodsmen searched the rest of the cave without finding anything. Alar slumped down upon a rock in the back of the cave. He rested his head in his hands. Out of the corner of his eye, a flash of color caught his attention. He looked closer and saw a purple splotch staining the floor. He scraped the stain with his fingernail. The stain's surface was dry, but it was wet and sticky underneath. He smelled it.

"This is the blood of that foul spider," he muttered.

Alar washed his hands in the waterfall pool. "There is nothing else that can help us here. Let us leave. There may be more traces of blood outside."

The woodsmen searched the mouth of the cave, and the rocks on either side of it. Marcus found a few bits of dried blood on a ledge a few feet from the mouth of the cave.

"Alar, I've found some more," he yelled excitedly, then realizing that his voice would carry, continued in a whisper.

"The spider must have gone this way."

Alar examined the blood stain.

"We are lucky to find this," he said. "I was afraid that the downpour might have washed away all traces of the spider's blood. Let's work our way along this ridge and look for anything that looks like the opening of a cave."

"Agreed," grunted Marcus, as he drew his sword. "Let's get the bastard."

The two men worked their way along the rock face. From a distant cave, hollow eyes followed their progress in the shimmering surface of a foretelling orb.

Catharvus turned away from the sphere and knelt before Avais' bony prison.

"They are coming," he laughed. "I watch their every move in the orb. They shall not surprise me, I am ready for them!"

Avais recoiled at his words and cowered in the back of her cage.

"Do not worry young sorceress. You are not going to die now. I shall keep you alive. I want you to watch as I kill your precious Alar. With the images this orb gives me, the advantage is mine. He is doomed. I cannot lose. I shall kill him and his woodsman friend. Alar's death will give me my freedom."

Avais inhaled deeply, then left the back of the cage where she had been cowering and moved to the center of the cage's floor. Her gaze met Catharvus' stare. She did not blink. She did not look away. Though her options were limited, trapped as she was in bird form, she was desperate to stop the sorcerer from using the orb to ambush her lover.

"You do not have a chance, you tired old man!" she spit out defiantly. "Your power is gone."

"My people could have killed you years ago, but they let you live. They treated you with both mercy and pity. We did not fear you, as you are far too impotent to ever escape from this prison!"

"Impotent!" Yelled the old sorcerer. "Impotent? I control both my destiny, and yours."

He grabbed the foretelling orb, and spat on the image of the woodsmen. The saliva boiled off the orb's white-hot surface. With a grimace, he grabbed the orb in his bare hands and walked towards Avais.

Ignoring the sizzling sound of his own flesh burning, he held the orb in front of Avais' cage.

"Take a last look at your boyfriend, for I shall soon slaughter him before your eyes!"

"No! No! No!" screamed Avais. "Take that orb away, it's image is making me sick.

The old sorcerer let out an evil laugh, then pushed the orb against the bony ribs that made up Avais' prison. She shrieked, then threw herself against the bars of the cage, and dug her beak into the sorcerer's knuckle. With strength driven by panic and love, she continued her attack, twisting until her beak struck bone.

Ignoring the pain in her fragile body, she writhed and pulled until she felt his finger snap.

Catharvus roared in pain, and jerked his hand away, bloodying Avais' face as she was slammed into the bony bars.   His reflex motion was so fast and uncontrolled, he lost his grip upon the foretelling orb. The sphere hit the cave's floor and shattered into countless pieces.

The old man's eyes glazed over in raw unfettered hatred.

"You will pay dearly for doing that," Catharvus screamed, as he ripped Bahaom's skull off of the cage's top and grabbed Avais by the neck.

"You will die now, you worthless animal!"

Avais fluttered in fear, battering her already ragged wings against his hand. He grabbed her body with his other hand and twisted her neck until it was on the verge of snapping.

Avais prepared herself to die.   Inexplicably, Catharvus stopped, then nodded his head.

Catharvus stared at the terrified dove for a moment, then threw her back into the skeleton cage. He slammed the skull atop it, again imprisoning her. Only then did the old sorcerer smile. He looked down at the wreckage of his foretelling orb. He smiled as he ground the shards of the crystal orb into the cave floor.

Shaking the diamond chain at Avais, he muttered, "Death now would be too merciful of a release for you. You shall watch as I kill your precious boyfriend, and as the prophecy says, be freed."

He rattled the diamond chain in Avais' direction.

"Once this reminder of the Air Children has been removed from my leg, you will be forced to observe as I destroy all life in this valley."

"Only then will I release you from your sorrows. First, I will rub your horrid bird body on Alar's cold corpse, then I shall crush the life out of you with my bare hands and eat your carcass raw! Your bloody feathers will be the only burial shroud the woodsman will ever have."

Avais turned her head so the sorcerer would not see the tears that spilled from her dark eyes.

Marcus and Alar moved along the trail of dried blood. Neither one could see the opening of the sorcerer's cave, but both sensed it was growing nearer. Their hearts began to pound though neither man was exerting himself. With each step, the air seemed to become more damp and chilled. Their nerves tightened as they passed splotch after splotch of purple blood.

The sky seemed to change as they advanced. It crackled and shimmered like a distant heat mirage. The hair on the woodsmen's arms stood up as they felt their skin begin to tingle. Gusts of wind whipped against them from all directions. Thunder shook the skies. The heavens turned blood red, then burst open, as a violent downpour started. The rocks grew slick, and mud began to slide down the slopes.

"We must get off this part of the mountain," Marcus yelled above the rain. "This storm is not one of nature, but is the work of black sorcery. We will be swept off this rock face if we stay here. Look, there is a ledge below us. Maybe we can find some shelter under it. Come on, let's go!"

Alar froze in his tracks. Marcus looked into his friend's eyes. A look of terror filled them that Marcus had never seen before. It was obvious that he was struggling against a storm of emotions that matched the arcane tempest that beat down upon them.

"You must move!" Marcus yelled over the din of the storm. "If you die in a rock slide, you will have done Avais no good. Now come with me, or I will pick you up and carry you to shelter."

As the wind howled, a lightning bolt split the sky, and struck the spot where they had stood only minutes before. Chips of rock flew in the air and rained down upon them. Sparks danced upon the cliff face as waves of lightning formed heat blasted against them.

"Now!" yelled Marcus as he shoved the younger man. Alar's feet did not move. Marcus pulled him around and shook his shoulders violently. He slapped him on the face once, then again harder. Alar blinked through the tears that welled up in his eyes. He was too choked with emotion to speak, but nodded, then silently followed the big man down the mountain.

The path widened as they neared the stone overhang. Alar pulled alongside Marcus.

"My dream starts with a storm like this," whispered Alar. "I am afraid, Marcus. Are you?"

"More than a little, my friend. No sane man wouldn't be. We are close to battle, and the enemy is strong."

"Though my fear of death is great, it is nothing compared to the dread I feel about Avais. This waiting eats at my heart. Each moment I delay may be Avais' last. That monster has her, and can do with her as he pleases. There is nothing I can do for her yet. I feel so helpless!"

"Have patience Alar," Marcus softly replied. "We will rescue Avais from Catharvus. That sorcerer's twisted brain is no match for us. You press on, driven by love, while he is consumed by hatred. It is on a matter of time until he is his own undoing."

They turned towards the ledge, each lost in his own thoughts.

Eyes half mad with pain stared out at them. The men were coming. There could be no escape. The creature lowered itself into the overhang's darkest shadows and prepared to strike.

Unaware, Marcus put his arm around Alar's shoulder and gently steered him towards the overhang. "Let's wait out the storm here. This place will be safe."

Alar saw something stir in the shadows. A tortured screech filled the air as a dark form lunged at Marcus.

"Look out!" he yelled.

Marcus stiffened and looked about, but could see nothing in the dark cave. He did not know which direction the danger came from. He froze.

"Get out of the way," yelled Alar, as he pushed the older man back. A curse escaped Marcus' mouth as he stumbled over a rock and landed in a muddy puddle. Though the big man was out of the reach of the lunging jaws, Alar was now directly in front of them. In as second, they were upon him. Alar threw up his hands, trying to fend off the claws that grabbed at him.

"Be gone, you foul beast," yelled Alar as he grappled with a set of snapping jaws that lunged for his face.

The creature paused for a second.

"I understand your words," it hissed. "Hear me now, you evil two-legged monster. I will not die without a fight. There is no honor in being slaughtered!"

Alar reached behind him and grabbed his pack.

"You speak the language of the air," he yelled as he pushed the animal away with it. "I do not wish to harm anyone, especially you, my brother. Why do you attack one of your own?"

The animal staggered back.

"I am sorry," it replied with a wavering voice. Alar noticed that it had begun to shake. "I did not know that you were different from the old one who did this to me. Forgive me, for I am not thinking well. My wounds are great, I suffer much pain. Even now, death closes in on me. It is not my way to surrender to it without a struggle. I have struck at you, I ask your forgiveness."

Alar knelt in front of the shivering animal. "Come out where I can see you," he said. "If you are wounded, maybe I can help."

Unholy lightening flashed in the distance. Its light illuminated a tattered hawk as it limped out of the shadows. It had been terribly mauled. A wing was missing. Where the wing should have been, now only charred flesh remained. The feathers that once covered the bird's right side were burned down to their quills. The creature looked at Alar through glazed eyes.

"Are you an Air Child?" it asked. Even as they spoke, Alar could hear its voice weakening.

"Yes I am. You are badly hurt. Let me tend to your wounds."

"It is too late for me," the animal whispered. Its eyes looked in Alar's direction, but no longer saw. The hawk's voice faded as it coughed and gasped for breath. Alar moved closer and cradled the animal in his arms.

"Life is funny," it murmured. "I always thought that the Air Children didn't exist. They were just a myth to me. I have never seen one. No one I know has ever seen one. On the last day of my life, I see not one, but three."

The hawk shuddered, then collapsed into the dirt.

Alar picked up the hawk and held it close to his body. "Do not die friend hawk. I will try to help you."

The creature closed its eyes. "It is too late for that. I will soon be flying on the highest breezes."

"What happened? Who did this to you?" said Alar, as he fought to hold back tears.

"An Air Child with feathers of the most beautiful white called to me. I tried to reach her, but the blue spirit flew too fast. I saw them disappear into the mountain. I flew to her..."

The hawk was wracked by a spasm of coughing. Alar stroked its head gently. When the creature resumed talking, its voice was halting and faint, its eyes opened, but it was beyond seeing.

"I found the white feathered 'Air Child'. She was imprisoned by a withered human who also spoke the tongue of the air. He insulted my honor, then hurled a ball of fire against me. The explosion threw me out of the mountain. I crawled along as far as I could. I stopped under this ledge to die. The storm pulled me from the sleep of the dead. That is when you approached."

"I am sorry that I disturbed you during this time of great pain," Alar whispered. He felt the hawk's body begin to twitch in his arms.

"Do you have the strength to tell me where the evil one holds the white Air Child?" Alar asked gently. "It is most important to me."

"She lies behind a crack in the mountain. A crooked tree grows above the spot." The hawk's eyes closed. "I shall soon soar among the clouds again."

Alar felt its body shudder once, then it was gone.

Alar smoothed the feathers on the hawk's body. He looked up at Marcus who was standing next to him, his head bowed.   He gently laid the animal on the ground.

"Rest in peace, my brother," he murmured.

Alar walked by Marcus, and stepped out into the storm. He scanned the mountain above him, his eyes squinting against the pelting rain. Lightening again flashed across the darkened sky. Near the top of the mountain, at the very limits of his vision, he saw it, illuminated by the brief flash. At the mountain's top, where the storm clouds swirled against the sheer rock face, a jagged crack was outlined. Above it lay the twisted trunk of a long dead tree, its form shaking like a fist in the swirling winds.

A clap of thunder shook the ground.

Alar's jaw tightened as he tried to peer into the night's darkness.

He turned to Marcus, "Come with me," he said.

Lightening again split the sky. Marcus hesitated.

Alar turned towards Catharvus' cave.

"Come with me or stay behind," he growled. "I am leaving now."

Alar charged up the mountain. Marcus followed behind him, struggling to keeping up with the pace of his young friend's frenzied ascent.

"Hide yourself, you fool!" hissed Marcus as he grabbed for Alar's leg. "If you climb straight towards the cave, you will run into the sorcerer's arms. Use your head!"

Alar paused for a moment, then nodded. He followed Marcus' advise, and began scampering from rock to rock, trying to stay out of the line of sight of the cave. In places, the rocks were too slick to climb. They were forced to veer to the east, in search of an easier route to the cave's opening. Eventually, the two came upon the path that Bahaom had followed. Alar drew his sword and prepared to step into Catharvis' world.

"No more waiting," he growled, "it is time."

Marcus grabbed him by the shoulder and pulled him back.

"What has come over you?" he whispered. "Has that bird tattoo's ink poisoned you brain. If we charge down the path and into the cave, he will see us coming. We will be mowed down like wheat before the cutting blade. Let us drop in on him from above the cave. If the gods are with us, the storm may hide our approach. Besides your spell book, surprise is the only ally we have out here."

Alar followed his friend's gaze, then nodded grimly. He knew that the big man was right

The woodsmen climbed the rock face and were soon fifty feet above the path. They worked their way west until they looked down on the cave's opening. There were enough hand holds to lower themselves to the tree that grew above the crack. The swirling wind howled angrily in the tree's branches as Marcus drew his sword.

"Ready a spell, brave friend," Marcus whispered. "I will swing down on the tree and draw the sorcerer's attack. You follow me and use magic against him."

Alar nodded and began to mouth the arcane words. This better be a simple spell, he thought. As if casting a spell wasn't difficult enough, I have to do it while clinging to a mountain in a thunderstorm.

Alar's shaking hands couldn't control the natural energies, and the spell fell apart. On his second try, the familiar form of the Magic Missile's energy packet appeared.

Alar looked at Marcus and whispered, "I'm ready, let's go."

Marcus smiled at his friend and pointed towards the cave. "Follow me, and this time try to make a spell that works!"

Marcus took a quick hit from his bottle, tossed it aside, and exhaled deeply. He grabbed the tree, and dove off the cliff. The tree bent like a long bow under the big man's weight. He had almost swung into the cave's mouth when the trunk of the tree snapped. As his support disappeared, Marcus was pitched forward into the cave.

The smell of the cave hit him before his eyes had time to adjust to the dim light. The air reeked of stale filth. Marcus heard a frantic fluttering and looked up to see a white dove throwing herself against the rib bones that imprisoned her. He waved his sword in front of himself as he glanced around the room. A blue sparkling chain stretched across the room, but its shackle lay empty on the floor near Avais' cage.

"I'll be damned," Marcus muttered. "He has already escaped."

The big man strode towards Avais.

"I will free you, little dove."

Avais screeched and beat herself against the cage of bones until blood splattered against their whiteness.

"Don't panic, damn it!" he yelled. "I will have you out in a second."

As Marcus grabbed the skeleton's skull, the air behind him began to shimmer, as Catharvus reversed the invisibility spell. Like a figure walking out of the mists of a deep fog, Catharvus' robed body appeared next to Marcus. The big man gasped as he saw the sorcerer's still shackled form materialize. Catharvus pulled a dagger from his sleeve and snickered as the blade began to pulsate.

Marcus let the skull go and whirled towards Catharvus. Before the big man could raise his sword, the sorcerer plunged the dagger into his neck. Waves of pain paralyzed Marcus as the blade pierced his flesh. His knees buckled, he slowly sank to the ground. As the dagger's blade twisted its way deeper into his body, Marcus' sword fell from his hand. The big man's eyes rolled upward, then closed.

Catharvus chanted the arcane words. Deep within his neck, Marcus felt the blades tip grow hot. A great emptiness filled him as his life forces began to slip away. The sound of Avais' cries faded into the distance.

The world blackened as Marcus slumped face first onto the cave's dusty floor.

The stone below Alar crumbled into an avalanche of dirt when the tree that Marcus was swinging on snapped. He lost his footing on the shifting rock, fell backwards, and began to slide down the cliff. Before him lay a five-thousand-foot fall into the valley below. As he desperately clawed at the rock, Alar's sword flew from his hand. The young sorcerer slid over the tree's roots, bounced into the air, then managed to catch hold of the cave's jagged lip with his now empty sword hand. Bolts of pain shot down his arm as the sharp rock tore into his skin. Alar held on with one hand, his body swinging wildly as he dangled. The spell, still clutched tightly in his right hand, crackled and buzzed. Despite his precarious grip, he had the presence of mind to keep the spell's primed energies from touching anything. He didn't want to set off the spell early!

He clung to the wall for a moment, letting the swinging stop, and catching his breath. Once his nerves had steadied, he kicked his feet forward, and when he had enough momentum, dropped into the looming darkness of the cave. He stumbled ahead, his eyes straining to focus in the dim light.

As his eyes adjusted, a nightmare vision unfolded before him. Avais, her feathers frayed and blood stained, cried out to him from within a skeleton's chest. Marcus lay on the ground before her. His skin was so pale, it looked blue in the cave's dim light. A withered, ghoul of a man, dressed in decaying rags, twisted a dagger in his friend's neck.

Alar lowered a shoulder and slammed into the man. The force of the impact knocked Catharvus backwards.

Catharvus' dagger blade was so deeply imbedded in the Marcus' neck that the sorcerer lost his grip on it as he fell.

The handle of the dagger immediately glowed an intense red. Marcus shrieked in pain. Blood welled up from deep within him, oozing around the pulsating blade. A pool of reddish mud began to expand on the cave's floor. Alar gasped, then grabbed at the knife with both hands. He strained for a second, then tore the dagger from Marcus' neck.

The uncatalyzed spell in Alar's hand touched the dagger and was activated by it.

A high-pitched whine filled the cave. Catharvus saw the spell energies engulf his dagger, and let out an unearthly scream. He rolled to his feet, hurtled the pile of blue diamond chain, and dove at Alar. With the strength born of a thousand dead souls, he attacked the young Air Child. He clawed at Alar's hands, knocking the dagger free. The knife, now enmeshed in Alar's spell packet, glowed an impossible shade of red. Crimson sparks ran across its surface as it began to catalyze the spell. The blade skittered across the floor, leaving a trail of melted stone behind it. It came to rest against the link that bound Catharvus' diamond chain to the wall.

An earsplitting roar filled the room as the dagger and spell reacted with each other.

"It's going to blow!" yelled Alar. He threw his body over Bahaom's skeleton to shield Avais. The old sorcerer let out an ear-piercing scream that eclipsed the spell's whining shriek and dove for his dagger.

The spell went off.

Alar clung to Avais' cage as the magical forces turned the dagger's mass into pure energy. An explosion rocked the cave. Visibility dropped to zero as centuries worth of dust flew off the ceiling and walls.

Then there was nothing.

Silence filled the cave, broken only by Marcus' moans, and Alar's rapid breathing.

Slowly the air cleared.

Alar forced himself to his feet in response to the raspy wheeze of Catharvus' voice.

"Help me," gasped the old man.

Alar watched as the hunched figure, its back turned towards him, slowly stood. Chips of blue fell to the floor below him as the once perfect diamond chain cracked and disintegrated. Catharvus staggered away from the explosion's crater. He collapsed on a rock. For the first time since the explosion, he turned to face Alar.

What Alar saw made him gasp and avert his eyes. Catharvus must have dove on the dagger as it exploded. The force of the explosion had torn away most of the old sorcerer's chest and face.

The old man seemed oblivious to his injuries. He looked around him in a confused manner. His remaining eye danced from the battered bird, to the pale bearded man that lay on the floor, to the dazed young man that staggered towards him.

"What is all of this?" he asked.

He blinked twice as the memories returned to him.

"Tell me that it wasn't me... No! It could not have been. Tell me it wasn't me!"

He looked at the tattoo on his arm. He fingered the dagger that impaled the Air Child bird.

"Please tell me that this was all a dream!"

He started to sob. "It all comes back to me now. I remember, oh, I remember it all now. May the gods forgive me for what have I done."

He looked down at his leg and kicked off the last tattered remnants of the shackle. It crumbled to dust. His eye focused on the explosion's crater. Ashes in the shape of the dagger were all that remained of his litch blade.

A warm gust of wind worked its way into the cave. The dagger's ashes scattered before it.

Once more, the old man began to sob. He reached out to Alar and grabbed him.

"You have done it, don't you see? The prophecy has been fulfilled. In destroying the blade, you have defeated me. In destroying the blade, you have set me free. The prophecy has come true."

Catharvus' eyes closed. The old man's hands slipped from Alar's shoulders. He sunk to the ground and breathed one last tortured breath.

A look of peace overcame him.

Alar looked down at the dead sorcerer. He gently folded Catharvus' hands over his mangled chest. Alar bowed his head, then stepped back. Catharvus' body seemed to shimmer for a second, then it dissolved into a cloud of smoke that lazily rose, then floated out of the cave, into the sunlight. A flock of birds gathered outside the cave. They wheeled and banked around the smoky cloud, helping it dissipate into the air.

When the last was gone, as if on cue, they separated into pairs, and dove towards the forest below.

Alar released Avais from her skeletal prison. Her body quaked as spasms of sobs racked over her. He held her against his chest until she stopped shaking.

"He is gone," Alar murmured. He stroked her feathers as he whispered to her. "You are safe now. We all are safe. Rest. I will tend to Marcus' wounds."

Alar put Avais down, then helped Marcus into a sitting position.

"By the gods, you're a mess," he said. "I guess the first thing to do is to get the bleeding stopped." Alar was applying a bandage of hastily torn cloth to Marcus's neck, when he heard the sound of a spell catalyzing behind him. He turned to see Avais' body materialize out of a shimmering cloud. Feathers dissolved into skin as the magical forces worked upon her. In seconds, the white bird had converted to human form.

"It was a little dirty, but the 'Air Child" seal on Catharvus' spell book did a fine job," she said.

Avais walked over to Alar and helped him care for Marcus. She cast a healing spell upon him and smiled as he responded to it. As the color returned to the big man's face, she reached into his pack and drew out a bottle of spirits.

"Drink this," she commanded. "It will speed your recovery."

"I would never dream of arguing with my healer," he weakly replied.

Avais turned towards Alar. They kissed, then clung to each other for a long time.

Marcus rose to his feet and staggered out of the cave.

"A man in my weakened condition can't be watching this," he muttered under his breath."

The rain had stopped, and the skies were turning pink as the sun pushed its way through the clouds. He looked back towards the cave in time to see Avais stoop and picked up Catharvus' spell book.

"This will be mine from now on," she said to Alar. "I wonder if there is any spell that will clean it up?" she laughed. "I hate to touch it. It looks like something that crawled from under a forest rock!"

"What about me?" questioned Alar. "The book that I have has been torn in half. Must I remain an incomplete sorcerer forever?"

"No, I don't think so," she said with mock seriousness. "You may copy the contents of my book onto a blank one. I shall never let my spell book get out of my sight again, I have learned my lesson."

Alar smiled.

"I guess this means that I will have to live with you while I copy yours."

"I believe that is the only way. I hope you are a good scribe."

"The book is huge, and I write very slowly," Alar said. "It will take forever!"

"I certainly hope so!" she laughed.

They walked arm in arm towards the cave's entrance. As they stepped out into the sunlight, a bright rainbow split the sky before them.

Peace had once again come to the valley.

www.ingramcontent.com/pod-product-compliance
Lightning Source LLC
Chambersburg PA
CBHW030910300726
48970CB00001B/92